King's Company

Books by Frank Ernest Hill

TO MEET WILL SHAKESPEARE

THE WINGED HORSE (*co-author*)

THE WINGED HORSE ANTHOLOGY (*co-editor*)

THE CANTERBURY TALES
(*translation into modern English verse*)

STONE DUST (*poems*)

WHAT IS AMERICAN?

THE WESTWARD STAR (*novel in verse*)

KING'S COMPANY

FRANK ERNEST HILL

Drawings by Addison Burbank

Dodd, Mead & Co., Inc.

New York ~ 1950

Printed in the United States of America
by Vail-Ballou Press, Inc., Binghamton, N. Y.

To R. A. N. H.
*who suggested the adventures of
Cedric, and thus started the book*

FOREWORD

Books are written for readers, yet in a sense each is also written for its author. *King's Company* happens to have been a particularly enjoyable adventure for me, for it has taken me to a corner of the world that William Shakespeare knew, and has permitted me to make a living picture of the play-house in which he worked and of the apprentices, hired men, actors and "housekeepers" or owners who worked there with him.

In the year 1600 England had already created a great national drama, but had yet to produce a notable artist. In a few years it did so, in the architect and designer Inigo Jones. He was chiefly identified with the Court masque, and thus indirectly with the English theater. He developed elaborate and realistic scenery (Ben Jonson described one set vividly in his foreword to *The Masque of Blackness,* for which he wrote the script), although the effect of such experiments on the popular playhouses was slight for some years to come.

In *King's Company* I have imagined a young Englishman who developed independently along somewhat the same lines as Jones. Led by accident and necessity to the Globe, the theater of which Shakespeare was part owner, he dreams of putting his ideas into practice there. Thus art and drama both find a place in this story.

As to history, the book makes some slight departures from

it. The Globe is represented in *King's Company* as opening for a few days early in March, 1604; actually it did not open until after April 9. The performance before King James at Westminster in Chapter XVII is an imaginary one. Naturally all the relationships or conversations of Burbage, Shakespeare, King James, Inigo Jones and other real persons with the hero and his companions are also fictional. However, every effort has been made to make an accurate picture of early seventeenth-century London and the Globe playhouse, as well as of such occurrences as the King's progress through London on March 15, 1604, which is described in Chapter XIV.

One word of warning: no attempt has been made here to fill in gaps in Shakespeare's own story. He is not a chief character, although he takes some part in the action, and I hope seems real as the busy but discerning and friendly person he undoubtedly was.

Frank Ernest Hill

THE CHIEF CHARACTERS

Imagined:

ROGER DARRELL:	The son of a nobleman, bent on becoming an artist, and furiously opposed in this by
SIR JOHN DARRELL:	his father, who disinherits him in favor of
ANTHONY DARRELL:	Roger's younger brother, who knows that two and two make four
RAPHAEL BARTOLOMEO:	An Italian-born artist and architect, and Roger's teacher, who believes he has a future in art
LUCY KNOWLES:	A neighbor of the Darrells, and almost the heroine
CEDRIC WALES:	who has run away from a hated guardian, and comes to the Globe playhouse with Roger, and gets the help of
EDWARD VANCE:	Roger's uncle, and a lawyer, who plans to protect Cedric from
GILES BRAGDON:	the guardian, and beyond doubt the villain, who keeps pursuing, as villains do, with the aid of
WICKARD:	a retainer, and competent swordsman, and
SEFTON:	a lawyer

TREVOR:
BARTON: Roger's friends, but not friends at Court
WAT SOMERS
JACK HODGE   Hired men and apprentices at the
BOB FAIRFIELD,   Globe
& OTHERS:
MRS. SLATER: Roger's landlady in London
SERVANTS, RETAINERS, PAGES, AGENTS, LAW CLERKS, ACTORS,
NOBLEMEN, MERCHANTS, WORKMEN AND OTHERS

And Real:
JAMES I: King of England, France, Scotland,
                           Wales and Ireland, etc.
NICHOLAS JOHNSON:
GARRETT JOHNSON: Artists and monument-makers, whose
                           shop is near the Globe
PHILIP HENSLOWE: Owner of the Fortune, rival playhouse
                           to the Globe
EDWARD ALLEYN: Part owner and chief actor at the same
RICHARD BURBAGE: Part owner and chief actor at the Globe
                           for the King's Men
JOHN HEMINGES: Actor at the Globe, and Manager for
                           the King's Men
WILLIAM SHAKESPEARE: Actor, part-owner, and playwright at
                           the Globe for the King's Men
INIGO JONES: An English artist and architect serving
                           the King

*The story begins at Darrell Manor, in Kent, shifts to the city of
London, to the Bankside, its southern suburb, and then to Westminster.*

Time: Winter and Spring of the year 1604

CONTENTS

ILLUSTRATIONS

King's Company

I

EITHER OR

SIR JOHN DARRELL came in with the look and abruptness of a man on an unpleasant errand. His two sons, Roger and Anthony, and the girl who was with them paused in their work as he entered.

Sir John gave only a glance at what they had been doing in the large bare room on the upper story of his manor house. Indeed, his eyes scarcely seemed to take in the purple throne spangled with golden crowns and the curtain of the same color which had been hung behind it. He turned to the older of the young men who stood with a paint brush in his hand.

"I have news for you, Roger," he said brusquely. "Sir Ralph Thorne promises you a commission, and you shall leave with him for Ireland come Twelfth Night and a week."

Roger Darrell looked at his father with astonishment.

"Sir, I think you have forgotten," he said courteously but firmly after a second's pause. "I am bound for London after Twelfth Night, to work for some months with Master Bartolomeo. You knew of this yourself, and approved it, and I gave him my promise."

His father flushed angrily and began to walk about.

"Why, then, you can take back the promise," he flung out as he paced, "for I have given Sir Ralph another that cancels it."

He looked at his son with hard eyes, and Roger stared

1

steadily back at him.

The two made a contrast. Sir John was not so tall as his broad-shouldered twenty-one-year-old son, but he was powerfully built. The chief difference lay in their coloring. It was said of the Darrell men that they were either reds or blacks. Sir John's complexion was fair and ruddy, and his hair and beard were sandy-red; Roger's smooth-shaven face was almost swarthy, with hair and brows to match. His darkness and size gave him a striking, even something of a forbidding air; although any discerning observer would have sensed a warmth and sensitivity along with the strength. Roger's gray eyes, the pupils clear against the light irises, only emphasized by a flick of difference that he was a "black."

"This business of daubing chairs and curtains," Sir John went on, glancing with angry contempt at what his son had been doing as if he now saw it for the first time, "can wait until we've made a man of you—"

He broke off and stared resentfully at the throne and hangings.

"What in the name of nonsense *is* this?" he demanded.

"Why, 'tis the throne for the Lord of Misrule in the Twelfth Night masque, Sir John," the girl answered quickly. "And the arras that will hang behind it." Although only sixteen, Lucy Knowles spoke with a poise and assurance that many older women might have envied. "Roger has devised it to fit into the great hall below. You can see how the fool's caps are entwined with the crowns. Isn't it a marvelous setting, Sir John?" Her blue eyes held his confidently.

"Very pretty, I dare say, very pretty," the other muttered uneasily, for Lucy was a favorite with him. Then he turned to his son again. "I tell you, Roger, that all this business of contriving and daubing, whether for mummery or monuments or great houses, can wait. You've wasted too much time with the

"When the two of you stand there like a pair of fighting cocks—"

Italian already—heard too much nonsense from him."

"But, sir—"

"Another month or two and he'll tame you to a pasty-faced artisan, and thrust papers under your nose to sign as his 'prentice."

"Why, sir, you seemed pleased to have me work with him all the two years and more he was here building the new manor house," protested Roger.

"If I was pleased, I am to blame for it," Sir John retorted, "and so will mend what I marred; for draughting and painting make a poor pastime for an English gentleman."

A wave of color darkened Roger's face.

"A better one, to my mind, than riding down half-starved kerns in Irish bogs!"

"So already you lack stomach for a man's work!"

"Few but you would dare say so!"

The two glared at each other, and Roger's younger brother spoke up quickly.

"Roger does not mean, Father—"

"This is no affair of yours, Anthony," Sir John snapped.

"Why, sir, I think it is," persisted the young man with a composure scarcely to be expected of his eighteen years. "When the two of you stand there like a pair of fighting cocks—"

"Enough! I'll manage this alone."

Anthony shrugged and was silent, but Roger spoke again.

"Sir," he said quietly, "Master Bartolomeo has said that I have a talent which I should use. And if there are few English gentlemen who can plan a noble house or match the Germans and Flemings as painters—why, sir, the more shame to England! I shall be ready to use my sword if my Queen—nay, I forgot, if our King James needs it, but—"

"No more!" Sir John broke in. "Make ready to leave with

Sir Ralph at the time appointed."

Roger struggled to control himself, like a man who has taken a slap in the face but does not want to strike back. Finally, having achieved a certain composure, he asked in a level tone:

"And if, being twenty-one, I do not leave with Sir Ralph?"

Lucy and Anthony gasped, and Sir John froze in amazement. Then he fairly swelled with anger, his hands twitching and his eyes seeming about to start from his face.

"What?" he shouted. *"If you do not?"* He lifted a hand before his son could reply.

"Aye, you're of age," he said, biting off his words with cold fury. "And you are heir to these lands. But I tell you this: you are so by my pleasure alone; and if you take your way against mine, you shall be heir to nothing. So mend your words and your ways, or leave this hall for good when you leave, and Anthony shall have your place. As I live and speak, he has a man's sense where your head is a muddle of folly!"

He turned on his heel and was at the door in three strides, but paused there for a second.

"Look to it!"

He sent the words like a sword-stroke, and turned angrily into the hall outside. The echoes of his steps, going away and down the oaken stairs, came back to the girl and the two young men, sharply at first, then muted by distance.

They eyed each other silently for a moment. Anthony let out his breath at last in a half whistle and grinned ruefully at his brother.

"Why, I thought it would come to blows between you," he remarked. "He wants managing, that father of ours, and you stood up to him like one of the King's mastiffs to a lion. Which you've done before, I know," he added, "and yet the time will come when you'll get mangled for it!"

"If he thinks he's finished this," growled Roger, "he'll find it's not so easy." His face was still flushed with anger.

Anthony shook his head. No clash between his father and brother had ever gone so far, and he was troubled. So was Lucy.

"But you heard what he said, Roger," she protested, "and you know that once his mind is fixed it's dangerous to bait him."

"Bait him!" retorted Roger. "It was he who baited me! I gave a promise—gave it with his own consent, and I mean to keep it."

"Not because it's a promise," Anthony smiled shrewdly, "but because all your mind and will are turned to draughting and painting."

His brother smiled back, half embarrassed, half defiant.

"What if they are?"

"But, Roger," persisted Lucy, "would you go against Sir John's express command?"

The young man shrugged.

"He blows hot and cold."

"I think not. I think he's resolved on it. And, Roger, while painting is a pretty pastime, he is right that gentlemen do not follow it as a profession."

"Nay, some of them do!" Roger objected quickly. He was no longer angry, but was still eager to justify his feeling. "I've heard Bartolomeo praise Thorpe and Smithson as good architects, and they are gentlemen. So is Bartolomeo himself. And in these arts, as I said, it's a reproach to Englishmen that we lag behind other lands where men win high honor in such fields."

"And so may you," urged the girl deftly, "but you need not hazard land and title, and—and—"

"And a wife fairer than an angel," murmured Anthony with

a grin. There had been talk of Roger and Lucy becoming betrothed.

The girl flushed.

"I didn't say that."

She sat down on a stool, frowning. Roger, who had been gathering up his painting materials, spoke casually now, as if he had not heard Anthony's gibe.

"I wonder at this talk about gentility," he remarked. "As I recall it, we Darrells are only three generations away from ironmongers, and the Vances from the wool trade." He referred to the family of his mother, who had been dead for several years.

"The more reason to guard what's recently won," said Lucy quickly. "Besides, as Anthony says, it only wants managing."

"Does it?" Roger glanced at her with eyes that were friendly enough, yet showed an underlying firmness. "Between you, Mistress Knowles, and my good father, I think I might be managed out of what I have most set my mind on."

She did not reply, but there was a set of stubbornness to her pretty face. Then suddenly she sprang up with an exclamation.

"The morning is well gone, and I shall be late to dinner if I stay longer!"

She picked up a hooded cloak from the table and put it on, for the January air outside was sharp. Then she came over and laid a hand on Roger's arm, looking up at him.

"Do nothing hasty."

He stood big and dark, looking at her. Then, as if amused by her poise and persistence, he smiled and gave a nod. Her face lighted at winning a commitment from him, and she hurried out.

Anthony studied his brother.

"How far do you mean to carry this?" he asked.

Roger lifted his shoulders.

"I may push off for London after Twelfth Night, when the mumming's over."

"If Father keeps his promise, you could be left there with a flat purse, and be forced to join up as a gentleman volunteer for Flanders or Ireland after all."

"My loss and your gain, then," said Roger with pretended nonchalance.

Anthony frowned and shook his head.

"I can't understand you," he complained. "You've a lifetime for playing painter and you handle a sword as if born to it. Why all this wrath against a year in Ireland? Why hazard everything?"

Roger put the last of his brushes in their box, and closed the hinged cover. He had never talked much with Anthony about painting, and it was difficult for him to do so now.

"I've asked myself questions like those before today," he said after a moment, his eyes on his brother but looking past him. "To tell the truth, I feared something like what happened a few minutes ago." He paused as if to find the words he wanted. "When a man would excel in any difficult field," he went on, "they say a lifetime is none too much. Does he dare lose a year or more at the beginning, when he learns best and most quickly?"

Anthony nodded, somewhat impressed. Roger sat down on a stool, frowning. He was fighting a battle he had fought with himself before, but never to a decision.

"So, you see," he explained almost as much to himself as to Anthony, "it's a question of how much I care about it."

"Do you care enough to throw away land and title?" his brother demanded.

"When you put it into one neat question it seems mad

enough," Roger agreed. "But then," he added, "you are one who sums up the yeas and nays of a matter and takes the sensible way, like an answer in arithmetic."

There was no reproach in his words; they were a statement of fact. Anthony took them as such.

"Do you know a better way of deciding?" he asked.

Roger sat for a moment, again studying how to say what he felt.

"Why," he answered finally, "you can follow something inside you. I suppose it's like a matter of faith that men have died for often enough when put to the test. Or, if you will, it's a passion like gaming—no—that's a poor way to describe it. Some will show such a zeal for arms and war," he went on, feeling his way, "and at the university I saw those who had as tall a one for books." He shrugged. "I can't find the words for it."

"I think you have, somewhat," Anthony told him, "although as to it's being a way for me, I don't understand it. And what if you end up in London as I say, with no money or any way to get it?"

"I don't think I shall."

"Uncle Ned? You think that old Puritan would help you?"

He spoke of their mother's brother, a lawyer in the city. Between him and Sir John, for various reasons, there was little love.

Roger laughed and shook his head.

"I hadn't thought of him. I meant Bartolomeo. Last year the plague took his wife and children. He has no helper he values. He counts much on my joining him. He's promised we shall soon work as partners."

"After you've thrown your heritage away?"

"We didn't talk about that, of course. It wasn't in question. But it would make no difference with Bartolomeo."

Anthony studied his brother, thinking over what had been said. Then, true to Roger's description of him, he put the yeas and nays together and came up with the common-sense answer.

"I'll grant it all," he conceded. "You'll have a livelihood. You'll not have to sell your sword for bread. But in the name of sanity, where will you be? You'll have cast away a title and taken up a trade. You'll work with your hands. You may be straitened for money. You'll have small time for pleasure or friends, and perhaps even lose the esteem and company of your old fellows. Or would Trevor and Barton and Johns find this a happy change?"

Roger laughed wryly, half conceding the point.

"I'll say nothing about Lucy," Anthony went on. "You can see she doesn't like it. I suppose there's nothing left for me but to hope you'll come to your senses. You have twelve days for it."

"No; only five."

"He said Twelfth Night and a week."

"The business would come to talk again during the week, and I want no more quarreling. If I go to London, I'll go on Twelfth Night itself, after the masque has been played."

Anthony gave him a long stare.

"So you're still resolved on it."

"I've never been resolved. I said, 'If I go.' I see how this looks to you," Roger said quietly. "You seem to have forgotten what I said of *my* feeling."

"I think you are mad," said Anthony.

The two stared at each other. In their instinctive difference of attitude the explosive nature of the situation was again clear. Roger looked tired and almost haggard. He spread his hands in a half-hopeless gesture.

"It's a hard choice," he said.

"It wouldn't be for me!"

Roger nodded and with a sudden smile flung an arm about his brother's shoulders, pulling him toward the door.

"But you see, Anthony," he said, "it's not you who must choose."

II

MASQUE AND MYSTERY

Roger seated himself on the throne in the great hall. Lit by the rush-lights that sputtered at either end, the place looked dark and almost sinister. Even the gold on the throne and hangings for the Twelfth Night masque, to be staged in less than an hour, gleamed with a kind of menace. It would be different, he told himself, when the many branches of wax candles were lighted, bringing out the bright colors of the trappings he had painted and the red and green of holly that festooned walls and ceiling.

He stirred, and the tinkle of bells on his own sleeve, for he was in costume as the Lord of Misrule, seemed strangely loud. He listened as their music subsided, and then heard faintly the sound of tankards and laughter from the nearby chamber where his father and some chosen guests lingered over drink and talk after their supper. In a moment Lucy and the bevy of girls whom she was to lead would come in for a brief final run-through of their pantomime. This was perhaps the last time that he would sit in the hall alone.

It seemed to him as if a gulf divided all the past from the future. London lay less than fifty miles from Darrell Manor in Kent, and yet it was the distance between two strange worlds.

Roger had left this more familiar world before. He had spent two years at the university at Cambridge, coming home

in his eighteenth year, after his mother's death. He had ridden
to London a good half-dozen times, fascinated always by its
shops, its street cries, its gilded processions, by its playhouses
and ships and contagious energy.

But always he had come back to the smaller, quieter world
of the Manor. Even what he knew of the building of buildings
and the painting of wood, cloth and plaster: this too had been
a part of his home. The blue-eyed, suave Bartolomeo, as fair
in his Lombard coloring as any ancient Saxon, yet warm with
courtesy and quick emotion, had come to Darrell Manor and
stayed there off and on for more than two years, raising a fair
new hall in what he called the classical style, laying out pavilions, stables, walks and gardens. It was Bartolomeo who had
praised the sketches that Roger had made for a little lodge by
the pond.

"What!" the architect had exclaimed. "It is *bellissima*—
most beautiful. You have been to Paris? To Florence, perhaps?
Or you have been taught by one who studied there? No? Then
it is the gift in you, straight from God! Color, line—yes, they
have the ease, the sureness!"

The words had warmed Roger, and sent his imagination
soaring. No one had ever taken seriously the many sketches
he had made during his boyhood years, or at the university.
But Bartolomeo was excited about what he did, and made
him feel like a god who could bring into being statues, pal-
aces, gardens at the wave of a hand.

The Italian had insisted that Roger make finished plans for
the little building, and for the paved walk and the stone stairs
descending to the water. He had shown the young man how to
use the curious draughting instruments that he lifted lovingly
from leather-bound, plush-lined boxes. He instructed Roger
in the preparation of paints: the dry colors dissolved in oil for
the frames of the windows outside and for the door and carved

lintel above it; and others mixed with the whites of eggs for the frescoes on the walls within.

From the time when the Italian had seen those first sketches, Roger had worked steadily with him on the hall and on the grounds.

"You will learn much. None in England will know what you will know," the artist had promised.

Roger shifted his position in the purple throne and sighed.

He *had* learned much from Bartolomeo—more, the latter had said on leaving two months ago, than an apprentice commonly absorbed in a seven-year term of service. But tonight, the Twelfth Night after Christmas, the fortnight of festivities which all men in England observed, would close in a burst of folly, and he would put his life at the Manor behind him.

He thought of the masque that Anthony and he had planned for the evening. The group of fifteen girls should delight the guests. Fourteen would be clad in yellow gowns with purple figures that reversed the color pattern of throne and hangings. Lucy, in a golden harlequin's costume, would lead them. All would be masqued, of course, as was the custom.

The same number of young men would appear later to join them in the dance. Yes, the little revel would be delightful.

Not, perhaps, so gay and wholly captivating as the Masque of Summer that he had arranged a year and a half ago for the Queen. Bartolomeo had been on hand then to supervise and correct. The royal guest had applauded the dance of the nymphs—a dozen girls from almost as many nearby halls whom Bartolomeo had taught some simple steps and the trick of moving together. After it was over Elizabeth had called for the poet who had made the songs—young Taversham, who had studied with Roger at Cambridge and died since of the pestilence. Then she had asked for the artist. Bartolomeo, bowing low, proclaiming a painter who might become England's

The Queen had said as he knelt: "Look up, Master Darrell! Come, you have done well enough to hold your head high!"

Apelles, had pushed Roger forward. And the Queen had said as he knelt:

"Look up, Master Darrell! Come, you have done well enough to hold your head high!"

He had lifted his eyes at the command. He hoped he had not shown the sudden shock he felt as he saw at this near view the dyed hair and painted, wrinkled face above the priceless cloth and welter of jewels that were an old woman's useless weapons against age. He had kissed her withered hand.

Well, she was gone now, and the new King had come down from Scotland. There was strange gossip abroad about this James I. They said—

A burst of laughter broke in on his thoughts, and he looked up to find the costumed girls about him. Lucy was shaking her fool's sceptre in his face and laughing the loudest.

"What! A brooding Lord of Misrule? Shake your bells, Prince, and be merry with your lieges!"

Roger rose, laughing as he was bidden, and thought: "Let her be gay now. I'm glad I made Anthony promise not to tell her. She'll be furious tomorrow, when she finds I'm gone."

He lit a branch of candles from one of the torches and put the girls through their dance: slowly at first, to make sure that their entrance was right, then faster. He went over Lucy's part with her alone.

"You come in by yourself—three steps, quickly, then a leap. Then the tumble."

The last was a difficult thing for Lucy. She was not a born acrobat. But she had been determined, Roger and Anthony had worked hard to teach her the trick, and now she did it passsably enough.

Immediately after the tumble the girls were to dance in, singing. It was an old song that they all knew: that was best for the occasion. They would kneel to him and he would speak the words that ordained the rule of folly, and after that the young men would come leaping in. They were well-rehearsed; from that point on it would be easy.

"Good," Roger said at last, when he had followed through with the entire routine again. "Let's get away before the guests come in from supper."

The girls skipped off, and he went to see how Anthony was coming along with the young men. They might want some taming down before the masque began.

It was a different hall now that the candles were lighted and the crowd was assembled. It glittered and flashed with color, and Roger felt a thrill of pride as the trumpet sounded and he stalked toward his throne with three clowns holding up his long purple robe and cutting capers that brought shouts of laughter from the audience. He stood beside the royal chair, one of his followers struck a gong, and the laughter subsided.

The prince stands by his throne, the hour arrives
When folly and free laughter take the world,

he heard Anthony intone loudly from behind the curtains.

Where are his people? Let all of them appear,
All who would make misrule their rule and kingdom!

Then a shining figure darted forward, lithe and sure. The three steps—would she manage the tumble? She leapt, rose into the air like a bird or gleaming golden fish, landed true, and did it again!

The crowd roared approval. *Why, the girl's magnificent!* Roger had not thought such ease and abandon were in her! She must have outdone herself in the excitement of the moment. The other girls danced in, their voices lifting sweet and clear in song, and it was his own turn to speak.

But before he could utter a word, Roger saw the line of standing guests at the farther entrance to the hall buckle and break, and with a sharp "By your leave, sirs!" a figure, booted and hatted, burst into the great chamber. The seated guests turned about, muttering or twittering at the sudden interruption. Four or five more figures joined the first, and all stood there, doffing their hats.

Sir John sprang up, and turned around to look at them. There was little good will in his eyes, Roger guessed from the set of his broad back. And why should there be? Who were these intruders who had burst in upon the Twelfth Night festivities?

"Well, gentlemen, what brings you here?" Sir John was demanding sharply. Then, as if recalling the tradition of hospitality which hung over the entire holiday season, "You interrupt our festivities. Will you join us and share them?"

One of the strangers spoke up—a short, bearded, rather sour-looking fellow.

"Sir, we are sorry," he said in a rusty voice. "We seek a runaway boy. We know that he turned in these grounds, and we believe he is here in this hall."

"A runaway boy?" echoed Sir John. "If he is here and yours, you shall have him." He glanced around, as did every man and woman in the audience. "I see none here but those who are of this place, or their friends," Sir John continued. "What kind of a boy do you seek?"

"A slight lad," came the reply, "of a sandy complexion, a little to red."

"Has any one of you seen such a boy?" Sir John asked his friends and neighbors.

Again there was a murmuring and much looking about, then silence.

Roger himself scanned the hundreds of people in the hall, seeing only familiar faces, and the masked girls. Lucy, he noticed, was standing foremost among these, with her head turned a little aside, and her fool's sceptre slanted across her knee.

Sir John spoke again. "Gentlemen," he said, "I will bid you join us here, or be about your affairs. As to those that are sandy and somewhat to red, I am of such complexion myself." There was a smothered ripple of laughter. "I dare say there are others of like features here," he continued, "but they are none of yours, I think."

The strangers looked at each other, and the leader whispered with one of his companions. Then he spoke to Sir John.

"We will be on our way. We mean no discourtesy to you or to this company."

"Then God give you good fortune and a brave year to come," said the host without much heartiness, and watched while the intruders filed out.

The masque went on. While it progressed, Roger felt a strange uneasiness, as if he had seen something that was not as it should be. But he threw himself into his lines, and almost forgot his feeling as the crowd picked up its shattered mood of gaiety. Yet throughout the mummery something troubled him and he thought vaguely that it had to do with Lucy. He could not tell himself what it was, yet it kept teasing at his mind.

Anthony was tugging at his sleeve.

"Where's Lucy?" he asked. "Have you seen her since the play?"

Roger shook his head. "She's not with the other girls?"

"No. None of them has seen her. Where did she change?"

"Why, with the others, I suppose, in the West Room."

"No. It was crowded. She went somewhere else. And she hasn't been seen anywhere since the masque."

The brothers worked their way through the throng, and two sober-faced girls joined them as they came into the deserted gallery outside the hall.

"Let's look in the other rooms."

Roger took a candle from a niche at one end of the long passageway. This taper with several others further along gave only a feeble light, but there was probably none at all in the chambers to right and left. He turned to the first door, which led into a kind of ante-room where women guests were sometimes taken to use the mirror at its farther end. The place was empty, but a single lighted candle stood on a small table beneath the glass, and Roger paused, wondering.

"Someone has used this room," he said half aloud.

Then his eyes caught a movement of the arras to the right of the mirror, and he strode over and lifted it. There, on a narrow bench that had been shoved back of the hanging, a slight figure lay bound. Two forget-me-not blue eyes gleamed up at him. Lucy!

Roger and Anthony pulled out the bench, undid the strips of torn cloth that bound the girl to it, untied her hands and feet and took a gag from her mouth. It was the lid of a little powder box that was on the table. A knotted kerchief had bound it firmly above Lucy's tongue.

She sat up, working her mouth and rubbing her wrists. She was clad only in what she had worn beneath her harlequin's costume.

"My gown!" she exclaimed thickly before any of the others could say a word. She dived behind the arras, which bulged and wavered for a few moments; then she emerged fully if hastily dressed.

The others crowded about her.

"Are you hurt?"

"What happened?"

"Who bound you?"

Lucy was angry.

"Didn't you miss me?" she demanded. "Must I lie here a full hour trussed up like a pig for roasting?"

"How could we miss you?" retorted Anthony. "You appeared, or seemed to, played your part in the masque—"

"But I didn't!" she protested indignantly. "He—he *couldn't* have played the part! How would he know it?"

"Well," said Roger, "someone played it, and played it well. I might have guessed from the tumbles that something was wrong. I thought the occasion had inspired you, for whoever it was did two of them, and as easy as the wave of a hand."

"I marveled at that myself," murmured Anthony. "But what happened? Who was it? Where is—is 'he'—you said? Where's he now?"

"How can I tell you that?" snapped the girl. "I dressed here because it was crowded where the others were. I stepped back into the room after rehearsal for a kerchief, and someone seized my arm, twisted it behind me, clapped a hand over my mouth. Then—" the tears filled her eyes—"then he swore to kill me if I cried out, pushed me over to the table, bound the kerchief about my mouth, and made—made me take off my jester's habit. Then he bound me and tied me to the bench, as you saw."

"You didn't get a look at him?"

"Not a clear one. His hat was pulled down low over his face. He seemed to be a boy, but monstrous quick and strong. I saw the hair on his wrist. It was golden-reddish."

"The boy the strangers were looking for!" exclaimed one of the girls, and the others agreed. They told Lucy how the masque had been interrupted.

"That's what troubled me!" exclaimed Roger suddenly.

"What do you mean?" Lucy demanded.

"Why, all through the masque I had a sense of something wrong, something about you, but couldn't tell what it was. Now—looking at your wrist—it comes to me."

"What comes?"

"Just what you spoke of—the golden-red hairs on the wrist. Your wrist is as smooth as alabaster. I know now that I saw the gleam of those hairs, without realizing what I saw."

"A pity you didn't," snapped Lucy, and the others murmured agreement.

"It's plain enough what happened," volunteered Anthony. "This boy came through the grounds to the hall, crept in—for the doors were left open much of the afternoon—and was hiding somewhere while you were rehearsing. He saw what was done. After all, it's a simple part to play—no lines to speak, just the entrance, the leap, the tumble. He—"

"But how could he know she would come to this chamber?" broke in Roger.

"He didn't," Anthony answered quickly. "He'd come into it himself, and when Lucy appeared, what could he do? The rascal made up his mind to seize her, get her habit, play her part, then slip away in the confusion afterward. He used his own kerchief for the gag—it's not Lucy's. He used hers, torn in strips, for her wrists and ankles, and—let's see—" he looked about quickly—"yes, a napkin that lay on the table, which he tore and knotted, to bind her to the bench."

Anthony stooped down and retrieved a strip of cloth from the floor under the little table where it had been tossed.

"I spoke to her—or rather to him," put in one of the girls, "just before we danced in. He laid a finger on his lips, as if he was waiting for a signal and did not want to be disturbed."

Anthony spoke up again.

"Perhaps we should ride out and look for him," he said slowly. "A runaway, and one that would commit an act of violence—"

"Look for him!" broke in Lucy with scorn. "Where will you find him in the night? Do you think such a scamp can be tracked easily? He has ears. He can hear the hoofs of a horse."

They stood uncertain.

"And what of me?" she continued. "Must this tale be tossed about the neighborhood? The five of us know what happened. But need others? Let it be thought that I took the part," she urged, "and went into the garden for a time when the masque was over. Otherwise the tale will run about the whole shire, and I shall be laughed at for a year to come, or longer." She flushed with vexation at the thought. "It *must* be kept secret. Promise!"

The others looked at her, at each other.

"Why, she's right," Anthony nodded. "There's no need to talk about this. We'll say nothing of it—nothing at all!"

It was much later that night when Roger slipped out of the garden and made his way toward the gates. He had given instructions to his boy, Dick, and knew that his horse would be ready. He had promised the lad to send for him later from London, if he could. The guests had gone, Sir John had retired. Roger had said a pleasant enough good-bye to Lucy, with no hint that it might be for more than a day or two. He had left a letter for his father on the chest beside his bed. As he stepped along softly now on the grass beside the road he could hear the servants in the kitchen wing, where they were drinking up the last of the cider and doubtless talking of how the Twelfth Night ox had tossed the cake from his horns right into the hands of Tom the blacksmith's boy from the nearby village.

In spite of what had happened, Lucy had played out her part in the hours after the masque with spirit, even with gaiety. Roger had seen her accepting praise with an easy smile for her part in the performance. And although Anthony had taken Roger aside and begged him to put off his departure for at least a night, he had refused. The occasion was too pat for getting away unnoticed.

As he walked along, Roger found himself wondering about the boy who had bound Lucy and taken her part in the mumming. Who was he? The strangers had mentioned no names, and he did not know them. Why should a boy be running away from what presumably was his home? *Why are you?* his mind mocked him, and he smiled. What a bold thing the youngster had attempted—and carried off! Of course, it had been easy for him to slip away after the masque, when everything had been laughter and confusion.

Slip away! His thoughts swung back to his own departure. He was leaving against all custom—all reason, most of his friends would say. Was it good?

He told himself that he didn't know. The strong arguments were all for staying at Darrell Manor. He knew, for instance, what his old companions at college would have said to him about anyone forsaking his lands and title to work with his hands.

There was Trevor, finished with Cambridge and now a man about town in London. Roger had heard recently that he had found a place at Court. A triumph, for his income was not high. And he thought also of Barton, who followed Trevor like a shadow. Well, what would they say? Roger could see the latter peering at him, that lazy smile of his freezing in surprise, then widening again, for Trevor would recover in a flash.

"The Darrell madness!" he could hear the assured, clipped voice, for Roger had had some reputation for wildness at Cambridge. "Ho, Barton, a rescue! Our Roger has parted company with his senses, and will be off completely without them unless we stop him!"

And Barton, earnest-eyed Barton, would be appalled. To him the nobly-born were gods and those who labored for them little more than sheep or oxen.

At certain moments, Roger himself was appalled. The life of wealth and power which his family led—not great wealth or great power, but enough of both—that was the existence he knew. The other life seemed unreal, except as he had touched it through Bartolomeo. Yet from that little-known world of craftsmanship came the only argument he respected against leaving the ease, the station, the future authority he could have at Darrell Manor. And the argument was this: that his gift was to work with his imagination and the hands that were skilled to express it. Bartolomeo had made him feel the force of that assertion. Indeed, without ever saying a direct word about it, the Italian had convinced him that merely to have this gift was so tremendous a fact that it carried its own obligations with it, as wealth or royalty were supposed to carry theirs. Perhaps, indeed, there was no argument here, but a conviction, a compulsion that swept arguments aside.

Why else was he leaving? He did not enjoy opposing his father. It hurt him deeply, and he knew that his act would age Sir John. Yet something commanded him to go.

Lucy? He was less troubled there. He had vaguely expected to marry her, yet sometimes he was not quite sure about his feeling for her. She had always been pretty sure about him, and generally he had liked her to be. Yet at times she annoyed him. She seemed to assume a title in his affairs which he was not ready to deed over just yet. Now, with all his mind and feeling turned toward his art, marriage would have to wait. His going to London might tell him exactly what he felt for this lovely and sure-minded girl. It might even show in the end what she was prepared to sacrifice, if anything, for Roger Darrell the man as apart from Roger the heir.

He approached the appointed place: a clump of aspens not far from the gates. As he drew yard-near to them, he saw the solid shadow of Dick and the horse among the trees, the boy's hand on the restless animal's nose. Then another shadow loomed up that took shape as Anthony.

"So you're going, then."

"It's best so."

"Give the business more thought. I'll do what I can with Father."

"It's past that now, Anthony."

Their voices were low, but the words were clear and hard in the otherwise silent night. Roger inspected his mount. In the two large saddle-bags that hung one on either side he could see and feel that Dick had packed the things he had laid out. The portfolio of sketches was there among a few books and changes of clothing.

"I'll send a letter when I can find someone to take it to you," he told Anthony. "I'll go to Mrs. Lowe's, but you'd best address me at Uncle Ned's."

Anthony nodded.

"I'll write," he said. Then he added, "It is a mad thing, Roger, and you'll think better of it."

Roger did not answer. He gripped his brother's hand hard, then swung into the saddle and fastened his cloak. The weather was mild for January, but a rider would soon feel cold. He walked the horse along the grass for the short distance to the gates, the two others pacing beside him. When he reached the entrance there were a few words of farewell, he

touched spur to flank, and waved his hand as his mount broke into a canter.

The road was just soft enough with travel to give back very little sound. He rode on through a night that was utterly quiet save for the muffled hoofbeats. Above, a few stars winked through a light overcast. He heaved a sigh that was half-regretful, half-relieved. He had been divided within himself. Now he was ending that division. Even if doubts might still stir in him, his father would know nothing of them, or care if he knew. To Sir John, the act would be everything. Like it or not, Roger was leaving Darrell Manor for good.

He shivered a little at the thought, then shook himself and urged his horse to a faster pace. Let the anger, the reproaches, the sweeping penalties sink behind him and away! There was a challenge in the days to come, and beyond it a glory as high as any men had achieved—the glory of great creation in art that no Englishman had ever touched. He, Roger Darrell, was taking the way that might lead to it. Perhaps he would be the first of his land to challenge the genius of the Germans, Flemings, Italians. At least he had the opportunity. As he bent forward in the saddle his eyes flashed and the dark road seemed to funnel out into patterns of radiant light.

III

IMPULSE OF THE MOMENT

ROGER woke two mornings later as the milky London sun slanted through the leaded panes of his window. He got up in a cold room. He had not found lodgings with Mrs. Lowe, but she had directed him to a Mrs. Salter, on Little Wood Street, and he had taken chambers there.

That is, if they could be called chambers. The two rooms were both plain and small. The one in which he slept was little more than a closet. The other, opening off it, was of moderate size, with small windows and a low ceiling. Yet everything was clean, the simple furnishings were of good quality, and he paid only four shillings a week for lodgings, breakfast and supper. He had come with a lean purse: three pounds and some silver, and did not relish seeing it go too fast, although he counted on getting more money as soon as he was at work with Bartolomeo. He had found a stable for his horse not far away, but beyond the city wall.

It was a good location, he thought as he splashed his face with cold water, hurried into his clothes, and put powder on a cloth to cleanse his teeth and take away the taste of sleep. He was within the walled city that was the heart of London and held perhaps half her people. From his lodgings it was a comfortable walk to St. Paul's Church and its bookstalls; in the Blackfriars district near by were shops that sold materials for drawing and painting. At the same time he was near Cripplegate, one of the eight towered entrances, counting that by the Tower of London, in the great wall. If the fancy took him he could stride past the watchmen at the three-storied gate, reach his stable, and be galloping into the country in a matter of minutes.

He was about to look for his hostess and ask for a fire when there was a light knock on the door and she came in with a pitcher of hot water, a little brazier of glowing coals, and some beef, porridge, toast and warm ale.

"I heard you stirring about, Master Darrell," she said.

With tinder and coals she soon had a brisk wood fire blazing. She was a pleasant woman—a widow with one child, a boy. Her husband had been a joiner, but she had sold the shop after his death. Now, Mrs. Lowe had said, she lived well enough on what she had realized from that, eked out by the rents from a few rooms in her house. Just now, Roger had learned, there was only one other lodger—a sedate young silversmith who, Mrs. Salter assured him, would give no one any trouble.

As he ate his breakfast, Roger re-read the last letter he had received from Bartolomeo. He also studied a crude map which the artist had drawn to show the location of his house in the Bankside, across the Thames River from the city, on the southern shore. The young man had thought of visiting his uncle first. While he had seen the grave lawyer only half a dozen times in as many years, he had felt an instinctive friendliness for him. Because of Sir John's discouraging contempt for his brother-in-law "—a book-slaving, close-mouthed Puritan," was the nobleman's phrase for him—Roger had never found an opportunity to know Edward Vance, but now he meant to make one. There was a directness and independence about his uncle that he liked, and Vance lived near Aldersgate, at no great distance from where he sat. But, he decided in the end,

Uncle Ned was probably busy during the day in one of the courts or at his chambers. Besides, the first thing was to see Bartolomeo. All the future rolled out from that meeting. The Italian should be expecting him. He had sent a letter to him five days ago, telling of his father's command and his own difficult but probable decision.

On this short January day London was a more sober place than Roger had remembered it from his other visits. Of course, the light had been longer then, and stronger, too, he told himself as he walked along the cold, cobbled streets, for he had always arrived in summer or autumn. Also, the crowds had been swelled then by thousands of others coming like him from the country. Still, with all this conceded, the thoroughfares seemed empty, the passers-by withdrawn and cheerless, and the shops short of customers.

Then he remembered: for almost a year the plague had been raging in the city. The new King, coming down from Scotland the spring before, had avoided the stricken capital and drifted from one great noble's country seat to another's, waiting. They expected him soon now, Mrs. Salter had said at breakfast, for plague deaths were few. Perhaps he would come by March.

Roger went toward the river by way of St. Paul's, and soon he entered a busier and more cheerful area. Just north of the great church, on Cheapside, the liveliest shopping street of the city, he saw two roped off areas that looked like the foundations of small but important buildings. Stones and timbers were piled there, and a group of workmen surrounded a craftsman who seemed to be giving them directions.

"Why, sir, it's one of the great arches," an apprentice told Roger readily. And seeing that this meant nothing to his questioner: "For the King, sir, when he makes his progress through London. All this was begun last April, sir—five arches to do him honor on his way. But His Majesty not coming to the city, it was all given over. Now they will begin again, and perhaps build seven instead of five. This one will rise twenty yards above the street."

Roger shook his head at the magnificent plan, and remembered that Bartolomeo had spoken of possible work on some structure to honor the new King. Would he himself have a hand in it?

He went on into the large churchyard, where the printers had set out their books on trestles, and apprentices were singing out the titles of recent volumes and pamphlets. Ballad-mongers, too, were crying their wares—printed sheets celebrating in rhyme the latest murders, voyages and wars.

"The true tale of the taming of Tyrone and the defeat of the Irish rebels!"

"The prodigious deeds of an English Captain among the islands of New Spain!"

"A ballad of the murderer of York, and a wife slain and fed to swine!"

Roger barely glanced at the wares they waved at him, turning instead to the cathedral itself.

He entered it and looked up the great central aisle. Here, in the open or by various pillars, men were promenading or standing about in groups, gossiping or transacting business. He knew that his uncle frowned on both customs, saying that the great church was no place for chit-chat or the striking of bargains. He spoke indignantly of the money changers in the temple, and would never meet a client at St. Paul's, as was the custom with many men of law. Well, thought Roger as he stood within the arched entrance, it was a just point, even though the changing parade of gallants, merchants, adventurers and food-vendors who thronged the aisle never failed to fascinate him with its preposterous color and variety.

It was at St. Paul's, he knew, that men made appointments, or came to find acquaintances by chance; for in the middle hours of the day most of London's men about town poured into the building for news or business. Bills were posted on pillars, some printed, some in flourishing script. Even as his eye swept over the great interior of the church this morning, he saw groups of curious loiterers bunched about these advertisements. And as he walked down the aisle, catching now a whiff of perfume, now the odor of an unwashed body, bravely dressed young men drifted past him, talking of the Court or the campaign in the Low Countries or of voyages to the strange new land of Virginia.

"—and so took three Spaniards, getting enough gold in ransom that a man might stagger carrying it away—"

"—stinking of myrrh and cassia. But catching a flash of her eyes above the fan, I went briskly to the attack—"

"—cargo of sassafras roots, which for the labor you shall spend are as rich a cargo as silver—"

And coming back on the other side of the pillars, Roger noted a weird variety of tradesmen or agents displaying cloth, laces, swords, or heard men taking notes for lawsuits, or talking of astrology or the new art of smoking—

"Oh, as to the lining, sir, absolute silk—"

"And having taken the goods does now deny and refuse all further settlement—"

"—and will predict for you, sir, by the stars, the perfect day and hour to commence your action—"

"—teaching the very best manner of taking this weed, as taught him by two Indian kings!"

In the midst of this hubbub of gossip and salesmanship Roger saw a staid clergyman with five or six fresh-cheeked choir boys pass on their way to some business presumably less of the world. It seemed as if he watched, played out in miniature, a drama of the teeming life of his land.

Finally Roger went on toward the river, to St. Paul's Gate, or wharf, where he bargained with a boatman, and was soon being oared across the clear water to the Bankside. The day was crisp and sunny, swans floated on the broad stream, he caught a glimpse of a brown fish darting deeper into the crystal flood beneath him. Before him, across the slow current, he could see plainly the trees and dwellings on the farther shore. There rose the crests of two playhouses, taller than the houses about them, and a little further to the right the Bear Garden, where trained mastiffs were loosed on snarling wild animals to the roar of crowds. Down river, to his left, loomed the arch of houses and turrets that filled the length of London Bridge, a little city in itself strung across the river on stone supports. Here men ground grain and kept shop and wives hung out their washings, while the traffic surged to and fro along the narrow passageway under their windows.

Roger landed and made his way through the houses and gardens, along ditches that drained the low ground near the stream, some of which not long since had been nothing but marshland. He followed Bartolomeo's map, and thought at last that he had found the house. It was a rather large one, with a garden at the rear. But it seemed strangely desolate, and he noticed with a start that the windows of the first story were shuttered. From above, others looked down on him coldly, seeming to stare blankly from their dozens of little square or diamond panes. Was Bartolomeo away on some commission he had suddenly received, or had he merely shuttered himself in for privacy's sake?

Roger mounted a short flight of steps that led to the stout door, and lifted the knocker. There was no answering stir from within, although he banged the iron hard against its base. He came down the steps after several attempts, and stood uncertainly in the lane before the house. A fresh-faced, sturdy fellow in a worn servant's livery lounged by the dwelling next door and stared at him. Then he spoke.

"Be you looking for the Italian?"

Roger nodded. "Master Bartolomeo," he said.

"Aye, that's him," the man agreed. "I could never keep the foreign sound of it in mind. You'll lose labor, Master, seeking him."

"But this is his house?"

"Nay, I think it be none of his," the other answered stubbornly with a shake of his head.

"It is marked here plain enough on the map he sent me," said Roger, studying the sheet of paper. "I had it from him only a fortnight since."

"A fortnight since," repeated the man, smiling in a secret fashion. "Why, then you had it right enough, and yet it is none of his, neither."

"What do you mean, fellow?" Roger asked sharply.

"Why, only that houses be owned by living men," replied the servant, "and this Master Bar—Bartolow, or whatever it may be, has gone his way, and owns no house but the narrow one we shall all get in our time, in the ground."

He crossed himself and eyed Roger with something like triumph.

"He's dead?"

"Aye, sir. Three days since."

Roger stared at the man, open-mouthed.

"Be you kin of his?" the latter asked.

"A friend only." The news had numbed Roger, but he fought against its paralyzing strength. "But who owns the house now?" he asked. "And how did he die? Of a sickness?"

The man shook his head as if he had no sure knowledge.

"A sickness they say it was. Some called it the pestilence. There's been much of that about. But I hear also that the doctor said it was none of the plague, but a kind of stroke. That's a natural thing, sir, for these lively foreign folk, forever waving their arms and talking like men possessed. But I know this: the provost came hard on the doctor's going, and with him a black-suited lawyer's man, and they locked and shuttered the place two days ago, and I've seen nor heard no more of them, nor of any other until you came a-knocking."

"Where's your master?"

"Gone to the city, sir; but you'd get less from him than from me. He was little at home, this Italian, since the plague took his wife and his two boys." He sighed. "There be many strange folk in the Bankside, sir," he complained. "I desire acquaintance with few of them. There's your boatman, ready with his fists and roaring oaths to make a man blench. There's the spendthrift sailors, and old soldiers quick to bully or rob. Players and painter-folk there are, and such as write plays or tracts and make a living from air and ink and paper, you might say; and there are rogues about the inns that live on the wrong side of the law. Between them they'll beat a man's body and abuse his mind, and I say that an honest fellow must look to himself if he walk among them."

Roger nodded. He knew that the Bankside had a poor enough reputation, but he was in no mood to discuss it with an ignorant and garrulous servant. He thanked the man and walked slowly away, as dazed as if he had just been knocked to the ground by a blow.

He trudged aimlessly along the river shore; he did not know for how long. It was no ordinary emotional shock that he was feeling; for that Roger would have found poise and control. But this event seemed to sweep away both the guide and the center for the life he had planned to lead. He could not believe it.

Bartolomeo gone! Yesterday the sense of him had been as bright and warm as sunlight; now it was out like a pinched candle flame. He remembered their long hours together, and these seemed somehow more a reality than the blankness of the present. Much of what he had become was Bartolomeo. What he had hoped to be began with this buoyant craftsman and teacher.

Bartolomeo explaining the principles of design: the central point of interest, the balancing elements, the simplicity of the classical style as against the lawlessness (or so the Italian had argued) of the Gothic. "You lead always back to the simplicity. That is the great principle. The color, ornament—they have a value, yes, but only to embellish, to make the important truth more vivid and important." Bartolomeo explaining the nature and proper treatment of colors: what agents worked best with each, how they should be mixed and applied to make them endure. There were secrets that few or none in England but Bartolomeo possessed; these Roger had been taught, himself in turn pledged to secrecy.

And now it was gone: the knowledge and force and splendid animation which had been this man. And Roger himself seemed to stand before some high, blank wall barring his way. Or was it a dense bank of fog in which sight and sense of direction alike were smothered?

More than an hour later he stumbled into an inn, toyed with food and drink, sitting near others who ate and talked and laughed as if this day were like any other. Once he noticed a group of four taking the new weed tobacco in silver pipes, and smelled the curious fragrance of its smoke. Again he roused himself when a quarrel broke out at the farther side of the room. At length the place was emptied of all but him, and he paid his reckoning and left his scarcely tasted food. The sun was low when he reached the river and took a barge for the city.

At the other side the boatman demanded double the fee Roger had paid going over, but he gave what was asked, numbly aware that he should have agreed upon a price before embarking. He climbed the stone steps and was back in the walled town, whose gates would close in half an hour, at sundown.

He stood at the top of the quay taking deep breaths of air. The stupor in which he had moved for the last few hours was lifting. His mind came back into focus and he felt the blood running freely in him again. But to what purpose? *You're in London, Roger Darrell, but why did you come to London? It was Bartolomeo, wasn't it? And Bartolomeo isn't here. He isn't here!* It was as if an audible voice spoke the words, and with it a gate clanged down before him. He shook himself, stubbornly pushing back the sense of defeat and futility, and started walking briskly, almost angrily, toward his lodgings.

He was passing a little alley when his eye caught a swift movement, and his ear a flurry of sound. There was a scuffle, and low but angry voices. A sturdy fellow with a sword at his thigh and the look of a soldier was stalking a boy, and had moved in as if to seize him. But as he did, Roger saw the boy make a swift movement and suddenly the man was hurtling through the air, to land on the stones of the street with a spatter of curses.

The boy was at Roger's side.

"Sir, help!" he begged. "As you are a gentleman, sir, do not let this man take me!"

The other was already up and at hand.

"The boy is mine!" he shouted angrily. "He comes with me, so stand aside, young sir, as you have regard for the law!"

"Sir, help!" he begged. "As you are a gentleman, sir, do not let this man take me!"

"The law!" exclaimed the boy contemptuously. "Sir, I never saw this man until now, and I think he is a cutpurse or hired ruffian. He forced me into the alley here and would have seized me!"

"Because you are my master's!"

"Sir, I think he is one that hunts boys for the players' companies!" the youngster protested quickly. "Not two years ago such a fellow was punished by the Queen's Star Chamber for seizing a gentleman's son, but now they have come out of their holes again and grow as bold as ever!"

"Why, you lying puppy!" cried the man with suppressed fury. "I'll teach you to sing a different tune! Stand aside, sir!" And he glared at Roger, who had moved between the boy and him.

"Wait!" It was a formidable Darrell, a black Darrell, who spoke. Roger had his doubts as to which of the two was telling the truth, but his impulse was to stand by the hunted one, the outcast. He knew that boys had indeed been kidnaped for the children's player troupes, sometimes even from gentle homes, to be trained as actors and singers.

"If the boy is yours," he told the man, "come with me to the nearest provost and put your claim to law."

"Why should I go begging to the law for what's already mine?" demanded the other with a frown.

"Why shouldn't you? If he's yours, you can prove it and have him. For all I know, your claim is no better than that of any other man who might step up and make one."

The stranger's frown deepened into an ugly scowl. He laid a hand on his sword hilt with an oath.

"I have no time for London constables! I'll take the boy, and no more words from you, unless you'll talk with iron."

Roger's own hand went to his sword. The calmness of a cold anger edged the words he found himself saying with an inner start of surprise.

"By your leave, it shall be my way or none."

The two blades exploded from their scabbards almost as one, and the stranger's leaped so fast that it nicked Roger's doublet as he shed his cloak and stepped aside. Then came the rasping clash of steel. Roger saw at once that he faced an adept workman, and he parried swiftly and vigilantly. He had had enough of sword-play—at home, near the university, and best of all with Bartolomeo. There were certain tricks in the Italian style— He gave ground under a furious assault, then launched one of his own. *Now wait him out, wind him, watch for the moment! Then try the Paduan Counter—it's unknown in England, Bartolomeo swore.* He stood on the defensive, while the stranger's attack came smooth and strong. *Blast the fellow! He pours it in like a torrent! The position of the blades must be perfect, the wrist steel-strong, the execution lightning fast—hah!* Suddenly the half-second of opportunity was there. He put all the force of his wrist into the parry, then lanced his blade up and out in a flash. He felt it going home. The lunging stroke not only pierced and paralyzed the stranger's arm, as intended, and sent his weapon clattering to the stones, but also drove him off balance, so that the man fell hard on the cobbles, his head striking against them with a thud.

There was a sudden stillness. Except for scratches in practice, Roger had never wounded an opponent before. He bent over the motionless body, half astonished and half appalled. He heard a groan. Down the alley a casement opened, and a man's voice broke the quiet.

"What's here? Murder! The watch, the watch!"

Roger felt a tug at his sleeve.

"Sir, he's only stunned. Quick! You can come to harm if you stay here."

Roger responded almost automatically, sheathing his

weapon and hurrying along the street with his urgent companion.

"This way, sir—to Cheapside. We'll be safe there!"

Rapidly they turned a corner, then another, then slowed to a walk as they found themselves among merchants closing their shops and citizens briskly making their way homeward. In a few minutes they were at the lower end of Little Wood Street.

"Come with me," Roger said on impulse. "I have lodgings on this street."

In the larger of the two rooms a fire was burning, and man and boy took off their cloaks. Roger motioned his guest to a seat.

"Now, my young friend," he said almost grimly, "off with that hat and let me have a look at you."

The boy took off the soft-brimmed headpiece which he had pulled down rather low and faced his host calmly. He had a mop of sandy hair and a complexion which would have seemed delicate except for the freckles that spattered his cheeks and nose. He flushed, then grinned a friendly grin.

"Thanks," he said in a low, pleasant voice. "I think Wickard would have made off with me if you hadn't stopped him."

Roger stared at the youngster. He had begun to wonder if the bold boy who had visited Darrell Manor on Twelfth Night was not sitting before him, but the other's words jolted the idea from his mind for a moment.

"So you know his name," he said accusingly. "You swore you'd never seen the man before."

"I hadn't," the boy retorted promptly, "except at a distance. He came just before I left—I mean, before I left the second time."

Roger frowned impatiently.

"This makes no sense to me," he pointed out. "Tell me a tale I can follow. Who are you, in the first place?"

"Cedric Wales," the other replied, with an air of being unjustly reproached. "And it wasn't true—what I said about his trying to seize me for the players."

"Then why did you say it?"

Roger spoke sharply. He was beginning to think that he had been something of a fool in acting on the impulse of the moment.

"Because you wouldn't have helped me if I hadn't," Cedric was saying with wide eyes. "I couldn't explain what had happened—not there. I had to get rid of *him* first. But I knew that if I *could* explain, you'd understand it soon enough."

"Explain it now, then, and see if I do."

The boy nodded.

"Sir," he began, "I ran away from my guardian. I ran away twice. The second time I got clean away."

"Then Wickard, as you call him, *did* act for your guardian, and had full right to take you into custody."

"No!" The boy was indignant. "If my brother had been there—my half-brother Ralph—it would never have happened. He'd have stopped it."

"Stopped what, in the name of patience?"

"He'd have stopped Bragdon from trading me off like a horse or an ox—from marrying me for a few hundred pounds profit!"

"Marry *you?*"

Roger looked with utter incredulity at the boyish face and slight figure before him. He knew, of course, that grooms who were even younger had gone through the forms of marriage. But that was mere policy—something for dukes or princes. Actually looking at a possible child husband, he felt a shock of disbelief and almost horror.

Cedric smiled a little.

"He hasn't done it yet, sir," he reminded Roger. "But do you not know what guardians in this land of England may do with their wards?" he continued with a boyish frown. "What force has one like me, without parents, against a stranger who rules him by the decree of a court—someone who thinks only of looting my inheritance for his own pocket, and tying me to one I could never cease to loathe?"

His eyes flashed and his lip quivered with indignation.

"Why, I *have* heard of such abuses," conceded Roger slowly, "although never yet—but why do you say 'a stranger'? Isn't your guardian a relative—an uncle or cousin at least?"

"He's no kin to me whatever!" snapped the boy. "Bragdon's not even kin to Ralph, being the husband of *his* mother's sister!"

Roger felt somewhat flustered with this flourish of non-related relationship. He looked at Cedric again. The large, gray-blue eyes met his own frankly, an honest flush seemed to darken the freckles on cheek and nose. He felt wholly convinced of the boy's earnestness, felt a thrill of admiration for his spirit. This lad would have had the audacity and resolution to manage the business of gagging and binding Lucy and taking her part in the masque, and Roger found himself ready to excuse that act, if it were indeed Cedric's, as the device of one in desperate straits. He was convinced that the boy's tale of his guardian's cruelty was true. He knew that the English law still gave guardians great powers with respect to their wards. Custom had established humane treatment as the usual practice, but an unscrupulous man could still make profit from a minor, and might resort to cruel acts which would be condoned or approved by a court.

"Let's look at this business again," he said finally. "Your

father and mother have both died, and this fellow Bragdon is guardian to your half-brother by right of a marriage relationship."

"And to me. Ralph would be my guardian if of age, but he isn't, and *his* guardian acts for him until he is twenty-one."

Roger nodded.

"You've the same father?"

"Yes. Ralph's mother was father's first wife. She died about a year after Ralph was born. Four years later, sir, my father married *my* mother. But she too died while I was yet a child. Father and Ralph reared me."

"That's hard—to lack a mother."

"I hardly knew one, sir. And they were monstrous kind to me. All that they did, I did. That is how I have more skill than most boys in wrestling and like matters. For as a young man my father had traveled in Eastern lands, and learned many tricks that few if any in England know. He was forever teaching us such sport, as he called it. That's how I learned to send a man flying through the air when he seized me."

"You sent Wickard flying quickly enough."

"Quickly enough," agreed Cedric calmly, "but not hard enough."

Roger laughed.

"You've a cold way of looking at things for one of—let's see —twelve years?"

"Thereabouts, sir," agreed Cedric. He did not respond to the laugh. "If I am cold toward another's hurt," he added, "it is because those who are supposed to protect me have taught me I had best be ready to protect myself, and not be soft with any who abuse me."

Roger thought of no answer to that, and shifted the talk.

"You say Bragdon would make an ill marriage for you. Why is it so ill?"

"Because he would mate me to one more than twice my age. And because I myself would have a voice in the business of my own marriage," answered Cedric composedly. "Had Ralph been here, he would have stopped the business."

"Yet it's lawful, isn't it?" Roger asked of the proposed match.

"I mean to find out if it is."

Again Roger felt a thrill of admiration for the boy's courage. But he kept to what was practical.

"Can you learn that in London?"

"Where else? Sir, my old nurse's brother is a serving man to Sir Thomas Cheney. I was bound for his lodgings, hoping for help. But Bragdon must have guessed I might go there. Wickard was waiting for me."

"So that's a closed door," Roger mused.

Cedric bent his head in agreement. His face was troubled.

"Oh, sir," he begged, "you have helped me already. Help me again. Bring me to a good lawyer. Don't take me to the provost!"

"Perhaps I *should* take you there," answered Roger without too much conviction. "But my uncle is a lawyer. A good man, although said to be of the Puritan faction, and perhaps over-scrupulous—"

"Yet he'd at least hear me!"

"I think he would." Roger rose and began pacing the room. *Confound the boy! He has claimed protection where it can't be denied. I've fled authority myself—first from my father's command, now from the law. How can I betray someone in danger for a stubbornness like my own?* He fetched up at last with a sigh, annoyed but baffled.

"I'll not take you to the provost," he said gruffly. He checked Cedric's glad cry, and began to tell the boy something of his own situation. He described his choice between service in Ireland and Bartolomeo, explained the probable penalty for the choice, related what he had found that morning when he went to report to the Italian in the Bankside.

"So," he concluded, "if it's any comfort to have the help of one with little in his purse, with no friends to count on, and no sure prospect for the future, that comfort you have."

"You'll find a way, sir," Cedric told him with admiring eyes. "And I'll not be a burden to you. I have gold—not much, but it will serve for a while. Cannot I be your page?" he continued, the idea coming to him as he talked. "It would be for a time only. Perhaps there's an attic room even in this house—"

"Why, you can sleep in this one," cut in Roger.

"Oh, I couldn't do that!" Cedric protested, vigorously shaking his head. "There's little room here, and you'll want no one in your chambers. If you brought friends here, it would be an annoyance were I about. No, I couldn't do it."

"Well, if Mistress Salter has a place for you, I dare say you'll be better in a room of your own," Roger agreed carelessly, glad to have his privacy. "I'll tell her you're to stay with me for a week or two."

"And to serve you."

"And to serve me," Roger agreed, "though you'd better keep to your room for some days, or at any rate to the house. If your guardian's man was looking for you once, he or others will be on the watch again."

"With his arm pierced through by the thrust you gave him, he will not watch for a week or two, I think," replied Cedric calmly. "But as for caution, sir, you yourself will do well to use some."

"I?"

"Didn't you come between me and my guardian's man, and oppose and wound him?" demanded the boy seriously. "The blame is all mine," he added apologetically, "yet it might be a serious matter against you, and Bragdon is vengeful."

Roger stared at his young guest.

"You have old thoughts for one young in years," he said.

Cedric looked at him calmly.

"They have a saying in my country," he remarked. "It goes: 'The motherless fox pup learns fast.'" Then when he saw that Roger had the point, "For that matter, it's easy to see you must go carefully now."

"I must find my uncle," Roger muttered. He knew that Cedric was right: if he had put himself where Bragdon could have the law on him, then he must indeed be careful as to what he did and where he went. He thought for a moment.

"I must run the risk of their knowing me," he declared at last, "and with Wickard abed for a week, the danger may be small. But let's study the tale we are going to tell about you, and then seek out our hostess." He grinned at Cedric. "We're in this together, lad, like it or not. And I don't know which is in the deeper."

Cedric flashed him an answering smile.

IV

"YOU YOURSELF ARE
YOUR FORTUNE"

EDWARD VANCE laid down the letter from Anthony which
Roger had given him to read, and looked at his nephew
soberly.

"You seem to have found a sure way to my brother John's
displeasure," he remarked dryly. "From this letter I should
say there was small chance of your making peace with him."

"That is only half of the trouble," Roger answered heavily.
"For even if he'd receive me again, I must ask myself if I
could and would return."

The two were sitting in a room of his uncle's house, a
spacious chamber furnished simply but with quality. The
chairs they sat in were finished with tooled leather. Instead
of the usual rushes, clean matting was spread on the floor—
a covering new in England, and expensive. In a case near
by against the wall stood an imposing array of books in leather
bindings of different colors. Roger noted Sidney's *Defense of
Poesie,* Holinshed's *Chronicles,* and Harington's translation
of *Orlando Furioso,* along with Perkins's *Laws of England*
and other volumes, some in Latin and French, bearing on his
uncle's profession. The sparkling sack which Edward Vance
had poured from a glass decanter—again a relative novelty
in England—into matching goblets was of the best quality.

The total effect was one of simplicity, yet it was an elegant simplicity; and Roger found himself thinking that if his grave kinsman was a Puritan he was an unusual one.

Roger had not found his uncle at home on the night of his encounter with Cedric. Perhaps it was just as well; for on the following day two letters had come for him: one from Anthony and one from Lucy.

The latter was a mixture of reproaches and cajolery: he was mad, she had written, and what he had done would require much undoing: "yet it is not past mending, Roger, and I will soon play your advocate with Sir John. I wait only until he has cooled somewhat, and regrets your going more than he is angered by it, and so will be open to reason." Roger had not shown this message to his uncle.

Anthony was less encouraging.

"He has cast you out, he swears, and will listen to nothing. I am to take your place with Sir Ralph, who tarries in War-wickshire, and does not purpose to lie in London until two weeks past the time he formerly set. I think our father has plans of betrothal for me, too; there also I am to fill your place—a matter not to my liking. On both points I will labor hard on your behalf as I have word from you that I may. Yet to be blunt, it will be a difficult business, for I never saw him more resolved."

Roger himself was still shaken by what had happened since his arrival in London. He knew that all common sense shouted at him to return and seek a reconciliation. His respect for his father, all his feelings as a son, urged him to do it. He was the heir. His defiance had wounded Sir John deeply—was against both love and duty as young men of the age understood these in the family relationship.

Yet the strong conviction that had brought him to the capital remained. It was even strengthened by what had happened since he arrived. A curious sense of obligation to Bartolomeo troubled him. *Now more than ever you are bound to justify his faith in you! If he was right when living he is right today!* And there was the mere stubborn desire to prove himself. *Why did you come? Was what you felt a flash of flame and smoke, ending suddenly like a piece of fireworks? Will you run back now with your first bad fortune?* These feelings sank and flared in him. He spoke the literal truth when he told his uncle that beyond any decision by his father lay one he himself must make.

Yet if he were to decide to stay, he was desperately uncertain as to what he could do. He had come to work with Bartolomeo, and Bartolomeo was gone.

Roger had brought a portfolio of sketches, and Edward Vance examined them with care. At times Roger thought he saw evidences of appreciation, but there had been no word as yet about that. The drawings lay on the table near which the two were seated. And now his uncle was speaking again.

"Yes, I suppose you find it difficult to put by your pride," he said in answer to Roger's confession that he was doubtful of returning in any case. "And also," Vance added quickly, "the love for the work you came here to do. For that must have been great indeed to push you into the course you took. And so far as I can tell, you have some cause for pursuing the work. But—"

"But I should be a fool, you'd say, to do it!"

The older man lifted a protesting hand.

"I have not said so," he answered. "It is true that to return and try to patch up a peace is what most men would call your only reasonable course. But most men would also have called your coming here in the first place an act of madness. However," he continued, weighing the factors in his lawyer-like way, "your position has now worsened. When you arrived you depended upon an assurance of work, further training, advancement, made by your friend Bartolomeo. Such prospects no longer exist."

Roger agreed gloomily.

"Therefore," Edward Vance went on relentlessly, "you are now left to your own devices. You yourself must be your own fortune if you stay here. I know little of what you can expect, for I have small acquaintance with such architects and painters as we have in England. Theirs is a profession followed mostly by others than our countrymen."

"But more Englishmen turn to it every year," Roger asserted.

"That may be," said his uncle dryly.

There was a brief silence. *You yourself must be your own fortune.* It was not a wholly comforting thought.

"You—you think advancement is all but impossible, then?" Roger asked at length.

The lawyer looked at him intently, as if asking him to see the outlook with complete honesty.

"I think it may be the extreme of difficulty," he answered, "and something that at first you may have to win by humble labor. I believe that for most of those who seek to prove themselves in painting or architecture, a long apprenticeship is required."

"But Master Bartolomeo said that I had gone as far or farther than most apprentices!"

"It is a point; but will others accept it?" His uncle looked at him sharply. "It seems to me that you must set all possible difficulties and impediments on the one side, to be weighed against your wishes and hopes on the other. You may be called upon to forget your gentility for a time at least, to assume the status of craftsman from which your great-grandfather rose."

Roger bowed.

"I've thought of that," he admitted.

"Think of it again." Edward Vance held his nephew with hard eyes. Then he reflected a moment, and his eyes softened.

"I will say this: there are great changes taking place today in England. The old forms of life are breaking down with the printing of books and the discovery of new lands beyond the seas. Men rise to eminence in new fields. They rise in old ones where once they could not rise. They are freer than they were, and they will win new freedom." His eyes shone as if he saw a vision. "There will come a day when rank and name will be small things compared with the talent a man can show, when we shall follow the spirit of our nobler laws and shake off a hundred, no, a thousand oppressions that are still practised by those in authority. God did not create man to be a tyrant over his brother man!" he concluded with a burst of conviction.

Roger felt a thrill run down his spine, then saw that his uncle was smiling a somewhat rueful smile.

"I speak of a golden day that is only in the grayest dawn," he remarked quietly. "Yet it grows, and you will mark the brightening in your time. And if you have the courage to follow such work as you will, I do not say that you will follow it in vain. Only you should face stanchly the hazards and labor which will surely be yours if you hold to such a purpose."

"I'll face a thousand hazards and unending labor if I can see where they lead!" exclaimed Roger. "But I don't know how I can come to them," he added. "I don't even know where to begin."

"Why, you can begin with those who practice what you would practice yourself," said his uncle calmly. "I had some business not long ago with one in the Bankside," he went on. "It concerned making a monument for the widow of a client.

I arranged to have this done by a Master Johnson, an Englishman, though his father, who still lives and works somewhat, is a Fleming. There are two of the sons, Nicholas and Garrett. They have done other work besides stone monuments—chapels, paintings, arches and pavilions. I could write a letter to Master Nicholas Johnson, with whom I dealt. If he can do no better, he can give you some advice."

"If you'll write tonight, I'll wait upon him tomorrow!"

Edward Vance nodded.

"It is possible," he continued, "that you could find employment at one of the playhouses. They come to my mind because the shop of the Johnsons lies close to the best known of them, the Globe."

"You—*you* bid me seek work at a playhouse?" Roger asked, thinking of the great hostility that had been shown by Puritan leaders in London to the theaters of the city and all who worked in them.

Edward Vance smiled.

"I'm not one of your ranting Puritans," he told his nephew. "My interest in reforming the Church is not to make it a bare and ugly thing, but one freer for the spirit. I'm not alone in that. Nor have I withdrawn from the Church because I dislike the course of its leaders. I am not a recusant."

This was news to Roger, but he nodded.

"As to plays," Vance went on, "I hold them to be instruments of good—if rightly used. Why," he exclaimed, kindling, "this same poet Christopher Marlowe, whom men call an atheist, wrote a noble warning to sinners in his *Dr. Faustus*. There is good doctrine in that tragedy. Faustus asks Mephistopheles how it comes that he is out of hell, and the fiend replies,

> Why, *this* is hell, nor am I out of it.
> Thinkst thou that I who saw the face of God

And tasted the eternal joys of heaven
Am not tormented with ten thousand hells
In being deprived of everlasting bliss?"

The lawyer recited the sonorous lines with relish, and smilingly pointed a finger at his nephew.

"If you look through all the tracts on religion published this last twelvemonth," he announced, "you'll find no words truer or more glorious than those!"

Then he burst into laughter as Roger stared at him.

"You'll change your opinion of me with better acquaintance, Nephew," he promised, still laughing. "And of many a so-called Puritan, for that matter. No, there will come a day when playhouses will be put to their true use of instructing the people, as they have been already in plays about English history written by Master William Shakespeare and others. Well, enough of that. Nicholas Johnson can perhaps tell you of opportunities at the Globe or Fortune or in connection with the Court entertainments they say our Scottish King enjoys and will provide abundantly."

He turned to the table, where an ink-horn lay, with several pens and some sheets of paper. He examined one of the quills, found it to his taste, and began writing.

Roger made his way home with a wary eyes for marauders that might lurk in the dark streets, marveling as he walked at the new glimpse he had had of Edward Vance. His earlier contacts with his mother's brother had been both brief and formal, and always with others present. He saw a new man emerging now. Perhaps it was from the same blood that flowed in this uncle that he had received some of his own stubborn sense of independence. He felt a warmth for the keen-faced, discerning lawyer. The latter had asked him casually about his supply of money, and hinted that at need a certain amount of help might be extended—"if you hold to your task, Nephew, and so prove that you deserve it." The world was suddenly brighter—until he remembered that in his concern for his own affairs he had completely forgotten to mention Cedric's. Well, the boy had the attic room he wanted, and, Roger recalled, he himself was to sup with Uncle Ned the following night.

Cedric's case was still on his mind as he neared Mrs. Salter's house. He pulled up quickly as he saw the cloaked figure of a man looking up at the building. The stranger turned and doffed his hat. Roger saw that he wore the dress of a law clerk. The sharp, white face that showed dimly under his landlady's lantern was unpleasantly rat-like. But the fellow was courteous.

"By your leave, sir," he began, "I am little acquainted in this neighborhood, and I seek the house of a certain Mistress Salter. Perhaps you know where it stands, and can direct me?"

"What's your business with her?" Roger demanded warily.

"Nay, it is not with her," answered the man smoothly, "but with one who I think is a lodger there. A Master Roger Darrell," he added, eyeing Roger as if he himself might be the man.

Roger was on guard at once. A lawyer's man seeking him! Why? There could be only one explanation. Bragdon had somehow tracked him to his lodgings, and meant to press a charge against him. Well, he would try guile against guile. He smoothed his features and shook his head.

"This is Mistress Salter's house, and I myself have chambers here. There's but one other lodger, a young silversmith by name of Woodley or Woodward."

"Are you assured of that, sir?" the man persisted. "My information is that this young Master Darrell came here only

a few days ago to seek lodgings, Master—Master—"

"Vance." The name popped out; thank heaven, he hadn't hesitated! "Why," he went on, "I myself came to Mistress Salter only three days ago, and perhaps cheated your friend of his rooms."

"Nay, he's no friend of mine," said the other quickly.

I'll promise you he's not, thought Roger, *nor you any of his.*

"Well," he replied aloud, "friend or not, it's as I tell you.

You must look elsewhere, I think."

"If your hostess is about, I might question her and get some news of him," persisted the man.

Roger put on an air of casual impatience.

"Why, it's close to eleven o'clock," he said severely, "and if I know her habits, she has been abed two hours. Wait on her tomorrow if you like."

"It's only that the matter has some importance," muttered the man.

Roger said nothing, and the stranger gave him a sharp look, thanked him in an abrupt fashion, and made off rapidly. The young man let his breath out in a relieved sigh. As he put his key to the lock, he congratulated himself on a narrow escape. He must rouse his hostess, if need be, tell her of his danger, and instruct her what to say if the fellow returned. He would have to look sharp now. Bragdon had been prompt to loose his dogs!

V

FOR HIRE AND SALARY

THE shop of Garrett and Nicholas Johnson stood almost under the shadow of the Globe playhouse. It was a large, barnlike building, facing north, with living quarters at the rear, and behind them a yard in which a washing waved in the wind. The studio was in front, where it received the northern light. It covered the space of several good-sized rooms. Here Roger found Nicholas Johnson. He was a sturdy, fresh-colored man who listened patiently while his young caller explained his errand, then took Edward Vance's letter and stood reading it with methodical care.

The night before when Roger had entered the house on Little Wood Street, he had found Mrs. Salter still up, and had explained his predicament to her. She had been alarmed, and protested that she could not give false testimony. But Roger had argued that so far as she was concerned there was no question of law involved. It was a matter of protecting him in a situation that was no fault of his. A quarrel had been forced upon him. She had merely to say that no man calling himself Darrell had lodgings with her. Finally she had agreed. Roger had told Cedric about the lawyer's man as the two had breakfasted. He had also apologized for not speaking with his uncle about the boy's case, and had promised to bring it up that very evening. So on Little Wood Street he was now Master Vance. But he could not change his uncle's letter to

Johnson; in the Bankside he was Roger Darrell!

Johnson finished reading the letter, and was quietly friendly. He looked at the designs Roger had brought. He knew Bartolomeo slightly, and spoke of him with respect.

"A good man," he said. "We work in different traditions, he and I, but I have seen certain things that he has done. They are well-conceived, executed with grace. It is a great pity, a loss, his going. But, Master Darrell," he added, "I don't know what I can say to you. I would gladly accept one of your talent as an apprentice; it would be for a short term only. But just now with my brother's son and my own both helping us, we have no room. And to set up a shop of your own—I think you are not ready for that."

Roger agreed.

"I haven't the experience for it," he conceded.

"Nor perhaps the money," said Johnson quietly. "For all this—" and his hand swept the shop with its benches, tools, canvases, stone and other materials—"has been the occasion of no small expense. But since you are a gentleman, you may have certain means—"

"None whatever, sir. I must find employment."

Johnson murmured understandingly.

"Your uncle asks about the playhouses," he continued. "There is no place in any of them for painter or architect. On occasion they need help from a painter: we have served them at times. But most of what they require is made ready by their hired men. Some have skill of sorts with a brush. At the Court it is different. The entertainments there are lavish; the King's agents employ men of skill. Yet you need reputation and influence to win a commission from them."

"I must begin where I can," said Roger stubbornly.

Johnson stood thinking about the matter.

"If you are willing to put your hand to such work as comes," he said slowly at length, "you can perhaps find employment as a hired man." He gave Roger a cautious glance. "We ourselves might employ you when our work crowds us. My brother is abroad this morning, looking to a possible commission. If he wins it, we shall have more to do for a week or two than we can manage, and can make a place for you." He paused briefly again. "The wages will be eight shillings a week —ten if you prove yourself as skilled as I hope."

The proposal was something like what Roger had thought of as a possible beginning. Yet he had a curious sense of casting aside not only his old life but the name and feeling of pride that went with it. A hired man! But quickly he checked himself. What were his uncle's words last night? He had spoken of humble labor. This was it, and it led toward the higher work he hoped to do. More than that, ten shillings a week would more than buy his food and lodgings. He spoke to Johnson with a smile:

"Sir, I will serve you gladly if you call me."

"Well said!" Johnson spoke heartily and put out his hand. As Roger gripped it he thought he saw a gleam of respect in the artist's eye.

"If you will leave these designs with me," he said, "I will show them to my brother. I think he will like their ease and boldness and feeling for color. And I don't doubt we shall call you, later if not soon. Come for the designs again tomorrow. Meanwhile I will think if there are other places where you might seek service."

"I thank you, Master Johnson."

"No thanks. It is a matter of common profit for us both. I can guess it is no easy thing for a nobleman's son like you to work for wages; you go higher in my esteem for the readiness you show to do it."

He lifted a forbidding hand as Roger would have spoken,

and stood for a moment turning over some idea in his mind.

"There is a young Englishman recently returned from abroad," he finally continued. "They say he has served as architect to the King of Denmark, who is our new Queen's brother. Before that, he studied and traveled in Italy on the bounty of my Lord of Rutland. His name is Inigo Jones, and there is talk that no Englishman was ever so gifted, and that he will manage certain entertainments soon for their Majesties. Now it may be he has not chosen his assistants for such ventures, and if you have friends that can bring you to him, lose no time in speaking for yourself."

"I'll do all I can," promised Roger eagerly. A name came to him like a shaft of light—Trevor! He must be in London, or soon would be. "I may have a friend here in London, now that I think again on the matter," he told Johnson. "One who might even have acquaintance at court."

"Good! Move him to help you. It is acquaintance and influence that count chiefly."

Roger was thinking of the young artist whom Johnson had described.

"Inigo Jones!" he exclaimed. "It's a strange name."

"You'll hear it often enough to make it familiar," promised the other with a smile. "Meanwhile I think you would do well to try the playhouses, if indeed you can find any men of consequence about them. The theaters have been closed for many months because of the plague, but it runs its course now, and they'll soon reopen. Master Richard Burbage might have some voice at the Globe among the King's Men. He himself is a gifted painter, although solely for his own pleasure."

"I saw him play Henry the Fifth, and do it magnificently!"

"Aye, he's a master on the stage."

Johnson went on to tell of Philip Henslowe, father-in-law of the great actor Edward Alleyn, and joint owner with him of the Fortune. This, he explained, was the new playhouse of the Prince's Men, chief rivals to Burbage and his company. "A hard man, they say," the artist remarked of Henslowe, "but always he has an eye to new talent." There was also Evans of the Blackfriars, playhouse for the children's troupe within the walled city, which was now the third theater permitted by the King's Privy Council.

"I don't know what you'll find," he said of all three places. "They may set you to turning a windlass or readying fireworks; you may now and then build and paint a grassy bank or a cloud, or daub a design on a curtain; they'll also have you fill in as a player in the crowd scenes, or even for small parts. Yet if you can pocket your pride as bravely as you did today, you'll have an experience of some value for one who hopes to devise costumes and design settings for a king's masque."

Roger agreed. He did not speak of his own masques at Darrell Manor. They had been arranged for private pleasure; the playhouses would teach him what was needed when a man worked with and against the best craftsmen in his field, for gold and later for fame.

He left his portfolio of designs and promised to return the following day.

At the Globe, familiar to him from his student days, Roger found no one but a caretaker. The man knew nothing of when the playhouse would reopen.

He walked back to the city by way of the bridge, crossing it from south to north, and passing through Cripplegate to Shoreditch, the suburb just beyond the wall. There he found the Fortune. He had never seen the playhouse before. He saw that it was a large edifice, perhaps larger than the Globe, and square in shape instead of octagonal. It had been painted recently, and looked smart and new.

A serving man lounged at the rear entrance. He agreed, for a sixpence, to take Roger's name to Master Henslowe. A few minutes later the young artist climbed the stairs inside to the second story of the building, and approached a neatly dressed man with a carefully trimmed brown beard who sat writing at a table. He was booted and cloaked, for the building was cold, and he swept Roger with sharp, small gray-green eyes. Yet he listened patiently enough to the young man's story.

"Have you drawings?" he asked in a tight, small voice when his visitor had finished.

Roger explained that he had left his designs with Johnson; he could return with them another day.

"No need, no need," chirped Henslowe. He smiled a wintry smile and pushed ink, pen and paper across the table, waving his caller to a stool.

"We shall save time," he said. "Draw me a design, Master Darrell, such a one as might fill a curtain at the rear of a chamber. Let it be—" he squinted and pulled an idea out of space—"one of St. George and the dragon," he finished with a cunning smile.

Roger was amused. He blocked out a sketch, but had not gone far with it before Henslowe stopped him.

"Enough, enough," he squeaked. "I see that you are not without skill in these matters. *Mmmm*—you understand the mixing of colors?"

"With oil or egg white or tempera," Roger assented. "I have painted costumes and hangings, and worked on wood and plaster."

"But cannot use a saw or a hammer, by the look of your hands and your habit."

"Why, I can do any kind of simple carpentry," retorted

At the Globe . . . Roger found no one but a caretaker

Roger, somewhat nettled, "and peg together a table or bench at need."

"Can you play a part on the stage?"

"I've played enough of them in such masques and revels as we arranged at home for pleasure."

"Well, well," temporized Henslowe. "We are idle now, waiting word from the Privy Council that we may play again. When it comes, we shall see, we shall see. I might find a certain use for you. I can pay—" he eyed Roger shrewdly, "perhaps five shillings a week."

"Master Johnson spoke of ten."

"You are green—a beginner. Men have won wealth on the stage, but you must prove yourself, then expect advancement. There is room for it," he assured Roger. "And if you do well, and your wages are not enough—well, for a time I myself might help a deserving young man—lend you something at modest interest. *Mmm*—six shillings a week let it be, and seven after two weeks if I like your work."

Roger stood fascinated by the man's cunning. He gave Henslowe his name, and the playhouse owner wrote it down, with the location of his lodgings, in a little book he drew from the folds of his cloak. "Fortune waits at the Fortune," he punned. *Not mine, I think, if there are other calls,* Roger told himself. Something warned the former heir to Darrell Manor that he would work long hours, and hard ones, to earn his six or seven shillings from that spidery little man.

Master Henry Evans of the Blackfriars within the walled city was the opposite of Henslowe in appearance—a dark, full-voiced, confident fellow with the bold carriage and gestures of an actor. He listened to Roger impatiently.

"We are servants to the new Queen's Majesty," he said, "and work with craftsmen that we know. What? Well, return when we are playing if you like, but I think you'll have your pains for nothing. We have those at call who know the stage and what we require. And now, sir, I have pressing business at hand, and I bid you good-day!"

Roger found Cedric waiting in his rooms. The boy asked what seemed like a hundred questions, and the seeker for work found himself going over the entire day in detail. He ended by talking of Inigo Jones as if the humble employment he had not yet found might lead him to this already somewhat fabulous person.

Cedric seemed more impressed by the immediate prospects.

"You'd paint curtains for the players and act with them?" he demanded.

"It will serve until I can win advancement," Roger replied defensively.

"It will be an exciting life and a merry one!" exclaimed the boy with enthusiasm. "I'll fetch for you and be your helper."

Roger laughed wryly.

"Hired men have no helpers." He looked at the excited boy and a thought flashed in his mind. "You yourself might find employment at the playhouse, taking women's parts, or a page's," he considered. "You have the voice and liveliness for it."

"I could play a milkmaid or a serving wench," Cedric conceded with a grin. "For such parts, red hair and freckles would suit."

Roger saw a chance to probe a bit along the lines of his suspicions. He had talked with Cedric only a few minutes that day, and had been too full of other matters to bring up the business of Twelfth Night at Darrell Manor. Now he had a natural opening.

"Why, I think you could do better than a milkmaid in a pinch," he said smoothly. "As a harlequin, perhaps, in a yellow habit tricked with purple."

Cedric stared at him with questioning eyes.

"A harlequin?"

The innocent gaze of the boy almost stopped him then and there. If Cedric was acting, he was a master at it. But Roger went on.

"Yes. One that comes in with a leap and a tumble. Could you manage that?" he asked with a smile, watching to see the effect of his words.

"Oh, I can turn a tumble neatly enough," replied Cedric carelessly. "And I can jig, too. Father and Ralph taught me," he added.

"By what road did you come to London?" Roger shifted his attack suddenly.

"By the Oxford Road, through Shoreditch."

That would be from the north and west, Roger reflected quickly, and not from the south and east, which was the way from Kent. Of course, the rascal could have cut over and reached the other route by a roundabout way. The questioner was baffled. He was all but sure that Cedric had been the intruder who trussed up Lucy and took her role in the masque, but he had no proof, and Cedric, if the feat had been his, clearly was not going to admit it.

"Well," Roger remarked with pretended carelessness, "I think you need to stretch your legs and get some air, and you shall come along with me to my uncle's. If you want his help, he will need to speak with you. You'll get a supper there, although perhaps not with us."

Cedric looked a little startled, but seemed pleased, and ran to his room for a cloak. The two were soon taking their way through the darkening streets toward Aldersgate.

"An infant," said Edward Vance, using the legal term for a ward, "is not without rights in English law against a guardian, if he can show abuse. He may appeal to the court through his *prochein amy*,* which is the French—long the language of our courts—for 'nearest friend.' "

The three—Vance, Roger, and Cedric, were seated in the same chamber where Roger and his uncle had conferred the night before. The lawyer had been friendly. He showed approval for what Roger had done; and when he knew the reason for Cedric's coming he showed an immediate interest in his case. He insisted that the boy sup with them, quickly made himself familiar with his situation, and was now explaining the possible grounds for action on the youngster's behalf.

"By this same device of *prochein amy*," he went on, speaking to Cedric, "you yourself may ask for a new guardian at the age of fourteen years."

"But Cedric is not yet fourteen," Roger broke in, "nor will be for more than a year."

Vance inclined his head.

"The right of appeal against manifest abuse still remains."

"Sir," asked the boy, "what is this 'abuse' of which you speak?"

"Many acts have been held to be such. The wilful or unreasonable waste of the infant's property is an abuse. So is a failure by the guardian to pay a debt owed by the infant or his estate, especially if the guardian keep for his own purposes the monies that should have been paid. The failure to school the infant properly, or to maintain him in a manner befitting his station is abusive, as is the effort to force upon him an unsuitable marriage."

---

* French remained the language of English law until the mid-fifteenth century. The spelling here is that of the courts of the time, instead of the modern *prochain ami*.

"The last he is surely guilty of!" exclaimed the boy, leaping to his feet.

Vance, who, of course, had already heard of the proposed marriage, shook his head.

"Is the person he seeks to match you with of mean birth? Is she without substance?"

Cedric tossed his head impatiently.

"Oh, the family is gentle," he admitted grudgingly, "and has a certain substance—"

"Then what we can do is most doubtful," broke in the lawyer crisply. "I should wish to study the matter with care before even making an attempt on such a charge, for age is not commonly a sound point for action. I should prefer other grounds. Where's your Master Bragdon's estate?"

"Near Holcome, in Surrey."

"And those of you and your brother are in the same vicinity?"

Cedric bent his head. He seemed to trace a design on the table, and such was his concentration that the others waited until he spoke.

"Master Vance," he said at last, "I sent a letter to my brother in Ireland only three days ago, and if he can come to England, I know he will. And perhaps, if we could find a way to know of his coming, all might be settled through him."

"You mean he has some power over Bragdon?"

"No-o; but he has shamed him before, and might again now."

Vance looked grim.

"It is not to my knowledge that such men are easily put from a wicked purpose," he remarked. "If it proves so in the event, I shall be glad of it. Meanwhile, let us put our trust in the law, if we have grounds for doing so." He thought for a moment. "I cannot act at once. I myself am engaged closely for a week, and meanwhile I must see if the agent I would like to employ is free for the task."

Cedric was surprised.

"What will he do?"

"Verify the appointment of Bragdon as your brother's guardian and yours, and determine if he stands so *in socage,* or by custom, or by statute. He can also look discreetly into the management of your estate. Have you ever been suspicious as to that?"

Cedric looked troubled.

"Suspicious enough, from what some have told me quietly. Yet I have no sure knowledge of anything, sir."

"We will go over what you know later. We may find a clue in it. Your brother Ralph is of what age?"

"Twenty, sir. Last April 24th."

"A pity. If your guardian holds office *in socage,* as I think, it is only because he is guardian of your half-brother, the next of kin that does not inherit directly from you. Therefore, when your brother comes of age, Bragdon ceases to have authority over you, and Ralph assumes it."

"Oh, if we could wait for that, sir—"

"We cannot. I must not keep you in hiding past the week or two needed to survey the case; it would go beyond any excuse we could make in court; besides, it is not safe. If we find we have grounds, we must go to court promptly. I hope we find them. I shall leave nothing undone to that end."

He spoke with an intensity of interest, and the reason for it came out with his next words.

"Each decision in open court," he declared, "that establishes more fully the just rights of man, woman, or child is a stone laid in the law that makes a stronger and freer England!"

Cedric frisked about like an eager puppy on the way home. "I shall be free, Roger—I mean, Master Darrell," he exulted. "No more insolence from that grasping and arrogant rascal, nor from any that serve him!"

"Easy now!" Roger warned him. "You were promised nothing."

"But he *wants* to help me," asserted Cedric. "And so I know he will!"

Roger laughed at this naive logic.

"You'd better hold your hopes down until Uncle Ned finds what he needs, if he finds it," he counselled. "And keep to the house meanwhile. With all Bragdon's bullies and law clerks ranging London, you're still in his shadow. Not that my uncle won't give him trouble enough if he gets the proof he needs."

"Oh, he's the prince of law-men!" cried the boy.

"Who's found nothing he can do to help you yet!"

"But who will." Cedric brushed the point aside. He paused and studied Roger as the latter laughed again.

"Do you know, Roger," he said, "you are marvelous like my brother Ralph when you smile. Though darker than he—and bigger and broader." The boy flashed what was close to a hero-worshipping glance. "But I don't know if *he* could have bested Wickard. That was a masterly thing!"

Roger warmed to the praise, chuckled, and gave his companion a push.

"Blood-thirsty little brat! Stop capering and talking and get home to bed," he commanded. "I'll be big brother to you, and make you walk a narrow path until you're safe." He added on impulse, "Come now, wasn't it you that trussed up Lucy Knowles at Darrell Manor on Twelfth Night, and played her part in the masque?"

Surely the boy would confide in him now!

But Cedric stopped short and frowned indignantly.

"I?" he demanded. He looked at Roger with something like contempt. "Why, I thought you favored your uncle somewhat, but now I see it's all bone and color, and nothing in the mind! What's this talk of masques, and how I'd play a part without training for it?" He stamped his foot. "Talk of masques to the watch and they'll understand as much as I do!"

"Now you grow saucy," said Roger, half-sharply, half-laughing at the mighty burst of indignation from his small companion. "Come along," he commanded, "and get to bed."

"Says the hired man!" retorted Cedric with a sudden grin, and darted from under Roger's hand and along ahead of him toward their lodgings.

VI

THE PORTRAIT

WHEN Nicholas Johnson came forward to greet Roger at his shop the next morning, the artist looked regretfully at his guest and shook his head.

"Bad news, Master Darrell," he said bluntly; "bad for us and for you. My brother had small success with the business I spoke of."

He hesitated a moment, then continued: "It's no secret now. No doubt you yourself have seen that the arches planned last Spring for the King's march through London, and given over when he failed to come, are now being built. We have already undertaken some paintings for the third arch, which the Dutch of the city are erecting near the Royal Exchange. But it has lately been decided to add two new ones, making seven in all, and my brother and I hoped to work on those."

"That would have been a commission indeed!"

Johnson smiled at Roger's enthusiasm.

"We hoped for a part of the work only," he explained. "Master Stephen Harrison has the general commission for all these monuments. There was the chance of winning a considerable assignment under him. But little came of it. Others had friends who could speak better for them than ours could for us. Friends and influence, as you have doubtless heard, count much in such matters."

He shrugged off his disappointment.

74

"My brother saw your designs, and likes them," he went on. He picked up Roger's portfolio, laid it on a table, and opened it. "He asked about your skill in catching a likeness. In the figures you have sketched to show costumes, like this one, he thought he saw a gift for that."

Johnson indicated a drawing in color showing the dress of a herald.

"My brother Anthony," explained Roger. "Why, yes, it is like him. I used to make drawings of Anthony and others, too, and not badly, I think. Later Master Bartolomeo taught me something of anatomy, and of portraiture, though these things were not his chief interest."

"I should like to see something of yours in greater size and detail," said Johnson. "We make portraits now and then. It's the fashion, and on a sudden every tradesman wants to see himself done in color as if he were an earl. I have little gift for such work myself. Possibly you could help my brother, who has more skill for it, and sometimes too many orders to fill."

"I'll see what I can manage," promised Roger quickly, thinking of his uncle as a possible subject for a painting, or even Mistress Salter.

"No hurry. Yet if you have time to do a bigger sketch, let me see it."

Roger bowed. He felt sure that Johnson would not make the request for nothing. He told him then about his visits to Henslowe and Evans, and of the empty Globe.

"Aye, I think the chief men are seldom there these days," Johnson agreed. "Yet try it again; the King's Men are the best of the player companies. Meanwhile I have the list of some other painters who came to my mind since yesterday," he added. "There are a half dozen or more: Hilliard, Oliver, the Segars, Thomas Bettes, Peake, Robert Cole." He gave Roger a leaf from a tablet on which he had scribbled names and locations. "You yourself are better taught than some of these," he remarked. "Show them your work and see if they have wit enough to value it. And don't lose courage. This business is likely to be slow, but it should come to something in the end."

Roger thanked him, and put the paper in his purse. So he was to begin all over again. He sighed as he turned toward the Globe. Sure enough, it was empty. Almost wearily he made for the nearest of the shops that Johnson had listed.

Master George Lyon was a sharp-eyed little man with only one apprentice. He was grudging in his agreement to look at Roger's designs, but when he had seen a few of them a kind of crafty alertness crept into his manner.

"Who was your master?" he demanded.

Roger told him, saying that he had worked with Bartolomeo for several years.

Lyon nodded.

"I see the Italian touch," he said. "Do you understand the preparation of colors in oil?"

He watched Roger carefully as he spoke.

"Naturally," the latter replied.

"It is a lead medium they use, is it not?" persisted Lyon.

"Somewhat so."

Roger saw clearly enough what was in the fellow's mind. He wanted to learn what he could of Italian formulae. What he would do for the man who taught it, once the knowledge was his, would probably be little. Nor, Roger guessed, was Lyon likely to make very good use of anything he learned. A half-finished portrait on a nearby easel, apparently of a London merchant, was wooden and lack-lustre.

"If there is work in oil to be done, I will bring such materials as are needed for it," he said coolly, to test the painter.

"Nay, such things must be done in the shop at my direction," Lyon answered sharply. "You are young, still need schooling." He licked his lips and measured Roger with a calculating eye. "For a certain sum I could receive you as an apprentice."

"For what term?"

Lyon considered.

"You do not lack skill, and have had some training. We might agree on three years."

Roger shook his head and moved to take up the portfolio.

"Wait. If you work well, we will make it two. But you must prepare your materials here."

"I am pledged to keep certain matters secret," countered Roger. He thought of Johnson. He felt willing enough to reveal to him any formula he knew. After all, with Bartolomeo gone, what Roger had been taught was his own now, to use as he pleased. He trusted Johnson. But the latter had never asked him about the Italian's methods.

"Think it over," Lyon was saying. "For two years and three pounds we might agree."

Roger took up his drawings.

"I must consider the matter," he said. "For one thing, it's a question if I can come by three pounds."

He left the shop with Lyon still expostulating. He had reduced the fee by a pound.

Roger walked slowly across London Bridge, jostled by the throng of people pressing in two directions. He was in a black mood. He thought he could see the life that lay before him. He might find a place with some third-rate dauber like Lyon, eager to squeeze from him what knowledge he had. Then in two years' time he would again be cast on his own resources, with prospects little better than he had now.

What had Bartolomeo told him? There were few in England beside the Flemings who knew the secrets men possessed on the continent—the van Eyck or da Vinci or Titian formulae. Roger was not even certain what the Flemings knew, although from some canvases he had seen in the Johnson studio he was ready to believe that those two artists commanded a technical skill that even Bartolomeo would have respected. Perhaps some of the English had it too. However, just now Lyon seemed a symbol. And for the moment Roger felt that even soldiering was a better hazard than drudgery with that cunning and ignorant man.

Then the thought of Trevor came again. It burst in on his dark thoughts like a flare fanning out through the night. What had he been thinking of? Trevor might open a path for him to the Court, even to Inigo Jones!

Roger had visited the London house of his Cambridge companion; he could go there that very day. Or better, St. Paul's! If Trevor were in London, he above all others would be likely to go to the church, to see and be seen. True, on his first visit there several days ago, Roger had not seen him. But he had not been looking for acquaintances then; and besides, with the decline in plague deaths the more fashionable elements were only now beginning to drift back to London.

St. Paul's would be better than the Trevor house. A meeting in the church would seem to be accidental, and his old Cambridge friend would respond best to an appeal if it were made casually rather than formally.

Roger quickened his pace, leaving the bridge and hurrying toward the cathedral. The time was the eleventh hour—right to the minute. As he neared the church, he saw to the west through Ludgate one of the seven arches rising beyond the wall, above Fleet Street—just the skeleton timbers of it, but the sight sharpened his purpose.

He strode past the noisy bookstalls to the entrance, passed in, and walked up the aisle, scanning the faces of the laughing and chattering crowd that passed him in twos and threes. No Trevor. He walked back on the other side, completing the circuit. Then he reversed his direction, for otherwise he would never pass those who were walking in the same direction as he. In a few minutes he spied his man.

Trevor saw Roger almost at the same instant, and hailed him with delight, pulling him from the throng to a nearby pillar. Hardly had Roger gripped his friend's hand when Barton appeared. It was all very gay and heartening.

Both young men were fashionably dressed, Trevor with taste and elegance. The plumed hat and the laced cloak were rich yet simple. The gold chain about his neck was of simple design, too, but made by no common craftsman. Barton's costume was much along the same lines. Of the two, Roger knew, the latter had more money; he suspected that Trevor counted on a certain financial support in return for taking his colorless companion in tow. But in spite of what had been spent on it, Barton's raiment missed distinction. Perhaps the man did not contribute enough to give the clothes a chance.

Roger stood a little awkwardly before his friends, conscious of his plain dress in contrast to theirs, and to the rich cloaks and doublets of the numerous dandies passing by. But Trevor at least seemed not to notice Roger's embarrassment, or the portfolio in his hand.

"So you're down to London!" he exclaimed. "You'll stay through the coronation at least?"

"Longer, I hope." Roger smiled, with a special meaning that Trevor could not know.

"Bravo!" cried his old companion, and Barton echoed the word. Then: "This calls for a long draft of the best sack and a longer talk. It's years since we've laid eyes on you, and we need hours to catch up. You're my guest for dinner: don't refuse me!"

"No, both of you are mine!"

"We'll cast for it," said Trevor, never too insistent on using his purse. "Come along. At the ordinary you must visit with us, it's well to be early. We'll dine on the stroke of noon."

The three were quickly out of the crowd and into the quieter streets. They chatted as they went, Roger telling the others that he had been about for several days and taken lodgings. Finally Trevor led him through the door of a tavern, quickly caught the eye of a serving man, and in a moment the three were seated at a table under a many-paned window. All was clean and well-appointed, Roger saw as he glanced around. Chairs took the place of the usual benches or stools, the rushes were fresh, and painted cloths hung across the end walls. On these were classical scenes—Mars and Venus, Apollo and Daphne, Pan and a horde of satyrs—skilfully executed, with rich color and a touch of the voluptuous.

Trevor called for dice and was soon shaking the ivory cubes in a gold-rimmed leather cup.

"If I have any favor with Fortune," he said graciously, "she will manage that you shall win and one of us shall pay," and tossed the dice.

Roger cast, with a guilty feeling about his slender store of gold, and the two others gave a pleased exclamation. He had cast aces, the best possible throw.

"The old Darrell luck," cried Trevor. "You'll never match it, Barton, though you should top my throw."

Then, while Barton was casting, he beckoned to a boy and asked for a special brand of sack. The boy nodded and went away. The cast made by Barton was the lowest of the three; he would pay and seemed pleased enough to do it.

The sack came, with sugar, then considered a refinement by many when added to wine; the others took it and Roger refused. Trevor asked then about life at the Manor, and Roger told them of the new hall, of Bartolomeo, and something of the work that he himself had carried on under the Italian's guidance.

Trevor nodded.

"I remember a likeness you took of me at Cambridge. It's a gift you could use among the Court ladies," he added. Roger was pleased at this faint sign of interest in his skill, but dropped the subject as dinner was served just then.

After they had eaten he asked about the new King and his entourage. Had Trevor joined it?

"I've spent the last six months in and out of His Majesty's Court," the other answered somewhat airily. "Now I have run before it to London for a few days of change. There's such a battle of aromas between rare perfumes and rare liquor (and some less fancy, too), that a man can't say which is victor, or if natural air exists in this world!"

Roger laughed as politeness demanded.

"Why, is the drinking heavy?" he asked. "I thought His Majesty was a sober and learned man."

"Oh, we shall be as learned a Court under our Scottish Jove as we were under our English Cynthia," answered Trevor with a shrug. "But we shall be much gayer. The King knows his Latin and is proud of it; but he pours out more wine than was ever drunk before at Westminster or any other royal seat, though perhaps that's the wish of his partner. Her Majesty loves a lively life, and, I promise you, could follow toasts while any could rise to propose them. Heigho! We shall have drinking, dancing, and masquing aplenty, I promise you."

"With a magician to devise the settings for the masques, I hear," probed Roger.

"A magician?" Trevor considered a second, then caught the point. "Oh, you mean Master Inigo Jones. Yes, he comes in on a legend, and from his talk, promises well."

"You know him then?"

"I've spoken with him. You've some special interest in the fellow?" he asked shrewdly, sensing Roger's eagerness. "Ah, yes," he concluded, remembering what had been said of Bartolomeo and the new hall. "You've been busy in the same world as his, and I suppose keep all the skill and interest there that you ever had."

"More skill, I hope, and much greater interest," said Roger, feeling that the time was favorable for bearing in. "Indeed, the two of them have brought me to London."

Trevor's eyebrows lifted.

"Does Sir John favor your following such activity?" he asked.

It must be the truth now, or quibbling and evasion. Roger decided to risk everything.

"He doesn't favor it at all," he answered. "In fact, Dick, my father and I have parted company, and he has cast me out."

His words might have been a bucket of icy water drenching his companions. Barton sat open-mouthed. Trevor's eyes lost their warmth and looked cool and hard.

"What are you doing in London, then?" he asked.

"Seeking my fortune." Roger grinned at him. Quickly he explained his plans for working with Bartolomeo, and the latter's sudden death.

"And you cast away a title for that?" demanded Trevor incredulously, going back to Roger's dispute with Sir John.

"They tell me I might pick it up again if I'd go back, ask forgiveness, buckle on a breastplate, and serve a year in Ireland," Roger conceded. "But—"

"But then by all means throw yourself on your horse and get

back to Kent as fast as you can," advised his friend. "That's my earnest word to you, Roger, and now go home and pray on it."

"Never was better counsel offered," said Barton feelingly.

"It has been offered me before," answered Roger, somewhat nettled. "My chief study now is to find how I can safely reject it."

"Are you serious?" demanded Trevor.

"Never more so. Some men long to excel in war, some in fashion, some in learning. My hopes lie with art."

"Heaven help you!"

"But even if you excel, Roger," objected Barton, "where will it take you? It is mere craftsman's work."

"Is Master Stephen Harrison no more than that? Or Sir Edmund Tilney, who has long managed the royal revels?"

"You've a point there," conceded Trevor slowly. "But Tilney at least is one who manages matters involving art, and plies no craft himself. Also, such as he have had substance of their own, and have risen by influence and favor. You've an income still—despite your father—through your mother, perhaps?"

Roger shook his head.

"But then what will you do?" asked Barton with real alarm.

It had come to the bitter point now, but Roger answered directly and with one word.

"Work."

Again the effect was all but catastrophic. The others stared at him without a word, seemingly paralyzed by the thought of a gentleman using his hands for gain.

"I may help an artist in the Bankside, or even serve one of the players' companies," Roger said defiantly, to break the silence.

"As a craftsman?" Horror edged Barton's voice.

"If you like. Until I find better employment." He paused and added, looking at Trevor, "I had some hope of your Master Inigo Jones—if I could meet and speak with him."

Trevor caught his meaning.

"With me as your sponsor?" he asked in a tight voice that carried its own warning.

"You could bring me to him. I want no further sponsorship."

Trevor shook his head.

"I cannot—I dare not do it. Go back to your father, Roger, meet his wishes, return as his heir, and for Roger Darrell the gentleman I will lend my full voice. But for Roger Darrell the craftsman, no."

"Do I cease to be gentleman because I use my hands?" Roger demanded, knowing the answer but trembling with anger and pushing the point to its extremity out of a stubbornness he could not control.

"To me, no," Trevor replied. He was white and edgy. "To all those I know in London and Westminster, yes."

"A man is no better, then, than the amount of gold in his purse and the cost of the doublet on his back," said Roger bitterly, although more as a statement than a question.

"The gold and the doublet are part of him, and you know it," retorted Trevor. Then as Roger eyed him scornfully, "In the name of reason, think what you ask! If it came to be known that I pushed a craftsman, even though gentle-born, into the Court, I should hazard all I have won there. I have labored long and most carefully to build it up," he admitted in the intensity of his feeling.

I can guess you have, Roger thought. He continued to look at the other, and said nothing.

"I'll not risk all I value to serve a stubbornness and folly such as I've never seen before!"

The words burst out suddenly, like a lash. Roger pushed up from the table.

"I might have known it," he said. "I'll leave you." He was so angry he could scarcely speak. He stood a few seconds, won command of himself, took out his purse and spun a gold noble across the table at Barton. "That will pay my reckoning here," he said. "I'll not be guest where I'm held so low!"

The others sprang up, angrily protesting. He couldn't do it! The act was an insult!

"Why, then, it's an insult," snapped Roger with cold fury, picking up his portfolio, "and yet you can't cross swords with a craftsman! So take the gold or leave it, and a long good-bye to both of you!"

He strode to the door.

"Heaven help him!" he heard Trevor breathe as he went.

It was half an hour later when he turned into Little Wood Street. He had made a wide circuit through the town to walk off the rage that shook him, but it still burned, though with lessening power. The door of the house was locked. He knocked loudly, but there was no answer. When he had found his key and entered, the place was empty.

He went through to the farther side and called up the stair-way to Cedric. No reply. Exasperated and fearful, he climbed the two flights of stairs to the garret room, found a locked door, and got nothing but silence for his knocking. A wave of the fury that had swept him half an hour earlier came surging back. Curse the brat! What had he been thinking of to run off and range the London streets alone? Or was the business worse than that even? Had Bragdon and his bullies watched until Mrs. Salter left the dwelling, then forced an entry and dragged the boy away?

Roger stamped down the stairs and up again on the other side of the house to his own rooms. Anger, exasperation, and sickening dread boiled in him as he paced to and fro.

Cedric came in not long afterwards, and faced Roger's furious questions and black brows with astonished eyes.

"I only went with Mistress Salter," he protested, "to fetch things from the market for her."

"And to walk into Bragdon's hands with no one near you but a woman!" accused the other fiercely.

The thrust went home; Cedric knew there was no real reply. But he muttered nevertheless:

"Am I to sit caged up like a dog or rabbit in a room three yards by four all day?"

"Yes!" exploded Roger. "What did my uncle tell you? Is Bragdon something imagined merely, or a man of straw to be knocked down by a finger-flick? You're to stay here and within until there's full safety in going out," he rushed on. "Or," he exclaimed with a gust of wrath, "you can go out and be taken and I'll wash my hands of you! What was all the talk and fearful care about Bragdon, if it meant no more to you than the rattle of so many words?"

The boy was silent, quite borne down by the sheer savagery of the attack. Roger suddenly felt his anger dying away into shame. His point was just, but he realized that he was using Cedric as a whipping boy for his own violent feeling. To sit about all day in a garret was a dull business for a youngster—for anyone. He himself might have been as eager to break out if he had been there, and as thoughtless of consequences. Yet, of course, Cedric must not go out alone.

"Well, no harm came of it this time," he said more kindly, "and if there's to be no other, we'll say no more about it." He passed a hand over his forehead. "I owe you some apology for the way I spoke," he added. "Certain things have happened that I found hard to bear. I was angry. Finding you gone was fuel on the fire. You must forget the heat and remember the point I made."

It was a difficult admission; but the change in Cedric made Roger glad he had spoken.

The boy's face brightened, then was all earnest solicitude.

"What happened?" he asked eagerly. "Didn't Master Johnson's brother like your designs? He's an ignorant fellow, then!"

Roger laughed in spite of himself at the vehemence of the last words.

"It's not that," he explained. He told of Johnson's suggestion as to portraiture, then of his visit to Lyon. Cedric listened with an occasional indignant exclamation. After a moment's hesitation, Roger told in full about Trevor and Barton and what had happened at the inn.

"They're no true friends of yours!" the boy exclaimed when Roger had finished. "I'd march up to the King himself for a friend!"

"I think you would," said Roger, watching the flash of indignant eyes.

"It's not as if you'd done a base thing," Cedric continued. "To give up land and a title to do a great work—that's a noble deed!"

Roger warmed to the words; praise and understanding were welcome at that moment, even from a boy. But he spoke the deepening discouragement that he felt.

"Noble or not, it seems to lead nowhere—not even to the tasks that Trevor despises."

Cedric nodded sympathetically, and sat thinking for a moment.

"But, Master Darrell," he pointed out, "I think it isn't true that there is no chance for the work you want. Did not Master Johnson hold out a hope? Didn't he bid you make a portrait for him?"

Coming with a kind of naive simplicity from the boy, the question gave Roger a curious lift of hope.

"Why, it's true," he answered slowly, "though only a thing of chance." He felt a surging back of his natural energy, and a sudden impatience with himself. "Why should I sit here talking a black mood blacker," he demanded, "when I can work myself out of it and at least see plain again?" An idea came to him, and he struck the table with his palm and stood up. "A portrait! What do you say to one of Master Cedric Wales, limned to the life by Roger Darrell?"

"You'll paint my picture?"

Cedric was delighted.

"Why not? There's still light to block it in, and tonight we'll grind and mix the colors. Tempera will do well enough."

Quickly he took a small board and posed the boy in a place where the morning light on the following day would not fall directly upon him. He was soon busy with pencil, while Cedric sat with a patience Roger had never seen him show before.

All the following day the portrait grew. As Roger had realized when once the idea had come to him, Cedric's distinctive coloring proved to be an advantage. The boy's eyebrows and lashes were dark enough to give definition, the features were clear-cut, the richly freckled complexion and the red-gold hair were distinctive. He knew that he had caught more than a fair likeness, and the tawny coloring matched well with the clear, gray-blue eyes and the boy's sky-blue doublet. Cedric marveled at the finished job, and swore that he himself would knock at

the door of Inigo Jones and win the great man's attention.

Roger laughed. "When you've shaken off Bragdon you may."

The work cheered him, but he could not put away a deep, underlying discouragement. At times he had to force himself to his task. It seemed as if he were a squirrel treading a mill in a cage, and all his effort was only empty gesturing against the tangled reality in which he seemed trapped and helpless.

The following morning he tacked little buttons of wood to the four corners of the portrait, laid a thin board across these to cover the painting, tied cord about the whole, and set out for the Bankside. It was a clear day. As he approached the river he saw that it lay almost as smooth as glass, the reflections of the boats and barges near the shore broken only slightly by the flow of water.

Roger had begun to bargain with a boatman when he glanced up and saw, not fifty feet distant, the form of Wickard, his arm in a sling. Had the fellow seen him? He did not wait for a possible answer to that question, but sprang into the wherry and told the boatman to push off and make speed. As they pulled well out into the stream, he saw Wickard and a companion getting into a boat, but his own had a good start, and he was soon at the farther shore, paying the boatman a stiff fee for having made the trip with a single passenger. He dived down a lane, twisted rapidly among houses and trees, came to Johnson's shop from the rear, and was soon inside.

Quickly he explained to the craftsman his earlier duel with Wickard and the possibility of his being followed.

Johnson heard him calmly, and took the portrait from his hands.

"If anyone comes here, I will deal with him," he said as he lifted the covering from the painting. He gestured to a pair of curtains framing an alcove. "Step behind those if you hear a knock."

He set the portrait on an easel and stood away from it.

"For something done in haste it is better than good," he announced. "I think it tells us what we wanted to know."

Roger sensed that this was high praise. He could not help admiring the calmness with which Johnson went about their common business, ignoring completely the possibility of an unwelcome interruption.

And the interruption came. There was a sharp knock on the door. Roger dived behind the curtains. Johnson took hold of the picture as he gestured his son toward the entrance, then seemed to reconsider, and stood away from it with a casual air. The boy returned to report that someone was asking for him, and before Johnson could reply a man pushed into the shop and confronted him.

He was dressed in livery—clearly a gentleman retainer.

"Master Johnson?" he enquired. The sign before the shop would, of course, have given him the name.

Johnson nodded.

Then the intruder caught sight of the portrait, and stood staring at it open-mouthed. Clearly he recognized the subject.

Johnson was regarding him calmly.

"Your business, sir?" he asked.

The stranger flushed, stammered, and said that he had come to ask about the making of a portrait for his master.

"Is this your work, sir?" he asked, gesturing toward the image of Cedric.

"No, sir," replied Johnson, "it is the work of a young friend of mine. And as to portraits, we do few of them, and are busy with such orders as we have. But if you will give me your master's name, and tell me where he lies, I will have someone wait upon him."

"Nay, he himself can come here," the other responded, "but—" he looked appraisingly at Johnson—"my master is in a hurry to have this commission executed and I think he would favor the work of your young friend which I see here. If you could direct me to him, it will answer."

"Why, as to that, I think he moves to new lodgings, but he will return here, and if I may know where to find *you,* I will tell him."

The retainer stammered, hesitated, and said that he himself

would return later. When would Master—Master—

"My friend will return at his own time," replied the craftsman stolidly, "so I cannot tell you when, and if you will not
leave word for him according to my invitation, then I think
we have no further business with each other, and I will be
about my work."

The stranger hesitated, then bowed and left, Johnson going
with him to the door. When he came back, he called his son.

"Cornelius, go lay a fire in the hearth outside, and tend it,
and if you see the fellow who just left lingering about, or another, particularly one with his arm in a sling, whistle a tune."

The boy gathered faggots and tinder, took a brand from the
hearth in the far corner of the shop, and went out. Roger
stepped from behind the curtains.

"Did you learn anything of consequence?" asked Johnson
with a smile. "I thought best to leave the portrait there, to see
the effect it would have upon our visitor, if any."

"I learned all that I wanted to know," said Roger.

"Then at your own time I will take you through the house
and show you how you can make your way to the river east of
the bridge without being seen. If you take a boat there, I think
you will get back to the city unobserved. Come again tomorrow," he added. "My brother will be here then. He will want
to speak with you."

VII

KING'S MAN

"Why did you not tell me these things before?" asked Edward Vance severely.

He faced Roger and Cedric that night in his home, his face set in austere lines. He had heard the full story of Roger's and Cedric's fears: of the wounding of Wickard, of the visit of the lawyer's man, of Roger's use of the name of Vance, of the visitor who came to Johnson's shop.

"Because, sir," answered Roger, truthfully enough, "you did not question me about the fight at the time, and we became concerned with other matters. I do blame myself for not telling you at once of the liberty I took with your name, which may justly displease you. But I did not *say* it was my name: I merely supplied it in the place he offered. And I *am* half Vance, at that, and so spoke with a certain amount of truth."

The lawyer smiled.

"So you did," he replied, "and all things considered, you managed well. The livery of the man who entered the shop today, as Roger described it, was that of your guardian?" he asked Cedric.

The boy nodded. "Yes, sir."

"Well, well, I think we can manage," Vance reflected. "If a charge were pressed against you," he told Roger, "we might enter a plea of service to the law; for your proposal was that all three of you go to a constable, and he refused it. We can also

93

plead self-defense, since he attacked you, and not you him. Yet it would be better to avoid the courts for the present. How did Wickard or Bragdon know your name?" he concluded.

"That's as much a mystery to me as to you," his nephew replied.

"But *did* he know it, sir?" spoke up Cedric. "Or did he know where Master Darrell lodged? For did not my guardian's man seek to learn both of Master Johnson?"

"Why, true enough," mused the lawyer, shaking his head. "This business becomes more and more tangled. They know you, yet don't know you. You'd never seen Master Cedric before the day you crossed swords with this fellow Wickard?"

Roger shook his head. He had decided to say nothing of the events of Twelfth Night and his suspicions of Cedric's part in them, since he was not sure that the boy had actually been there.

"No, I had not seen him—nor Wickard me, I think," he added.

"Strange," murmured the lawyer, "for seemingly he knew both your name and where you lodged—unless you have been in another difficulty?"

Roger denied this vigorously.

"*Hmmm,*" continued Vance, "this lawyer's man was not by chance the same person who visited the shop this morning?"

"They were as little alike as a rat and a weasel," said Roger.

"A flattering comparison," Edward Vance remarked, his eyes twinkling. "Well, I had thought to bring both of you here to my house to stay if there was need, but I think that as yet there is no occasion for it. You had better make for the Bankside early tomorrow and breakfast there. They will hardly be stirring so early. And keep to the house, young sir," he added to Cedric, for Roger had reported the boy's foray to the market. "I myself will come to you when our agent is free, which will be soon, and we shall push this matter fast, once we begin. It is no sure thing," he warned them both. "Indeed, we work against custom and a vested right. A guardian takes his powers by process of law, and cannot easily be parted from them. But all that can be done we will do."

Roger reached the Johnson shop not long after seven o'clock the following day. In the studio he found Nicholas Johnson and two others. The craftsman introduced one as his brother, and Roger noted a family resemblance, although Garrett was younger and had more the air of a man about town than did the rather stolid Nicholas.

The latter turned now to the third in the group—a supple man of thirty with a proud, easy carriage that might have graced a nobleman of rank and authority.

"And here, Master Darrell," he said, "is one you have been seeking these last few days—Master Richard Burbage of the King's Men."

The actor took a quick step forward and grasped Roger's hand.

"I hope we are well met," he said, with a voice that was strong and musical. "I came to ask Master Johnson's aid, but he tells me that you can serve as well or better than he."

Roger murmured something between thanks and protest.

"In a word," Burbage went on, "we of the Globe can use your skill with a brush. There will be other tasks on occasion —speaking a line or two on the stage, helping with machines and properties." He looked at Roger questioningly. "Master Johnson tells me you may agree to such service."

Now that the opportunity lay before him, Roger had a curious sense of being trapped. Nevertheless, he bowed.

"I know it is work scarcely suited to your station," Burbage said, as if he read the young man's feelings. "But you'll find it lively enough, and I think will learn something from it. The man we have used most for the decorating of curtains and the readying of other properties has worked under my direction. Now he lies abed with a broken leg that may keep him there a month. Meanwhile we play a week from tomorrow for my Lord Nethereaven, and we must furnish costumes, settings, and properties all new. We meet at the Globe for rehearsal in half an hour, which was the cause of my coming here so early. I hope to take you there with me."

"You'll find the work of some practical value, Master Darrell," spoke up Garrett Johnson, "and will draw top wages for it—ten shillings a week."

Everything was settled in a matter of minutes. It was as near to his hopes, Roger told himself, as he had dared to think of during the last few days. Yet some remnant of feeling in him which he shared instinctively with Trevor and Barton, and which his meeting with them had stirred up in spite of his anger at their attitude, worked in him and troubled him. *It's a carpenter's place you're to fill.* No one of his station in England of that day would have failed to have such a thought in such circumstances. But he thrust it aside. This, he reminded himself, was the humble beginning his uncle had talked of. If there was a way for him to something better, this might be it. *I'll fill the carpenter's place, then, and climb over it to an architect's.* Yet he could not lose the sense of being pulled down.

But he forgot it as he walked with Burbage toward the eight-sided playhouse—a building more than eighty feet in diameter and about half that in height. They made for the stage entrance at the south side.

Roger had never entered this part of the theater. Several times he had paid his penny at the regular entrance gate to the north, then gone up to the second gallery, which cost an additional penny. He knew the Globe well enough as it appeared from a seat there.

He remembered the stage; the "pit" before and partly around it, open to the sky; the galleries lining the encircling edges. It was somewhat like a Greek or Roman amphitheater, he had thought. Of course the ancients, as he had seen in drawings, had used the slope of an encircling hill for their seats. The stage was at its base. But in London the spectators either stood in the "pit" or sat in the galleries. These served the same purpose as the tiers of stone benches on the hill, but men had built them up from the ground with beam and plaster.

Burbage led the way to the rear door. He and Roger entered, coming into a kind of lobby that lay behind the stage areas on the first level.

In this place a few actors were already sitting or standing about, studying their parts. At a table sat a man who, Roger guessed, was the Company's prompter. He was reading and marking a manuscript. Against the walls were stacked a few furnishings—stools, pewter tankards, rapiers, curtains. Several boys about Cedric's age were sprawled on the floor near a window, studying their parts. All the actors were hatted and cloaked, for the unheated playhouse was chilly.

"We are to play *The Merry Wives of Windsor* for My Lord," explained Burbage as he stood with Roger in the cluttered little lobby. "The roles are new to some in the Company, and we shall rehearse the play this week, along with several others, for word comes that the ban on the theaters will be lifted soon. But here's the thing that concerns you— My Lord is new to his honors, and counts much on making a brave showing—braver even than My Lady Pembroke at Wilton, where the King tarried. He demands new costumes and properties entirely, and all of the best."

"What kind of a stage will you play on?" asked Roger.

"Why, one that will be set up in the great hall of My Lord's estate," answered Burbage. "It will be much like what we have here, but smaller. Come out onto the platform with me."

Passing through a massive oak door at one side of the vestibule, they stepped out onto the main stage. Burbage walked briskly to the farther edge of this large platform, which was broad at the end toward the lobby, and narrower as it ran out into the pit.

Roger stood for a moment looking out. Below on either side lay the empty floor around which the playhouse was built. It was open to the sky, paved with brick, and sloped upward slightly toward the galleries. These, following the eight-sided shape of the playhouse wall, loomed high and bare. Roger stared at the skeleton-like theater, imagining it filled with men and sound: the bawling apprentices and sailors and workmen in the pit below, the lively law students and tittering Court gallants in the galleries, with a few masked or unmasked ladies. Burbage guessed what he was thinking, and smiled.

"You've never stood here and looked out," he remarked, "and I've seldom sat out yonder and looked in. But turn about and I'll show you what kind of a playhouse we'll have at My Lord Nethereaven's."

Roger faced in the direction from which they had come. The whole front of the tiring house, containing stages, dressing rooms and storage lofts, loomed before and above him.

The general effect was that of a three-storied house, as he already knew, with the two upper stories projecting forward a few feet over the lower one. But there were points of difference. For instance, from places well forward on the main stage two pillars rose upward for more than thirty feet to support an overhanging roof which covered a considerable portion of the stage. And on the ceiling which they upheld was a blue field covered in gold with the signs of the zodiac. Again, at the rear of the main platform hung curtains, which, he knew, masked an inner stage where a scene could be set while action went on outside. Directly above them were more curtains, hiding an upper stage of similar size, and across the front of the third story were curtains also, to conceal the musicians who played in a gallery behind them.

"We'll have something much like the stages on the first two floors here, though smaller," Burbage was saying. "Heminges has the dimensions. The play has enough changes of scene, but a number of the settings are used several times. We'll have five stages counting the two windows in the upper story, and we'll be able to run along without a pause at any point.* But, as I say, My Lord will have everything new, and you must devise such curtains and properties as we require. Johnson says you have the skill for it."

"I hope so. Master Johnson has seen my drawings. I've managed the settings for some masques at home—"

"I take Johnson's word for what you can do," Burbage assured him, "and the one thing of yours which I saw shows your skill, for that matter. You'll have help enough; several of the men can lay on colors, and I'll lend a hand myself if there's trouble. I have some skill in painting and find a pleasure in it."

He rubbed his chin thoughtfully, then shrugged.

* Altogether, the Globe could provide seven playing areas. On the first level were the main stage and an inner stage now commonly called the Study; on the second level there was a total of four. Directly above the Study was another stage of similar dimensions, now called the Chamber, and in front of it, when the curtains were closed, a strip about four feet wide, and extending across the width of the back wall, called the Tarras, was used to represent the top of a wall. On either side were the two window stages. The seventh stage was a space in front of the music gallery on the third story, and was used when a character was supposed to stand on a high tower of a castle, or was clinging to the mast of a ship. This stage and the Tarras were not needed in *The Merry Wives of Windsor*.

"We could have put the entire business into the hands of a good craftsman," he added, "but, to be frank with you, there's a profit in doing it ourselves, and we shall get more what we want." He thought a moment and then said: "Let's see if I can find a copy of the play for you. You've never seen it played? No—well, read the play, and you'll begin to understand what's needed. Then we can talk of materials and sizes, and you may find time to pencil in a few ideas this afternoon."

Before they went backstage again, Roger told the actor briefly about his fight with Wickard, and his desire to stay unknown for a while. Could he be booked as Roger Vance, and be called that about the playhouse?

Burbage lifted an eyebrow and then gave a chuckle.

"You're starting well," he told Roger. "A dash of dueling is almost the mark of respectability among the players. Marlowe, Marston, Spencer, Johnson and others have drawn swords and sometimes gone to prison for it. I've been close enough to it myself. Why, yes," he agreed, "I'll put you down as Vance, and you shall be called so."

"It's my uncle's name."

"If you drew it out of the air, it's the same to me. Vance you shall be. But let's get a copy of the play."

They returned to the crowded lobby, and Burbage with an exclamation moved toward a gentleman of easy but dignified carriage who was drawing off his gloves.

"Will," he said, pushing Roger forward, "here is a lad who will more than take Ward's place. The Johnsons both speak for him, and I have seen a portrait of his that would have puffed me big with pride if I'd done it. Master Roger Vance, Master Will Shakespeare."

Roger looked into friendly hazel eyes and felt the grip of a firm hand. So this, he thought to himself, was the Master

Shakespeare who was the idol of many at Cambridge. He was a poet, Roger knew; some young men at the university considered his *Venus and Adonis* more important than the plays, which they did not regard as literary productions. But chiefly the students knew him as the creator of characters that were the talk of town and Court: Richard Crookback, Romeo and Juliet, Shylock, Portia, Falstaff, Harry the Fifth, and now the still sensational Danish prince, Hamlet, brooding amid ghosts, dreams of revenge, and pretended madness.

As he took Shakespeare's hand, Roger saw a rather meditative face framed in dark auburn hair, with a shadowy mustache of the same color. The general appearance was one of quiet and composure, yet the new hired man felt a power behind the steady eyes that held his own.

"Since Master D—er—Vance will manage our settings and properties for us," Burbage was saying, "he'll profit by knowing the play. Have you a copy he can scan for an hour?"

Shakespeare hesitated a second.

"I shall need my own," he said then. "I've scribbled some notes on it. Get Vincent's. We shall all be reading today, and he'll have no prompting to do. Meanwhile, welcome to our fellowship, Master Vance."

He smiled and moved off. Burbage took Roger to Vincent, the Company prompter, and after a brief argument took his playbook, led Roger upstairs to the second story, and called to a young man in a leather jerkin. He explained what Roger was to do.

"Fetch Master Vance a table and stool and set them under the window yonder," he directed. "If he needs anything more, see that he gets it. For a beginning, find a slate and some crayon, and paper and pencil."

"Yes, sir." Wat Somers, the hired man, bowed bashfully, and followed Burbage with an admiring glance as the actor clapped Roger's shoulder and hurried away.

"I think I'm filling the place of your friend Ward," Roger said to the young man.

"Oh, if you're to design for the stages, it's more than he could do," the other answered. "I'll get the table."

"Have you served here long?" Roger asked.

"A matter of two years and more," Wat replied, flushing. "It's—well, I'd hoped to win a place as an apprentice," he confessed, "but to speak the truth I'm ill at ease on the boards." He sighed. "But it's a lively life."

He seemed to talk with difficulty, yet to be glad of a chance to do it.

"They're not a bad lot, the lads here at the playhouse," he finished with a kind of a rush.

Roger nodded, and Somers went away. The new hired man opened the playbook, finding a clearly written script that was easy to follow. He glanced at the cast of characters and saw the name of Falstaff. It was one known throughout England, and he bent to his reading with quickened interest. Outside on the main stage he could hear someone calling the roll of Company members, then Shakespeare speaking with quiet authority. For a few minutes he was vaguely aware of the others as the rehearsal commenced. The voices of the boys, playing the women's parts, rose flutelike above the bass or baritone of the men. But soon he was lost in the story of Sir John in love, with the merry wives leading him from one preposterous humiliation to another.

When Somers returned with the table he hesitated for a moment, then asked Roger if he had made plans for dinner. The latter shook his head.

"We have a pasty brought in, and bread and ale," the other explained, "and it's thruppence if you'd like to join us."

Roger decided quickly that he would, and said so, and Somers looked pleased.

When he had left, Roger went on with his reading until he had finished the play, then busied himself with making some sketches. Finally, when it was almost noon, he went downstairs and out onto the platform, where the rehearsal was going forward. He watched and listened, fascinated by the skill with which these men and boys brought the comedy to sparkling life. Soon the scene they were rehearsing came to an end, and the company broke off for dinner. Burbage asked Roger if he would come with him, but when the latter told him he had accepted Somers's invitation, the actor hesitated, gave him a sharp look, and nodded.

"You'll get acquainted better that way," he said with a twinkle in his eye, "and perhaps it's best you should. I'll come back early and talk with you."

Roger guessed from the actor's manner that dinner with the stage crew and apprentices and hired men might not be a wholly pleasant experience. He waited with interest to see what would happen.

He followed several of the apprentices upstairs, where he found that the stagehands had set out a large table and some benches. Almost as if on signal a stout serving man in a stained apron came up the stairs from below, carrying an enormous meat pie, apparently sent in from a nearby tavern. A boy followed him with a huge pitcher and several loaves of bread, while another trailed him with a dozen pewter mugs and hacked wooden trenchers. Food, drink and utensils were flung upon the table and those who had brought them disappeared as a spate of youths and men swarmed about the board. There was a din of voices in which Roger caught half a dozen different English accents. There was also a smell of not too lately washed bodies. The hungry crew attacked the pie with their knives, scooping portions of it onto their trenchers.

"Fight for it, lad, if you'd have any," an older man advised Roger, and the latter managed to get a scanty portion of meat, onions, and turnips, using his dagger. Someone handed him a hunk of dark bread, and he helped himself to ale from the pitcher.

He had seen rude eating before, but had never been thrown into a scramble for his food, or sat next to men who speared chunks of meat with their knives and carried them dripping to their mouths, instead of taking a moderate morsel with the fingers and using a napkin afterwards when needed. He seemed to be among guzzling pigs or dogs. Somers and an apprentice or two ate with a certain amount of restraint, but the others flung their food in, or leant to take it from the trenchers, literally lapping it from these receptacles. When they used hands to help a too hasty knife, they licked the gravy from their grimed paws. As to their ale, they gulped or guzzled it. Roger had seen hounds that ate with more restraint. The scene ground into him the fact that this was the new life he had accepted and would share. It was almost as if he had fallen into the mud and stench of a stye—and knew he would stay there.

All this bore in upon him in spite of himself. With his entire mind he thrust it away and began to eat. Then as he cut a piece of meat and lifted it to his mouth a big lout of a fellow across the table from him guffawed. His eyes had caught the silver haft of Roger's dagger.

"Bid the cook bake tomorrow's pasty in a dish of gold!" he bawled out to the group. "We've one with gentleman's tools among us!"

He gestured toward the silver hilt, and there were smiles
and laughter from the boys and men.

Roger flushed, but said nothing. He wanted no trouble
with any of his new companions.

"And he eats dainty with his fingers," went on the other.
"What, ho! A napkin for my lord! A napkin!"

He glared about as if to summon a serving man, and managed to convey an immense astonishment that none was at
hand. Some of the crew guffawed, but, "Let be, Hodge, let
be," said the one who had spoken to Roger earlier.

However, Hodge was enjoying himself.

"A gentleman's habit, too," he continued, with a pretense
of immense astonishment. "How is this? Ah, we've a fancy

one! Yet he must feed at the trough with the rest of the beasts, like it or no!"

It was an accurate shot at Roger's state of mind, and the latter winced.

"And he doesn't like it!" proclaimed his tormentor, seeing that his shaft had gone home. "Who dragged this fine one into the mire? How came he among a rascally lot like us?"

The man was a natural comedian, and half the table was now convulsed. Somers leaned over and whispered to the fellow, who laughed with satisfaction.

"Ah, Master Burbage brought him," he continued, not dashed in the least. "Sir," he said to Roger, "I salute you. You're a dauber and tacker and hammerer, and will belike wear down to the rest of us. Or be taken down. There are ways for that—aye, ways enough!"

He chuckled. An angry retort was on Roger's lips, but he thought of Burbage, who would scarcely like his quarreling with one of the men, so he grinned what he felt was a haggard grin, and said nothing.

Then, to his surprise, Wat Somers spoke up.

"It's no fault of Master Vance's," he asserted, "that he came to work dressed as he was when—when Master Burbage found him and asked his instant help. For there are s-settings and—and p-properties to ready for the performance, and we had none to do it."

He flushed and stammered, but said his say earnestly. It was an indirect appeal to the loyalty of the crew as King's Men, and it succeeded. There was a murmur of assent.

Hodge himself was impressed, and nodded, but had a parting shot.

"Why, if that's it," he remarked, "good speed to you with your task, Master Vance. And I'll have a napkin for you tomorrow."

Everyone laughed, and Roger joined in.

"No, I'll bring my own," he retorted, "and one for you too, Master Hodge."

It was the right touch, and the crowd approved it, breaking up good-naturedly. But Roger went back to his table feeling strained and shaken. He was sure he had not heard the last of Hodge.

Somers, who had fetched crayon and a slate earlier, now brought some scraps of paper and a pencil, and Roger thanked him for speaking up on his behalf. Somers was pleased.

"Jack Hodge is a trouble-maker of sorts," he said, "and rules the roost among the rough ones here. But I think you could manage him if it came to a brawl."

"I'm not here for that," objected Roger.

"Nevertheless you may come to it," the other assured him. "He loves to lord it, and will try a fall with any man on half a chance."

"Then if he does, I'll give the best I can," promised Roger.

Somers was cheered by this assurance.

"It would be a brave thing if he were taken down for once," he remarked with satisfaction as he went away.

Troubled, Roger turned to the playbook, studied it briefly, rubbed his slate clean, and began a more detailed sketch on paper. It was for the Garter Inn, a setting which required the rear stage on the first level of the playhouse. While he was working at it, Burbage appeared with an actor whom he introduced as John Heminges, manager of the Company. Heminges was a sturdy, clear-eyed fellow in his early thirties. He had a hearty manner.

"Jack has the measurements you need," Burbage said, "and will talk with you about the costumes."

"Aye," said the other, "we must put the tailors to work."

He gave Roger the dimensions of the three main stages,

and explained that sketches for the costumes could be sug-
gestive rather than detailed. "We'll need but the idea—cut
and color—the tailors are skilled at this work and will carry
it through with no trouble."

The three talked of the play in general.

"It's simple enough," Burbage declared. "You are in the
town of Windsor, or in the park near by, or in a field, or you
go to the inn or the house of Master Page, or Ford, or Dr.
Caius. The outer stage will serve for town or field or forest.
You'll need a grassy bank, as I told you, and a few bushes on
board frames, and we'll deck the posts with greenery. For the
inner stages, above and below, there will be curtains for the
rear wall and sides, and, of course, the properties. All that
you must study out."

He looked at Roger's sketch.

"It's good," he said, "but give it more of a rustic air. A
touch of comedy in the setting will make the lords and ladies
laugh. But keep it simple. We spend most on the costumes."

"Make a beginning with them," urged Heminges. "We'll
need all the time we have to get them ready."

Roger nodded, and the two actors left him and went downstairs to resume the rehearsal. He realized fully now that the
possibilities for designing anything of distinction scarcely
existed. He would be mostly a handy-man. Contrivance, not
art, was his task. Contrivance, and the labor of helping to
carry out the routine tasks it involved with his own hands.
Well, he would bend his skill to that. After all, there were
effects to be achieved, and they offered a few possibilities.
Somewhat doggedly he set himself to deal with them.

He had hardly made a beginning—sketching several
costumes and the inn scene on paper—when the rehearsal
ended, and Burbage and Heminges returned. Heminges made
some suggestions about the costumes.

"For Falstaff, it's close to what we want," he said. "Make the cut somewhat more ridiculous, and when you come to the colors, make them strong and ill-matched. Yet keep it a gentleman's habit, though fantastic. A bit ruder for Master and Mistress Page. They're country folk—what you have here smacks too much of the fashionable."

It was sound criticism, and Roger promised to carry it out.

"I'll do them in color tonight," he assured Heminges, "and more besides. And a scene or two, I hope."

"Then gather in all your landlady's candles," advised Burbage, "and stop now, for the light's going. Are we fully cast now as to parts?" he asked Heminges.

"I've cast Master Vance for one of the serving men who carries out Falstaff in the basket of clothes," the other answered. "He seems to me to have the thews for it. And—ah yes, we need another boy or two in the final forest scene, where the fairies dance about the fat knight. But I can find them, I think."

"You want a boy?" asked Roger. "May I bring one? He dances easily, and is a lively youngster."

The two others exchanged glances.

"Who is he?" asked Heminges. "Someone from the house where you lodge?"

"He stays there," replied Roger, "but he's not of the household. He's gentle-born, speaks well, if you value that. He's been serving me as a page."

"Why, then," decided the actor, "if you'll bring him along, I'll look at him and hear him."

Roger thanked him. This, he told himself, would get Cedric out of the garret, and keep him busy.

"I'll bring him tomorrow," he promised. "And when you see him, you'll want him."

VIII

LADY WITH A PURPOSE

MAKING his way up Little Wood Street forty minutes later, Roger moved through the failing light of the late afternoon by habit alone. Wickard or Bragdon might have leapt upon him, for he scarcely noticed the street or the people who passed him. He was busy in his own mind.

Two sets of images struggled there. Now the tiring house of the Globe flashed in: the scene at the noon meal and his sense of strangeness and even of degradation; Heminges and Burbage appeared, too—*I've cast Master Vance for one of the serving men who carries out Falstaff in the basket of clothes.* Then the realization that he was a handy man—most of his work with a saw, hammer, or paint brush—was sharp and relentless. It gave him a sense of moody unrest, almost of hopelessness.

Then he pushed the feeling out, and was happier in the hoped-for future. He was soon imagining himself setting up and taking down curtains and properties in the playhouse, or trying costumes on players who strutted before the backgrounds he created for them.

At the door of his house he came out of this dream world with a jolt. A boy stood by the stoop in the livery of Sir Hubert Knowles, Lucy's father. The youngster bowed and smiled. Roger had seen him before, and nodded. He mounted the stairs, and in his room, sure enough, sat Lucy herself, chaperoned by a serving woman. She rose with a smile and offered him a cheek to kiss. Then she turned to her maid.

"Wait for me downstairs the next ten minutes, Alice," she said calmly. "I must speak with Master Darrell privately on certain matters."

The woman started to say something, for in those times to leave a young woman alone with a man in his rooms was scarcely an approved practice. But it was a tribute to Lucy's poise and character that Alice changed her mind, and left without a word. When the door downstairs closed audibly, the girl seated herself with a considerable rustling of taffeta and starched linen.

Or the woman, rather; for Roger noted with a slight start that she had an air of full maturity. A jeweled hat sat sedately on her brown hair, which was done up with assured style. The rich little cloak about her shoulders, the rustling dress bulked out according to current fashion with the fabulous framework of wire and whalebone called a farthingale, the white starched ruff that projected at least six inches from under her chin, setting off pink cheeks and sparkling eyes— all might have been the apparel of a woman who knew the city and the Court. A breath of subtle perfume came to Roger as she settled herself in her chair.

He cast his hat on the table, took off his sword and laid this with his afternoon's sketches on a chest against the wall.

"Welcome to London," he said with a rather grim smile that reflected the contrast between his plain quarters and the costume of his guest.

Lucy caught his feeling.

"Why, you lodge well enough here, Roger," she said pleasantly. Then she added with a slight edge to her voice, "That is, the rooms are well enough. I wish only I could say the same for your page."

"Cedric?" he asked.

"Is that his name?" she said indifferently. Then with a frown, "You must teach him manners. Never have I seen so much rudeness in so small an amount of boy."

"Why, what did he do?"

"He met me at the door and said pertly that no Master Darrell dwelt here," she replied, her indignation mounting as she spoke. "I said then I would speak with Master Vance, for I had that name too from your uncle, who directed me to you. Nay, he told me, Master Vance was abroad. I asked, when would you return? He had no knowledge of that whatsoever. I said I would wait in your chambers. He answered he knew not if it was fitting I should!"

"Amazing!" Roger exclaimed. Nevertheless he felt a certain wry amusement, for he could imagine Cedric delivering these shots with complete audacity and sureness.

Lucy continued her recital.

"I told him then to call the mistress of the house, or lead the way to your rooms himself. He gave me such a glance as he might fling a kitchen wench; but he brought me here, leaving without a word. And here I have sat more than a hour!"

"I'll speak to the rascal about it in a way he'll not forget," promised Roger.

"Where did you find such a monster?" demanded Lucy. "If it were not the wildest of improbabilities, I'd say that you had caught up with the creature who bound and gagged me at the Hall on Twelfth Night. The coloring is like."

She looked at Roger with something like suspicion.

"Nay, he came to me here in London," he replied as carelessly as he could. "I thought of the boy at the masque, too, but what I learn of him doesn't fit."

He felt enough obligation to Cedric to stretch the facts a little. He wanted no further complications. But Lucy seemed

*Roger realized with a slight start that Lucy had an air of full
maturity*

to dismiss her suspicion as quickly as it had come.

"No matter," she went on. "I have much to speak with you about, Roger, and all of far greater moment than this brat of yours."

She fixed him with earnest, troubled eyes.

"I hear amazing things of you."

Roger seated himself, smiling.

"What do you hear of me?"

"That your master Bartolomeo is dead, and that you seek employment, even of the meanest kind."

Roger shrugged his shoulders.

"Why, as to Bartolomeo, it is true, and much to my surprise and sorrow," he answered. "But as to your other news, it is wrong on two counts. But tell me of matters at home," he broke off urgently. "What of my father? Of Anthony? Why are you here yourself?"

"Your father professes to do well enough, and Anthony also," she said somewhat stiffly. "As for me, I have come with my father who had business here, and am even now supposed to be with the dressmaker, fitting a gown for the King's progress, which we heard yesterday will be scarce three weeks away."

"So soon?" Roger asked. Then he added: "You'll look well in the gown to judge by the effect of your present habit."

Lucy flushed, and smiled a little, pleased.

"Thank you, Roger." Then her eyes grew harder. "But matters at Darrell Manor are not good. And yet might be very good, I think. Roger, all depends on you. That—that is why I am here. One move from you, one happy move—" She paused and broke off quickly. "But what *are* you doing here, if you do not seek employment that is beneath you?"

"I *have* employment."

"Of what kind?"

"At the Globe Playhouse."

"As a player? Oh, surely not."

"Surely not," Roger echoed, but in a positive tone, smiling. He indicated the sketches he had thrown on the chest. "I am designing certain properties and costumes for them. And since you will know it in the end, as a hired man."

Lucy's face showed something close to horror.

"Are you mad, Roger?"

"I think not. It is work that may lead to what I want."

"But Roger!" she protested. "To work for hire! What face can you put upon it? Have you told your friends?"

A suspicion came to her and she struck out sharply.

"Have you seen any of them?" she demanded.

He hesitated, and she spoke before he could answer.

"No!" she declared. "And what is this business of a new name? Are you ashamed of your own?"

"There's a matter of having wounded a fellow who forced a quarrel upon me," Roger answered shortly. "To be plain, I'm liable to arrest."

"Arrest! Why, this is the very fantasy of ill fortune! And all the time you might step out of it as easy as waking from a nightmare. Roger! Have you thought of your father in these weeks?"

"Often and much," he answered grimly.

"No—I do not mean have you thought of him to blame him. To pity him, rather. Don't you know, Roger, that under his bluster he suffers—that he's a lonely old man, eager to see his house well ordered, eager for love—that you, his oldest son, have hurt him?"

Roger nodded.

"Anthony says he isn't himself at all," she continued. "He

stays much apart, in the house, walking to and fro. He barks or snarls at the servants. Sometimes he's not been abroad the whole day."

"I know what's happened has been a blow to him." Roger frowned as he spoke. "I've thought of how he might take it. I didn't want to cause him pain, and I'm sorry for it."

"Sorry!" Lucy exclaimed scornfully.

"I am, Lucy," he assured her. "Most deeply sorry. I'd give much to see him happy."

"Why, you can!" she pounced on him. "No father likes to lose his oldest son," she went on swiftly. "He talks of Anthony, but that's only to put a good face on his bluster. He's proud of your energy, your bearing, your talent. Why, he loves the very fire in you that made him cast you away!"

Roger nodded, for he knew pretty well that it was true.

"But he'll have the fire out—that's his price," he objected, nevertheless.

Lucy laughed at him.

"Have it out!" she scoffed. "Why, you know yourself that he'd only give it a chimney. And you know that in short time you'd be at whatever you want to do, and have your way wholly in the end. Think of *that* for a change," she urged. "And," she added softly, "it is not your future only that hangs on a word, an act, from you. I wonder sometimes if you give any thought to *my* feeling, and of what this could work against me." She lowered her eyes. "Or perhaps you have thought and didn't care."

"You know better than that. You know that I've thought of you. But there are certain things—if a man doesn't stand for what he feels he must do—"

"I know, Roger. I do understand your opposing him. But it—well, I'm afraid. It's going faster than you thought. It's gone to the point where something must be done." She looked up at him with distress in her face. "Already Sir John speaks with my father about a match with Anthony."

Roger picked up his hat and pulled at the plume. He had not really supposed that matters would whirl along at such a rate. But he spoke with a shrug.

"Why, if it's a question of fathers, it can be a question of daughters as well as sons," he said, meaning that she could leave her father as he had his.

Lucy looked at him reproachfully.

"As if I wouldn't, if it were possible!" she exclaimed, answering his thought, and making him feel that she counted this step—a fearful one for a girl in that day—nothing to hesitate about at all.

"But I think you see what we face as well as I, Roger," she continued. "You are desperate now to win bread for yourself. If there were two of us instead of one—" she lifted a hand to indicate the complete helplessness of the situation. "Besides," she went on, "it isn't necessary. Indeed, it's as needless as—as leaping off a cliff or into a fire. You have the whole remedy in your hands. Wait, Roger," she said as he moved to interrupt her. "What have you found here in London? You hide from the law. You labor for wages, like the commonest workman, go under a false name. And what lies beyond? Is there something better you can hope for?"

"There may be."

"But when? Tomorrow? Next month? This year?"

"I don't know."

"But, Roger, there is so little time. Oh, believe me, to stay on here, hoping for some miracle of fortune—it's to bring everything down in ruin on us both. Complete ruin. When one act, one word—"

"I know it!"

He pushed back his chair, rose, and began pacing the room.

She had pulled back all the doubts and fears that had dogged him for a week.

"Do you suppose it was easy for me to take work as a hired man?" he flung out. "Do you think I haven't searched for a hole in this tangle, like an animal in a cage? Do you imagine I like the look of what I see ahead?"

"Then why not change it?"

Lucy's words annoyed him with their quickness. He frowned at her.

"It isn't as simple as that."

"Look into it, and you'll see it is." She bent forward pleadingly. "Oh Roger! Don't let your pride fool and blind you! It can be managed, I know it. If you— Oh,— Help yourself! Help —us! Write to your father. Give Anthony leave to work for you. Let *me* do it. One word, and I will!"

Roger looked at her and was shaken. He took her hand, sighed, then smiled, and an answering smile lighted her whole face. *You're a fool! She's as beautiful as an angel. What are you doing here in London, skulking about, playing laborer, dreaming of the impossible?* His mind taunted him and he almost said the words she wanted to hear. Then something in him steeled against it.

"I can't leave the King's Men with this task unfinished," he said slowly. "But—well, that is a matter of days only, it's true—"

"You could write your father meanwhile."

"I'll think about it."

"No. Do it, Roger."

"I'll think about it."

Lucy's lips opened as if to take up the fight again; then, as she saw the stubborn set of his jaw, she closed them, and beamed at him instead.

"You'll think about it *and* do it," she assured him buoyantly.

"You will! I know it, Roger."

Roger smiled at her, really uncertain, and said nothing. But she read his feeling.

"And write to me," she urged him. "We leave town to-morrow and spend a week or more near by, with my father's friend, Sir Hubert Lane. Then we shall return. The house lies up the river." She took out a little tablet with a tiny gilded pencil attached to it, wrote the address, and laid it on the table. "A man will bring a letter there for sixpence." Then she lifted her face to Roger's.

A little later, as they went down the stairs, Roger could have sworn that someone had darted ahead of them only a moment before, to disappear into the other wing of the house to the right. He thought at once of Cedric. It seemed quite of a piece with what the young scamp had done before, and what Roger knew he might do.

"I'll read him such a lecture as will leave him dumb for a week," he muttered to himself as Lucy and her two retainers moved down the street. She turned just then and gave him a dazzling smile.

At the moment, she was a symbol of what he had left in contrast with the drabness, perhaps hopelessness, of what he had. The playhouse seemed a cold, dismal and tawdry place, its limitations real, its promise as a path to a better future slight and pathetic. Perhaps Lucy was right. Perhaps he *could* have both his natural place in the world and the work he wanted. He stood for some time looking down the street to the corner where she had disappeared.

IX

THE CHALLENGE

No CHOIR boy with eyes fixed on heaven and lips making sweet
harmony of a Latin hymn could have looked more innocent
than Cedric as the two sat over their supper before a cheerful
fire that evening. Roger ate in silence, and the boy never
offered to break it. But his almost angelic appearance seemed
a silent reproach to his new friend. *I'll change that soon
enough,* thought Roger grimly.

"Well, sirrah," he said when they had finished, "so you
make it your business to be rude to my guests. Is this Bragdon's teaching or your own nature?"

Cedric looked at him calmly.

"I knew of no guests you expected," he replied, "and was
ill-prepared to welcome any."

There was good enough sense in that, considering that
Roger's only other visitor had been the weasel-faced lawyer's
man who came asking for him at night.

"If your friend had been courteous enough herself to tell
me who she was," the boy went on, "I should then have been
more to blame for *my* discourtesy, if any. But one who insists
and commands without showing any right to do so runs, I
think, some risk of being suspect."

"Suspect!" shouted Roger. "Why, she is—"

He broke off suddenly, arrested as he awoke suddenly to
the meaning of a phrase in Cedric's speech.

"You say if you had known who she was," he said slowly, "you might have behaved better. If she didn't tell you, how do you know about her now? By heaven, I think you listened at the door! I had everything but the sight of you as I came out."

"Then you had nothing," retorted Cedric with a faint grin.

"You were there!" accused Roger sharply.

Cedric shrugged.

"Her manner set my back up like a file on a saw," he confessed. "It's true and I admit it. And as for the eavesdropping —well, I still don't know who she is, though I caught the better part of what she said. Are you betrothed to her?" he asked innocently. Roger gasped at his effrontery.

"No!" he shouted in reply before he caught himself. Then he growled: "Though what concern of yours it can be, I don't know. Merciful heaven!" he exclaimed, "I ought to beat you until you howl! Have you no sense of manners whatever?"

Cedric looked distressed.

"I'm truly sorry, Roger," he said, "and if I had known she was your betrothed—"

"She isn't, I've told you!"

"If indeed she isn't, I cannot be sorry for that," the boy declared, flushing with a curious defiance, "though I would have shown her courtesy enough if I had known she was a friend from near your home."

"Well, she *is* that," retorted Roger, "and although I am not betrothed to her, I was close enough to being, and may actually be so at any time. And I am mightily displeased with you."

"I'm sorry for it."

"You don't look very sorry to me."

"I'm not as sorry as I might be if—"

"If what?"

"If she had more regard for you than she has, or you for yourself," the boy blurted out.

Roger stared at him.

"In the name of patience," he demanded, "tell me who you are to judge what she feels for me, or what I do about my own affairs."

Cedric shrugged, but evaded the demand.

"I see no regard for you in seeking to pull you back to your father like an ox with a ring through his nose, which seemed to be her whole effort and design."

Roger noted the unflattering comparison, but grimly decided to ignore it.

"And what if it *was* her design?" he asked. "Is there any good reason why I should *not* go back to my father?"

"Only that since I have known you, you have seemed to think you had good reason to leave him."

Roger marveled at the neat retort. By heavens, when the boy became a man he'd likely go far, with all the energy and shrewdness he had.

"Lucy and I were not wholly of a mind on my going back to Kent," he conceded. "But what if she were right?"

Cedric looked at Roger steadily.

"Right or wrong, were *I* a woman," he declared, with an owlish gravity that Roger might have found amusing at another time, "I would think long before I tried to force the man I loved away from the thing he did best and wanted most."

His eyes held Roger's own, and he spoke with feeling.

"Why, Cedric," Roger protested, "you yourself heard her say that she would defy her own father to come to me at need."

"I heard her say nothing like it! She shook the possibility at you, and then told you it was madness."

"Was she wrong about that?"

"Yes. If one has no will or intention to do a thing, it's a trick to say he will." Unconsciously or intentionally the boy shifted from the practical question to the more vulnerable one of Lucy's character, and then faced Roger defiantly. "I am sorry if I speak too plain," he said, "but I must speak as I think. She neither regards you as she should, nor lets you so regard yourself."

"So *I* come into it!"

"Do you not, Roger?" Cedric asked with earnest eyes. "Did you not come here for a purpose? Have you not worked and suffered for it, and are you not thinking now of leaving off what you began as if it were nothing at all?"

Roger sat amazed. What kind of a boy was this that was so wisely and clearly telling him his duty? And feeling deeply what it was, too. He sat staring at Cedric and felt a sudden revulsion against what he had half set himself to do. He remembered what he had told his uncle—he would work and suffer endlessly if he could only see that it might lead him toward the career he wanted. And now, when he had made a beginning of sorts— Yes, it was true that he was a hired man and had been made to feel like one. It was true that the tasks he faced were more contrivance than art. But what did he know yet of where they would lead? Hadn't he half surrendered to the idea of being a mere carpenter, when he might become something more if he worked the vein of slight hope that was offered? He felt a sudden revulsion. *Why, you are a turn-tail! What have these difficult days here meant to you? Why did you quarrel with Trevor? For what have you been laboring this very day? Are you quitting the fight when it's hardly joined?* He sat for a moment in silence, feeling ashamed before the memory of Bartolomeo, before his uncle, Nicholas Johnson, himself.

"Nay, Cedric," he said at last, gruffly, "I've made no promises and no decision. And I will say this: you speak to the point. I have obligations, it is true. On your account alone I should be slow to think of leaving London now."

"On my account I would not have you stay one hour!" flashed the boy. Then he added more quietly: "I do not mean that I would not wish you to stay, that I don't value your help. But if there is a good for me that goes against what is best for you, I do not want you to think of staying. If you stay, it should be because you find it the right and true thing for you."

Roger sat thinking. The boy had flung down the very challenge that had led him to London. He felt again its moving power. Yet there was a point also in what Lucy had said. For an instant the gentleman stood up as if to do battle with the hired man, but Roger knew that it was a gesture only, and that he was moving toward a firm decision. But he spoke cautiously.

"I shall do nothing hasty, Cedric," he announced. "You are right that I came here for a good reason. I'm not yet ready to forget it. I'll not be leaving you or my work until I see more clearly than I do."

Cedric looked at him soberly.

"If you stay, it must be for yourself, not for me," he declared.

Roger nodded.

"Thanks for that, Cedric. It's well spoken and I'll not forget it. Meanwhile, I *am* staying. And," he said with a start of remembrance, "I have a night's work to do."

He went over and picked up his sketches. Then he remembered his last words to Heminges.

"By the way," he added, "if you still fancy a life at the playhouse, you shall go there with me tomorrow morning."

"What do you mean? Have you spoken to Master Burbage?

"I know they'll take me! They must!" he cried

Am I to have a part in the play?" Cedric leaned forward with kindling eyes.

"If they like the look and sound of you. Heminges has told me to bring you, and he'll decide."

Cedric clapped his hands, bounded up, and began to jig.

"I *know* they'll take me! They must!" he cried. "What kind of a part am I to play?"

"Some imp or fairy, I believe," Roger answered, "and it seems to suit you famously. Save the dancing for tomorrow," he admonished with a grin. "I have a mountain of designs to turn out and need a quiet room for it. Not but what you're welcome to stay if you like. I'd enjoy company, but I'll be too busy for much talk."

He began to assemble the materials for his work. Cedric looked at the sketches, exclaiming about them, then as Roger began to draw, sat silently for a time, watching. But before an hour had passed he began to yawn, and finally rose, murmuring a sleepy good-night, and left Roger busy with his pencil under a cluster of candles.

X

BABES IN THE PLAYHOUSE

"JIG, then, lad, while I hum a catch for you!"

Heminges stood with Roger, Shakespeare and Cedric on the big platform of the main stage of the Globe in the early winter morning. It was a friendly gathering. Cedric seemed to have made a good impression upon the actor and the playwright so far as appearance went; now they were testing his skill. And as Heminges carried a lively air in a pleasant baritone voice, the boy shook his legs in a brisk tattoo, changing from slow to fast and back again.

"Bravo!" exclaimed the actor at last.

Roger sighed with relief. He had brought Cedric out early that morning. The youngster's eyes had been heavy with sleep, and turned dully when Roger pointed to the workmen gathering at the foundations of the arch near St. Paul's, and at the stone and lumber assembled there for building the huge structure. On the river there had been a cold, thin fog that seemed to numb the boy. It was only after breakfast in a Bankside tavern that he had warmed into something like his usual self. Then the sight of the playhouse, the first he had ever seen at close view, seemed to pull him completely out of his daze. Now his face glowed with color and his eyes shone.

"Can you speak as well as you can jig, Master Cedric?" asked Shakespeare. "Do you know some lines of verse by heart? If you do, speak out—and say them loud enough to knock against the gallery wall yonder."

Cedric studied a moment, then smiled at Roger and began. He threw out his voice, yet seemed to keep it low and intimate:

> My true love hath my heart and I have his,
> By just exchange one for the other given:
> I hold his dear, and mine he cannot miss;
> There never was a better bargain driven!

He continued on through the sonnet that had been on many men's lips during the past twenty years, delivering it with a lightness and tenderness that suited the lines, and finishing in a tone that was almost casual, yet somehow grave and impressive:

> Both, equal hurt, in this change sought our bliss:
> My true love hath my heart, and I have his!

"A hit, a hit!" fairly crowed Heminges. "Will, you gave the lad a target and he's planted an arrow in the very center!"

Shakespeare smiled at the other's enthusiasm, but seemed well pleased himself.

"Who taught you to say the lines, lad?" he asked kindly.

"No one, sir; though I heard my father recite them often, and perhaps I say them as he did."

"Well, Master Cedric," remarked the dramatist, "Sir Philip Sidney himself would know some small pleasure in heaven to hear his words so sweetly rendered. I think we may call you one of us."

He looked inquiringly at Heminges, who spoke up vigorously, "Aye, what else?"

"I may have some lines for you, young master," Shakespeare continued, turning to Cedric again, "for this play calls so loudly for boys, what with three women and many youngsters pushing into it, that I who wrote the comedy often wonder how they all got there!"

"Aye," agreed Heminges, chuckling. "That first performance before the Queen at Windsor sent us scurrying about for
an extra boy or two. I remember that. Lad," he said on impulse
to Cedric, "the play would never have been written except for
the Queen. Master Shakespeare had dragged this fat fellow
Falstaff through two long histories, and planned then to kill
him off, but Her Majesty sent word he was to write something
more about the mountainous rascal, showing him in love!"

"Is it so, sir?" asked Cedric of the playwright.

"The truth itself," Shakespeare agreed. "But, Jack," he
said to Heminges, "we have a full morning's work waiting for
us, and Master Vance I think has designs he must show Dick
Burbage."

"I must see those, too," said Heminges. "Master Vance,
come along; for I and even you must join in the rehearsal
later. I'll send out the Company to you, Will," he said to the
playwright.

And soon, as he conferred with Burbage and Heminges in
the space behind the stages, Roger could hear the prompter
calling the roll, and Shakespeare speaking briefly before the
run-through of the first scene.

But when he laid the sketches on the table, first displaying
those for the costumes, he forgot the rehearsal completely.
The two actors were apparently as much interested as he. They
studied closely what he had done, and offered objections or
suggestions freely.

"More color and frills for Dr. Caius," Heminges pronounced. "He's a comic, Master Vance, and a Frenchman.
Dress him to the part."

He liked Roger's flamboyant suggestions for Falstaff, and
approved the costume for young Fenton, the hero.

"You've the right touch there. He's well-born, and deserves

a dress that smacks of the London mode."

Burbage made a sensible suggestion about the habit of a hobgoblin: instead of brown, why not a glossy purple-black for his cape and doublet, and a helmet-like black cap to match, then red for the under-side of the cloak, for the hose, and the buttons? The effect would be something like that of an exotic beetle.

Altogether half of the ten costumes sketches were taken by Heminges for immediate dispatch to the tailors; the others Roger was to re-do.

"We can alter some of our old costumes in certain cases," the company's manager remarked. "They're of the best materials, and with some cutting and trimming and additions My Lord will never know them for anything but new."

"See that he doesn't!" warned Burbage. "All must look as fresh-turned as new sovereigns."

Heminges nodded.

"Never fear! If a player and a tailor together can't fool a lord, then there's no living for an honest man in England!"

"Or a dishonest one!" Burbage laughed.

"No dishonesty!" Heminges retorted. "Every stitch of what's worn will be tailored for the play. What's new on the boards is what *looks* new, and everything will!"

Roger was now ready to show the scenes he had finished— three of them. He wondered with an anxiety approaching anguish what Burbage would think of one in particular, for it was a daring experiment. The idea for it had come to him late the night before, as he worked in the complete silence of his room. He had perceived suddenly a possibility for more than contrivance—a chance for art!

It had to do with the forest scenes. Burbage had said that all these would be played on the main platform. Yet Roger noticed that several times in the course of the play one of these followed another—two woodland settings in succession.

This pratice was an inheritance from the old miracle plays, which often used three or more "stations" on their simple stage—a manger to indicate the interior of a stable, a throne to suggest a palace, a bush and a bank of turf to represent a hill where shepherds sat. These were, of course, mere symbols of scenes: in each case the spectator had to fill out the picture for himself. And, of course, no full scene in the modern sense could be set on the outer stage, for perhaps a third of the persons watching any play stood or sat at the sides of the projecting platform, and did not get a front-on view of it.

But what, Roger had asked himself, if he set the second scene of the two in the inner stage instead of on the outer? *It would be an easy thing,* he thought eagerly. *A forest background can be painted on a curtain wholly covering the rear. On each side, farther forward, trees painted on canvas and then cut out and stretched on frames. Two on each side, one nearer the audience than the other. All will be seen only from the front—it will show a forest glade receding into the distance.*

He remembered then that Bartolomeo had told him of such settings in Italian theaters. They were prepared with great care and expense, and remained during the entire performance, for one scene and one stage only were used in those theaters. In this respect they were at a disadvantage as compared with English playhouses. But the latter in turn suffered in quality: the settings were never notable as art—a rear wall always much the same, side curtains, a few properties. *I can combine the two! The advantages of our theater will remain —the various playing areas. Yet for the rear stages, something better is possible. By devising fuller and richer scenes for them, I can approach the quality they achieve in Florence and Padua!*

Immensely excited, he had bent eagerly to the task of creating a design that would show his idea. While he was busy with it, and even when he had completed his work, it seemed a triumph to him. But now, as he prepared to show the two actors his sketches, he had a strong doubt if Burbage would regard it as one.

He took out first that for the Garter Inn. Quickly he explained to Burbage how he had carried out the latter's instructions of the preceding day. The walls and door were a neutral color and unadorned. The properties used for furniture, and the curtains covering part of the rear wall (the usual arrangement in settings for the inner stage) and certain removable objects hung upon that wall—these would provide the means for transforming the set completely when it was needed for another locale. For example, bring in a different table and chairs, take down the deer's and boar's heads, remove the shelf with tankards that stood beneath them, bring in a new arras, hang a picture where the shelf had been, and the Garter Inn would change to Ford's house. Burbage was pleased, and Heminges echoed his approval.

Roger now brought out his design for a room in Dr. Caius's house—a setting for the upper stage. With only a few suggestions for change, both accepted this. They were appreciative of the imposing flasks Roger had drawn—receptacles of exaggerated size and shape which he had modeled on the equipment of a chemist's shop he remembered near the university. They liked the ponderous medical books in colored bindings.

"Good!" exclaimed Heminges. "You've done for the doctor's chamber what you failed to do for his costume!"

Then Roger laid the sketch for the forest on the table for inspection. He could hear both of them gasp as they saw it.

"Why, what's this?" demanded Burbage when he had

caught his breath. "We play most of the forest scenes on the main platform, or against a curtain if on the stage behind."

"Yet in several places one follows another," Roger pointed out, "and to show something closer to nature—" He broke off. "Do you think the design fails?"

"Why," answered Burbage slowly, "as a design it's good enough. But to use it in playing the play—well, I am of two minds about that."

"And what's this that multiplies your thinking, Dick?"

All turned to face Shakespeare standing near them. He was ready for his chief actor and had declared a break in the rehearsal in order to come and get him.

Burbage moved to one side so that Shakespeare could see the design, and explained how Roger had planned to use it.

"It's well done," he finished, "but we've seldom set an outdoor scene in the rear stage, and never against a pictured background."

Shakespeare stood looking at the sketch with evident interest.

"It's really a perspective scene, such as I understand they make in Italy," he said at last.

"It is, sir, it is!"

Roger spoke up eagerly. To be permitted to carry out this design, the one piece of complete art that he had been able to devise for himself, seemed of greater importance to him than ever.

"My teacher, Master Bartolomeo, told me of such settings," he went on quickly, "and in this recess it is possible to use them, for all the audience sees the scene from the front only. And since you play for one who wants richness and novelty, will it not please him and his friends to see a change from one part of the woodland to another flash before their eyes as the curtain is drawn?"

The others murmured an appreciation of the point.

"It is easily done," Roger urged. He explained how he would paint and set up the rear curtain and the trees at the sides, and concluded, "And when the scene has been played, all can be removed in a few minutes."

"Well, I am more than half persuaded," said Burbage.

Shakespeare took up the design, holding it at arm's length, then laid it down with an air of decision.

"I am wholly so," he declared. "Dick, such things have been done in a fashion at Court, though never, I think, so boldly. For they use real trees for the most part, which are heavy and to my mind out of place. It's an effort toward copying nature, but patched up, and not art. If we can show a new and ingenius device, we better our craft. So paint your forest, Master Vance, and we'll play before it gladly."

Later that afternoon, called down from his hammering and painting in the loft, Roger rehearsed his own part in the play. As Heminges had said, he took the role of a serving man. The scene was in Ford's house, and the latter's wife arranged to have Falstaff carried out in a basket under a heap of soiled linen, thus tricking her husband, who suspected that the fat knight was about. Hodge and Roger bore the basket. They were instructed with care as to gait and posture, but the action was simple.

The rehearsal moved on to the final scene, and Roger watched to see how Cedric would perform.

Here the tricks that the two housewives had played on Falstaff came to a climax. Although the ingenious ladies had led him from one humiliation to another, he still believed that he would win the love of one or both, and came to a rendezvous in Windsor Forest. There all had been prepared for his final punishment. The two husbands had been informed of the plan; they, the wives themselves, the serving boys, pretty Anne Page—all were on hand. Disguised as elves, goblins and monsters, they were ready to pay the fat old rascal off.

The fairies appeared first, and at the sight of them Falstaff fell flat and pretended to be asleep. He had heard that mortals risked death if they were caught watching the revels of the elves.

In the rehearsal of this scene, Anne Page as the fairy queen summoned her subjects for a consultation. When they had assembled, a hobgoblin called the roll. This sprite later had a few additional lines to speak, and then led the others as they danced, singing, about the prostrate Falstaff, pinching him and burning him with their tapers while he endured the torture for fear of losing his life if he cried out.

Shakespeare was dissatisfied with the way the scene was played. He seemed particularly concerned about the hobgoblin.

"Come, Harry," he told the boy who took the part, "put life into your lines. You're not reciting to a master at grammar school. It's an imp you play. Dance and swagger through it!"

The youngster tried earnestly to respond, but could not shake off his stiffness. The playwright stood thoughtfully after a third attempt, apparently baffled.

"I can do it!"

Roger started, for it was Cedric's voice. Everyone was staring at the boy. He had committed a breach of playhouse etiquette.

He himself quickly saw this.

"I ask your pardon, sir," he said to Shakespeare. "I spoke hastily."

The actor nodded, but looked at his new boy actor with appraising eyes.

"Yet I think I shall put you to the test, young sir," he remarked.

"Oh, no," protested Cedric, fully conscious now of his discourtesy. "I should not have spoken. I could not take another's part when—"

"You're welcome enough to it," muttered the baffled Harry.

Shakespeare smiled at the two, and spoke quietly to the boy he had been coaching.

"Let him have your script."

"Nay, I know the lines," Cedric said quickly, waving the paper aside. "But—if I could have the cue?"

He looked at the boy playing Anne Page, and meanwhile retreated to the group of those playing the fairies.

The other youngster complied. "Crier Hobgoblin, make the fairy oyez!"

At the words Cedric took a step forward, did a tumble, and bowed low to his queen. Then he turned and called with a sweep of his arm:

"Elves, list your names! Silence, you airy toys!"

The fairies called out their names, and Cedric went on, the others responding to his bouncing liveliness. The scene suddenly sparkled and leapt, was elfin and fantastic. When he had finished, Shakespeare nodded with approval, gave him a few suggestions, and asked:

"Do you know the song, too? Can your carry the air?"

Cedric answered that he could, and soon was leading the elves in a dance step about the cowering Falstaff. His feet seemed scarcely to touch the stage. As he pinched the cringing knight, or set a candle to arm or knee, each motion matched the rhythm of the chanted words:

> Fie on sinful fantasy!
> Fie on lust and luxury!

Lust is but a bloody fire
Kindled with unchaste desire,
Fed in heart, whose flames aspire
As thoughts do blow them higher and higher!

And now the fat knight, desperately keeping silence, was heaving and shuddering to the song:

Pinch him, fairies, mutually!
Pinch him for his villainy!
Pinch him and burn him and turn him about,
Till candles and star-light and moonshine be out!

Roger chuckled. By heaven, the boy was a jewel of an antic! They were both of them babes in the wood of the playhouse world, but it was a magic wood, opening up a hundred possibilities. Now that he had won permission to paint his forest scene, he seemed to be on a path leading straight to the Court and the fabulous Inigo Jones. As for Cedric, the Globe was a miracle of deliverance. Here his bubbling energy could run free. He would have work and enjoyment in one, without the ghost of danger from Bragdon and his menacing retainers.

XI

THE THIRD HUNTER

A WEEK later Roger sat in the playhouse lobby, waiting for Heminges, and jotting down some notes about the condition of the properties he had been looking over.

It was the second morning after the performance at My Lord of Nethereaven's. The company had spent the better part of the preceding day in getting back to London. Today, Roger had come to the playhouse earlier than usual, and made a hasty survey of the curtains, costumes and other materials stored in the lofts of the third story and in the basement. He knew that the week would be a busy one. The Globe was opening in four days. Between now and then the paraphernalia for five performances must be assembled and put in order. In some cases the plays were recent ones, and everything needed for their presentation was in fairly good condition. But several were older, and costumes and properties for these demanded overhauling, with some repainting and repairing, and even replacements.

Roger sighed. The work was interesting, and yet he realized that all of it would be routine hand labor. The rear walls for the stages of the Globe were set pieces which remained the same always except as new curtains or properties were used. And even if a curtain showed wear, the answer was some fresh paint. With stools, tables, altars, grassy banks, only some carpentry, or some new cloth, or a daub of color would be needed.

There had been little in the settings of *The Merry Wives* to challenge him as an artist—only the forest scene, really. But he saw now that his work for that play had been an orgy of originality compared with what his future tasks would be. There was nothing about them that required an artist. They didn't even require much in the way of skilled craftsmanship.

The Merry Wives! Yes, the play had been a success. My Lord had been pleased, his guests had applauded with abandon. Cedric, who dozed now on a bench on the other side of the lobby, had played quite up to the promise he showed in rehearsal. Roger felt that his own work on the staging of the comedy had been done well, yet as his mind flicked back to it he had a wry sense of disappointment. It was as if he had made exciting progress with some Court belle, only to see her whisked off by a more dashing cavalier, the very sparkle he had kindled in her eyes mocking him as she went. For as the play had begun that night the actors had swept onto the stage, magnificently uproarious, and the costumes, scenes and properties on which he had labored became mere background—the necessary but scarcely noticed setting for a flashing jewel.

He heard the door close, and looked up. It was not Heminges, but Shakespeare. The playwright drew off his gloves and walked over toward Roger. Cedric sprang to his feet and bowed. Roger rose too. Shakespeare waved the boy down and turned to the young man.

"You're early, Sir Artist," he said pleasantly, "and I'm glad of it. I wanted to tell you that your task the other night was discharged better than well."

"I—I thought it was scarcely noticed, sir," stammered Roger. "The comedy was so successfully played that I fear little account was taken of the scenes and properties."

Shakespeare shook his head, smiling.

"You wrong yourself," he insisted. "I can tell you that My Lord was as delighted with the dress of the play as with its voice and gestures. And when the curtains were drawn to show the forest setting for the inner stage, I heard a gasp of pleased surprise. Of course," he added quietly, "a performance pleases or displeases as a whole rather than in parts. Each of us counts his own work well done when the play succeeds."

Roger bowed, recognizing the truth and personal point of the final words. Shakespeare came over and sat on the edge of the table, motioning Roger to resume his own seat.

"I've been watching you with a certain personal interest, Master Vance," he said, "for there was a time when I filled a post somewhat like yours. Yes," he nodded as Roger showed surprise, "I was a very humble beginner when I joined My Lord of Leicester's players seventeen years ago. I did not step down as far as you, I think; yet my family had won a certain distinction in Stratford, and I myself had served as a schoolmaster, associating with gentlemen and exercising some authority. I didn't find my tasks as a man of all work easy at first."

Roger nodded again. He felt an understanding and sureness in the other's words that seemed to leave him nothing to say.

"But I learned this," Shakespeare went on: "A man is foolish who does not make himself see honestly the hard, cruel, despicable, yes, even the malignant things in the life he lives; but he is yet more foolish to see nothing else." His eyes glowed with a light that seemed to reveal an inner power. "He may proclaim these ills," he continued, "speak out against them, as often I have set myself to do. He may even feel, as I have felt at times, that for most of us they tip the scales against the bright and good. Yet he will do well to accept them as there, and go on with what he sets himself to do."

He looked at Roger steadily a moment, then shrugged and laughed.

"A sermon after breakfast," he said lightly, "and you have a busy day before you—a day of patching and contriving."

Roger smiled somewhat sheepishly, for the words hit his feeling exactly.

"It's in the run of your work," the playwright remarked calmly, "and yet your hopes are for something very different. You are an artist; you would like to practise your art—just as I, as a writer, like to practise mine. I'd be sick at heart if I came here hoping to make plays, and were set to copying or tidying other men's words. Yet the plays we prepare for now will give you no opportunity to do much more than carpenters' or house painters' tasks."

Roger perceived with a start that this man saw into his mind as if through a window. Yet he realized that the very fullness of Shakespeare's understanding gave it a warm friendliness as well as point. He asked impulsively: "But, sir, will there be other plays—later ones—that will offer a greater opportunity?"

Shakespeare shrugged.

"I've followed playhouses and players' companies more summers and winters than I like to count," he answered, "and always I've seen them grow and change as if they fed on magic. And if we who manage the theaters and make plays for them don't betray our quality, there will be changes with every tomorrow, and opportunities with them, for Dick Burbage and you and me. But I don't know what they will be, Master Vance," he concluded, "or if you can seize them and use them."

"I can wait—and try."

Shakespeare nodded, and sat quietly for a moment. Then

he said casually:

"To tell the truth, there's a play already written that none has read but me. I have had it in mind since seeing your work, for there are certain possibilities—" He broke off. "Would you like to talk with me about it?"

"Would I!" Roger jumped up from his stool, his eyes shining.

The other checked him with a gesture.

"It may mean little or nothing," he warned. "You have lodgings in the city, I think?"

"Yes, sir. On Little Wood Street."

"Why, then I'm a stone's throw from you—at Silver and Monkwell," said Shakespeare. "If you have the leisure this evening, we might spend an hour together. I am not sure but our writing and acting could profit more than they do from the way we dress our stages."

"I'm sure they could, sir!"

"Be sure, by all means." The playwright smiled. "And yet," he warned Roger once more, "even if betterment is possible, I can't say if our Company would approve a bold venture toward it. My voice is only one of a number. Yet you and I are free as the winds to talk about the business."

He described the location of his house.

"It's the shop and dwelling of one Christopher Montjoy," he explained. "He's a Frenchman, a Huguenot, and expert in his trade of hairdresser. You'll find me there."

He broke off as Heminges and several others came in, and Roger had a chance for no more than an exchange of glances with a delighted Cedric before he was deep in a discussion of his work with the Company's manager.

Some of the plays needed very little work. *All's Well That Ends Well,* for example, was a recent production, and almost everything required for it was in order. Ben Jonson's *Every*

Man in His Humor called for rather simple settings and costumes. But *As You Like It,* which was the opening piece, was an older comedy, and so was *Twelfth Night.* Costumes for these needed to be repaired or replaced; an arbor which Roger had found in the basement (it was raised from there through the large trap door in the main stage) would have to be rebuilt.

Heminges went over all that needed to be done.

"Devise something new and different," he urged. "Do what you have time for if you are pressed. Smith can help you. You've a lively mind and a good eye for color. We make our bow to London after more than half a year of idleness. We should step out bravely. Yet the expense must not be great," he warned. "By heaven, except for our bounty from playing before the King, and a few pounds picked up playing from town to town in the country, we'd be beggars now," he concluded.

Roger, Smith, and a number of others spent the morning gathering together the costumes and properties needing to be freshened or replaced, and doing carpentry work and painting where these were required. Hodge, who had been fairly quiet during the preceding week because of the urgency of the task of getting everything ready for the play, was readier now with provocative remarks. Roger took them in good part or ignored them. His talk with Shakespeare had given him a hope which made such annoyances seem trivial. When he stepped down from the loft at noon he was in a good humor, and very hungry.

The actors were just leaving, and the boys, shepherded by Wynn the prompter, were ready to set out for a nearby private house where they were being fed. Cedric was with them; and Roger saw that young Fairfield, who seemed to play most of the heroine roles, was leading a not too quiet attempt to haze the new boy.

"The part fits him like a glove, for the girl's a stupid slut," he was saying.

"Who gets wed to a fool in the end," put in another boy.

" 'An ill-favored thing, but mine own!' " quoted a third.

Roger did not know the exact occasion for the gibes—actually, it was Cedric's being cast for the part of Audrey, a more than simple country girl who gets the jester Touchstone as a husband in the last act of the play.

The new boy was shrugging off the chaffing good-naturedly, but Roger guessed that behind his assumed indifference he was annoyed with his sharp-tongued companions. The youngsters went out just as the servants from the inn entered in their usual slap-dash manner, the cook's man carrying a huge fish.

Roger followed him upstairs. He had his own share of badgering from Hodge during the meal, though it was nothing like the first day's. The new hired man was dressed for his work now, with a carpenter's apron and a plain sheath knife, and he knew that in the past week he had won the respect and friendliness of a number of the men. But Hodge took no account of this, and mimicked Roger's well-bred accents and his gentleman's manner in a fashion that brought more than one laugh. Roger managed a good-natured retort once or twice, and when Hodge twitted him with having shirked carrying his full part of the load when the two had borne Falstaff out in the basket of soiled linen, he merely shrugged and laughed:

"Each thinks he has the heavy end. Sometimes I wondered if you'd climbed in on top of him."

This sally was greeted with a titter, and Hodge glared.

As they finished eating and rose, and Roger passed by him, the fellow shot out a foot quickly.

It was too late to avoid it, and Roger felt himself falling, but he seized the other's calf as he stumbled, and pulled him off the bench, so that the big fellow landed with a thump on his posterior. He sprang up cursing.

"Let be!" Roger warned him. "You bid for it, and got a fair exchange."

A few of the others murmured agreement. "Let be, let be," they echoed.

But Hodge had made his opportunity and did not intend to be balked.

"Nay, I'll try a fall with this cockerel," he insisted, and most of the men, willing to see good sport, called out: "Make room!" "A fall, a fall!"

Smith, the older man who had given Roger a friendly word the first day, seemed to be the arbiter. He hesitated, looking toward the stairs that led below as if some of the housekeepers (men like Shakespeare and Burbage who owned the playhouse) might be around. Then he gave a gesture of assent.

"One fall, then," he agreed. "No biting or gouging, but clean sport. You hear, Jack?" he demanded of Hodge.

"Nay, I'll do no more than maul him and muss his hair," the latter agreed.

"Stand back, then," Smith told the others. "Tom," he ordered one of the younger men, "go down and stand by the door and keep a sharp eye and call out if the masters return."

The young man nodded, and reluctantly descended to his post. Hodge dove in while Roger hesitated.

The rush backed him up and almost downed him, but he went with it four or five steps, and then twisted suddenly, so that Hodge and not he was against the wall. He wanted room to maneuver. He made a feint and felt the other's strength, which seemed as great as a bull's. They thrust this way and that, but at length Hodge got a leg behind Roger's, tripped him, and both fell. Roger rolled, sensing that if he were once to let himself be caught in the grip of those enormous arms he would have a hard time of it. He tried deftly for a hold he had learned in wrestling at the Manor, but Hodge blocked him neatly. *He has skill as well as strength. Keep moving.* Roger did, and for a time it was any man's battle, for the new hired man had power enough of his own, and was a shade the faster of the two.

Then for a second he was off guard, and the great arms closed about him. He remembered the advice of the forester who had taught him wrestling. "If you're caught, Master Darrell, and like not to break out, throw a fit!" He had been shown how to throw one, and he did it now, writhing and contorting and bucking and shuddering with an explosive energy that caught his opponent by surprise, and in a minute he had broken the grip and was on top of Hodge. The group cheered, and Hodge grunted: "Well done, Master Dainty, but not again!" and they were rolling once more, each furiously seeking an advantage. Roger got one, but lost it; Hodge almost caught him again, but the grip did not quite close, and Roger broke it. Then they twisted and blocked, each wary for an opening, when the lookout below suddenly called out a warning.

"They're coming! I see Master Burbage!"

"Break, lads!" commanded Smith quickly, and pulled them to their feet. "It was good sport, and no man the master."

"In another minute I'd have pinned him," panted Hodge. "And will yet, don't doubt it," he flung at Roger, and made off.

Roger had hardly brushed himself off before he heard the actors opening the downstairs door.

Wat Somers sidled up to him.

"*Would* he have pinned you?" he half whispered with a concern that made Roger laugh. He wiped the sweat from his cheeks and forehead, and a little blood with it, where he had been scratched.

"Not if I could have pinned him first," he answered. "But he doesn't down easy."

Somers nodded.

*He made a feint and felt the other's strength, which seemed **as** great as a bull's*

"It was a famous thing the way you broke the one good hold he got!" he volunteered, and seemed to be comforted.

Roger had a long and busy afternoon, and was late coming down from the loft where he had been working. He wondered if Hodge would be waiting for him; but the rest of the stage crew seemed to have left, and he took off his work clothes, donned his good doublet, and threw a cloak about his shoulders. Cedric was there, ready, and they started for the door.

Roger opened it to face a man who had lifted his hand to knock—a responsible-looking person in the dress of a lawyer's clerk. As the young man eyed the stranger, he heard Cedric skipping to the far side of the lobby, where the wall of the inner stage hid him.

"Sir," said the visitor courteously enough, "a word with you."

He offered to enter, and Roger stepped back.

"I seek a Master Roger Darrell," the other told him composedly, meanwhile studying his face with sharp eyes. "I have important business with him."

"Of what kind?"

The question popped out before Roger realized that he had asked it. The stranger smiled.

"He is here, then?" he asked. "Else," he pointed out, "why should you inquire as to my business with him?"

"For the same reason that I would ask the question of anyone who came here," answered Roger with a quickness on which he congratulated himself. "As to the person you name, I am new with the Company, and do not know all those who serve it. But I haven't heard the name spoken about the playhouse," he concluded.

The visitor eyed him sharply. *This is a fox, not a weasel,* thought Roger. *Or better than a fox, for he has an honest and responsible look, though he's shrewd enough.*

"If you yourself do not know a Master Darrell," the other was saying, "perhaps there are some about who do. Yet you bear a marked resemblance to him, as he was described to me."

He studied Roger closely again, and nodded.

"I have heard no one here speak of a Master Darrell as serving the Company," Roger assured him stoutly.

"I am told he has some gift for painting," persisted the other, "and may be employed in the capacity of a hired man."

Roger smiled as disarmingly as he could.

"Why, I myself have such a gift and am so employed."

"And your name, sir, is—"

"Vance."

Roger thought that a flicker of satisfaction passed over the man's face, and he wondered if the visitor were associated with the other clerk who had come to Little Wood Street, and knew the name that Roger had taken there on impulse. But if the man had such knowledge, he said nothing of it.

"I most earnestly entreat you, Master Vance," he said gravely, "that if you can help me to find this young man, you do so. It is a matter of more importance to him than to me."

"In what way, if I may ask?"

"I cannot tell you." He measured Roger shrewdly, as if about to make a test. Then he said calmly: "Even should you yourself confess to being the man, yet I must first be well satisfied that you are before I state my business."

He watched to see the effect of this stroke.

Roger gave him no satisfaction.

"Confess!" he exclaimed. "But I have already told you who I am!"

"I do not know what reason a gentleman of family like you, for clearly you are such, may have for wearing another name," the man persisted quietly. "Yet he might have many. Such, for example, as unwillingness to associate his family with an occupation which might distress them."

Roger flushed, and felt all but cornered. But just then Burbage and Heminges came down the stairs, and he turned to them.

"This gentleman makes some question of my name and identity," he announced. "He seeks a Master Darrell, and seems to believe, in spite of my assurances, that I am he."

"Nay, sir," Heminges spoke up promptly. "This is Master Vance, and no man by the name of Darrell serves the King's Men. All matters of this kind are in my hands, and I would know. John Heminges, sir."

The stranger bowed.

"James Fenwick, at your service," he replied. "But may I ask, Master Heminges, and with no disrespect to Master Vance, if you have more knowledge as to his name than his giving it to you?"

Heminges colored.

"Why, sir, indeed, sir—"

"I have such knowledge." Burbage stepped closer to the stranger. "I brought Master Vance to the Company, and he is well vouched for by friends whom I trust. And I myself have some knowledge of his family."

"Master Richard Burbage, sir," said Heminges, gesturing toward Burbage.

The lawyer's man bowed again. He was impressed.

"Sir, I have seen you on the boards," he told the actor, "and have heard also of your good character."

Burbage acknowledged the compliments by inclining his head.

"I must be satisfied with what you tell me," the lawyer's man continued somewhat hesitantly, after a pause, "though considering certain facts—" He broke off. "No matter. I am sorry to have intruded here. It was a business of some importance. Gentlemen, good-day."

He turned to the door. Roger sprang forward to open it for him.

"If this proves to be the end of my search, it will be a matter of some loss to Master Darrell," Fenwick said in a low voice as he went out. His eyes held Roger's a second, and he shook his head.

"Strange, very strange," he muttered.

When the door had closed and Fenwick's steps could be heard receding, Burbage looked at his hired man with a quizzical smile.

"I did my best for you, and no untruth. I *have* one small piece of knowledge of your family. So the hounds keep after you," he mused.

"What, what?" demanded Heminges. "Hounds—and your doing your best for him? *Are* you Darrell and not Vance?"

"It's a matter of some sword-play," explained Roger, "and possible jeopardy from it." He told quickly of his fight with Wickard, and of the two other men who had sought him.

"The third hunter, then," murmured Burbage.

"Yet he spoke strangely at the end," puzzled Roger, shaking his head. "In passing through the door, he said it would be a matter of some loss to me. How could that be?"

"When your curiosity conquers your caution, haunt Paul's for a few noontides, and when you find the fellow again, ask him," suggested Burbage.

"Nay, I'll keep my curiosity to heel," Roger retorted.

"Tush—it's a great packet of trouble about someone being merely pinked," snorted Heminges. Then as he saw Cedric, who had come forward and stood watching them with an anxious face, "It's no great matter, lad. The fellow's gone and I'll lay odds the chapter is read through and ended. Put off that long face, and think nothing of it!"

Cedric smiled wanly.

"If you tell me so, I shall believe it, sir," he said with an attempt at brightness.

But when the two finally left, his eyes kept seeking Roger's with grave concern. He knew that the visit might be a very different matter for both of them from what the honest Heminges supposed.

XII

THE VOICE OF ROSALIND

CEDRIC and Roger ate a hurried supper that night. Both were excited. On the way home they had noticed that all seven arches had now shot up to their full height; they could be seen plainly from the river. These monuments and the busy and startling day at the playhouse seemed to quicken the whole pace of living. London was coming out of the dark of winter and pestilence into glittering life, and their own life seemed to be quickening, if perhaps dangerously.

Roger had decided that he must report the visit of the new lawyer's man to his uncle at once. He could stop at Edward Vance's house before going to Shakespeare's. Meanwhile, the encounter with Fenwick had started his own mind, and Cedric's, puzzling over the whole train of events which had troubled and alarmed them.

All through the meal Roger worried and talked by turns of this mysterious succession of visitors and pursuers.

"I don't understand any of it," he told Cedric. "First comes a man who knows my name, but not me. I give him a new name, and he's baffled. Next, one appears who seeks me, but can't name me or tell where I dwell. Then the third: he has a description of me but little more; he claims to seek me out for my own gain. Where did they pick up their scraps of knowledge? Why haven't they more? What drives them to all this effort for a word or a shadow?"

"The last one may have come from your father."

"Impossible. He knew nothing of him, as you heard yourself."

"Yes, he spoke vaguely of your family. But where would he get a description of you?"

Roger struck the table sharply with his palm as a thought came to him.

"Master Johnson!" he exclaimed. "I think he knows me only as Roger Darrell, and he knows surely I am with the King's Men. He could describe my appearance. Yet I told him of my fight with Wickard," he recalled, "and if he would talk freely with a stranger, he is less my friend than I thought him." He sat baffled for a moment, then shrugged. "Yet, if he did, it is all still a mad business," he muttered, "and the more menacing because it *is* mad."

He hurried off to Aldersgate, found his uncle away, called for paper and pen and scribbled an account of what had happened, leaving it with a servant. Then he turned back toward Silver Street.

With an effort he thrust aside the sense of exasperation and danger which haunted him, fixing his thoughts instead upon the more pleasant prospect of things at hand. What did Shakespeare have in mind? It must be of some importance, or the playwright would not propose to spend an evening on it.

At the juncture of Silver and Monkwell Roger had no difficulty in recognizing the shop of Christopher Montjoy, which occupied the corner. The windows and doors of this were shuttered and locked, but there was an entrance to the side with a lantern above it. This, he concluded, must be the house, and he lifted the knocker that hung at its center.

He heard steps within; then the click of a little wicket in the upper part of the door. Behind the six-inch aperture a girl's face appeared.

"I seek Master Shakespeare," he told the watchful eyes that looked into his.

The wicket closed; he heard low voices; then one: "You may open, Joan."

The door swung in, and he saw a serving girl holding a candle and staring at him, then behind her a dark-haired young woman simply but becomingly dressed.

"Master Shakespeare told us that he expected you, sir," she said with the trace of a foreign accent, "but I had forgotten to tell our maid. I am Mary Montjoy. I will take you to his chambers."

She lifted a candle from a niche in the wall and led him upstairs. There she knocked on a door which was opened promptly. Shakespeare faced them.

"Ah, Master Vance," he said; and to the girl, "Thank you, Mistress Mary."

She curtseyed, turned, and descended the stairs. The playwright drew Roger in.

"A comely and responsible young woman," he remarked. "These French Protestants are a gain to England. They bring skill and charm linked with sobriety. I am as well cared for here as in my own house. Although," he added with a hint of pride, "in Stratford I could show you a more spacious dwelling and a much more pleasant landscape about it. But come, be seated."

He motioned Roger to a chair near a plain but well-shaped table on which stood a branch of candles. The playwright himself took a seat on the opposite side. Roger's glance swept a large, clean, simply furnished room, on one side of which was a case filled with books. Shakespeare's eyes followed his guest's.

"I have only a few volumes here," he explained, "some of which I bought hoping to find matter for a play."

He stepped to the shelves and drew out a book.

"This is a tale by Geraldi Cinthio, an Italian, which has been Englished and was used for a play more than twenty years ago," he said. "The story is not a pleasant one, but it has a certain fascination."

He laid the book on the table.

"I've used it for the new play I spoke of," he went on. "I have called it *Measure for Measure*. It is comedy, yet bitter. The scene is in Vienna. The Duke of that city lets it be known he will make a journey to Poland, but disguises himself and remains in his capital instead. He wishes to see how the young deputy he has left in power will discharge his task of reforming the morals of the city. In part, you may call the play a tale of what power does to men who suddenly have it placed in their hands."

"If I know men at all, sir, they abuse it."

"Most men will," agreed Shakespeare.

He went on to tell briefly of Angelo, the Duke's deputy: how he revived an old law which made death the penalty for lovers who lived together without marriage; how he arrested and condemned a young man named Claudio for this crime; how Claudio's sister Isabella, about to become a nun, pleaded with Angelo to spare her brother; how he fell madly in love with her and offered to pardon the prisoner if the girl would become his (the deputy's) mistress.

"That's the situation, Master Vance. It's of a kind, I think, to please those about the Court, where already manners are freer and tastes run more to scandal than under the late Queen. Well, as to the peril of young Claudio and the passion of Angelo—the Duke becomes aware of both. By a trap which he sets, Angelo is exposed and punished, Claudio goes free. There's something of our King in the Duke: I think this will be seen. There's a purity and eloquence in Isabella that should move those who hear her. It shines like a light against a dark background of vice and cruelty."

He took up a manuscript that lay on the table.

"Here she pleads with Angelo," he said, and read a few lines:

> Oh, it is excellent
> To have a giant's strength, but it is tyrannous
> To use it like a giant. . . .
>   Could great men thunder
> As Jove himself does, Jove would ne'er be quiet,
> For every pelting, petty officer
> Would use his heaven for thunder, nothing but thunder!
> Merciful heaven!
> Thou rather with thy sharp and sulphurous bolt
> Splitt'st the unwedgable and gnarled oak
> Than the soft myrtle; but man, proud man,
> Dressed in a little brief authority,
> Most ignorant of what he's most assured,
> His glassy essence, like an angry ape,
> Plays such fantastic tricks before high heaven
> As make the angels weep!

Roger murmured his praise, and showed in his kindling eyes more than he spoke.

"You like it?" Shakespeare tossed the manuscript aside. "I fear that's the best of it," he remarked. "But you see the nature of the play. It's set in the city. The scenes are in the palace, on the streets, in the nunnery, Angelo's house, the prison. Well, your inner-stage setting for that forest scene has been teasing at my mind. Could we give more reality and force to the backgrounds for this piece? I'd have gates, perhaps, instead of those curtains forever closing off the inner stage from the outer. I'd have a prison more like one than we commonly contrive. I'd have settings built into the mood and action of the play. What do you say? Could something be managed?"

"It could be, sir, it can be. Could—may I have the play to read?"

"I'm to get it copied tomorrow; then you can." He looked at Roger with something like severity. "I think you understand that you must show it to no one. There's been too much stealing of our plays by London printers."

"It will be safe, Master Shakespeare."

"I believe you. Well, turn the matter over in your mind. And remember, what's done must be simple. No devices that encumber or halt the play. If the action breaks, it breaks an expectation in the audience, and we lose them."

"Yes, sir. When I've read the play, I'll make the designs. They will show what's needed for changes of scene, and how each can be managed. Sir, this is more than the opportunity you spoke of."

"Is it? Then I'm glad, Master Vance. But remember, my voice is only one. This may lead you to nothing but a week or so of labor by night—the planning, the pictures—no more."

Roger walked home intoxicated with possibilities. In spite of Shakespeare's warning, in spite of his more cautious self, his whole mind and imagination were singing with hope. Already ideas for what he could do crowded in upon him. By heaven, he'd give Shakespeare and Burbage something to marvel at! It seemed to him that at last he had before him the kind of thing he panted to do, that his hand had already closed on a latch and that he would lift it and swing open the door to a shining future.

The rehearsal was going forward on the main stage. The play was *As You Like It,* and there was a full cast for the particular scene being played: that in which the usurping Duke and his court watch the bout between Charles the Wrestler and the young hero, Orlando, who has challenged him. Roger was a walk-on for one of the attending gentlemen. Somers, Smith, even Hodge had been impressed to fill out the crowd. As the wrestling went forward, the latter was standing near Roger, and grunted his contempt.

"I'll show you better play than that, Master Dainty," he said in a hoarse whisper as he watched.

"You have already." Roger grinned at him, and got the nearest thing to a kind look that he had won from his quarrelsome fellow-worker.

He himself was ready to agree that the heavy John Lowin as the professional and Burbage as the hero might have managed a more exciting and expert performance.

However, the struggle was soon over, with the mighty Charles thrown and knocked speechless. The Duke, discovering in Orlando the son of a man, Sir Rowland de Boys, whom he counted a former enemy, spoke his displeasure at the discovery and moved off. "I would thou hadst told me of another father." Celia, the Duke's daughter, and her cousin Rosalind exclaimed with the indignation of idealistic young girls against the ruler's discourteous action.

> My father loved Sir Rowland as his soul,
> and all the world was of my father's mind,

declared young Bob Fairfield in the person of the heroine.

Had I before known this young   *son—*
                      his
       MAN

Suddenly his voice dropped to a bass and then shot squeaking up to a treble, and he stopped, white and confused. A kind of gasp came from the actors. Their leading lady was becoming a man, and his voice had split in one of those freakish changes common to boys in their early 'teens!

It was a possible calamity. Shakespeare and Burbage rushed over to the boy.

"What's this, Bob, what's this?" asked the Company's chief actor. "Has it broken like that before?"

"Never, sir, never," young Fairfield assured him earnestly. Then with a lift of the head, "and will not again!"

"Can you be sure of that?" asked Shakespeare doubtfully.

"Yes, sir. I'll watch it now," declared the boy.

"Well, let's get on with it, then," said the playwright.

The boy looked at the others about him, who had left their places, and they hastily grouped themselves again. He began:

> I should have given him tears unto entreaties
> Ere he should thus have ventured.

The words soared smooth and flute-like, and everyone breathed more easily. Celia came in with her lines, telling Orlando he had done well, apologizing for her father's abruptness. Rosalind took a chain from her neck, and stepped close to the hero.

> Gentleman,
>
> Wear this for me, one out of _{SUITS} with FOR- *tune—*

Again the break! There was no doubt of it now. Tears stood in the boy's eyes.

"I—I can't manage it, sir. It plays tricks with me," he confessed to Shakespeare miserably.

The playwright patted his shoulder.

"No fault of yours, lad," he said kindly. He looked about, studying the other boys. "We can't hazard a breakdown during the performance. Someone else must take the part."

"I know the lines, sir," ventured the boy taking the part of Celia.

"You know your own lines," Shakespeare told him quietly,

after only a second's hesitation, "and you suit the part you have. I don't want to change you. Dick," he said, glancing at another boy, "does a stately woman or a sharp-tongued one, but lacks the liveliness and charm we need here." He hesitated again, then smiled broadly as he saw Cedric's eyes fixed eagerly upon him.

"Do you know the lines, too, Master Cedric?"

"For the most part, sir."

"Step out then, and let's see how you give them."

The youngster bounded up to Fairfield and took the chain which the boy had failed to hang about Orlando's neck, and waited while Celia repeated her speech. Roger thought that even before Cedric spoke a change had taken place in him. The pert, eager youth had suddenly melted into a young woman falling in love. His voice came low in contrast with Celia's soprano, and there was a curious sense of something more than the simple words as he spoke them—

> Gentleman,
> Wear this for me, one out of suits with fortune,
> That could give more, but that her hand lacks means.

The new Rosalind bestowed her gift, and moved away with her cousin, looking back for a second at Orlando, while the young man muttered desperately at his own inability to thank her. The girl turned, sensing that he wanted to speak.

> I'll ask him what he would. Did you call, sir?

Then, while the hero remained tongue-tied:

> Sir, you have wrestled well, and overthrown
> More than your enemies.

The words conveyed their veiled confession delicately, but with a kind of brave frankness, and the entire troupe stood silent a moment, recognizing with the speech that they probably had a better Rosalind than they had lost. Then Celia picked up her cue, "Will you go, Coz?" and the two girls left. A brief talk between Orlando and the courier Le Beau, and the scene closed.

Shakespeare walked over to Cedric and nodded approvingly.

"You gave the lines well," he said. "They are only a few, but not easy ones. We'll try the next scene." Then as an afterthought, "What about *your* voice?"

" ' 'Tis in grain, sir; 'twill endure wind and weather,' " Cedric grinned at him, quoting a line of Olivia's in *Twelfth Night*, which they had rehearsed several times the week before.

"I hope so," the dramatist sighed with a faint smile.

He watched carefully while the scene between the girls in a palace chamber went forward. It showed Rosalind in the double role of wit and young woman in love. Cedric was using the written part for his role. Distracted somewhat by glancing at this, and by the novelty of his new assignment, he did not manage too well the mixture of mooning and lively nonsense that the part called for. But he worked toward it deftly under Shakespeare's direction, and at the end of the day carried off the part to study.

As Roger dressed, the playwright came by and told him to call for the script of the new play that night.

The boat nosed across the river in the fading light, and Roger sat in silence, pondering the sudden change in the fortunes of his young companion, and feeling somewhat dazed still by the impact of what seemed to him the boy's amazing ability to act. Cedric sat watching him with the ghost of a smile.

"Did I manage it well? I was no discredit to you?" he demanded at length.

"You know you weren't," Roger told him. "Where did you get the trick of it?"

"The trick of what?" Cedric was the perfect pretence of innocence.

"Of acting like a girl—nay, of *being* one," Roger replied. "I never saw the like of it. I'd have said *no* boy could mimic a girl to the life like that."

"Oh, I've taken girls' parts in pageants and festivals," Cedric shrugged carelessly. "I've played about with more girl cousins and their friends than I can count. I've heard them sighing over their sweethearts and seen them trying their tricks on them, and heard them giggling confidences in the chambers or by the garden walls."

He spoke somewhat scornfully.

"I'd have been a dolt if I didn't know their shifts and sighs and glances backward and to," he added.

"Well, you've learned them," Roger assured him. "But I think tonight you must be all boy. For if my uncle doesn't come to Little Wood Street, we must seek him in Aldersgate." He sighed. "I'd meant to spend the evening with Master Shakespeare's new play. There are a dozen things that need doing. Ha!" he exclaimed, recollecting, "I must write to Lucy again, or she will be out of all patience with me!" He had written her a short note three days before.

Cedric made a face at him.

"You let that vixen manage you out of your peace of mind."

Roger grinned at the boy. He knew that Cedric had no love for Lucy, and tried to pass the matter off.

"Not so. My mind's quite at peace, but I want hers to be, too. It will cost only a sixpence."

"And dear at the price!" Cedric muttered.

"The money's not yours," Roger retorted. He looked at his companion and was amused. "I think you're jealous of her," he chuckled.

Cedric straightened up, his eyes snapping.

"I jealous? And of her?" He swept Roger with a contemptuous glance. "Nay, for all of me the pair of you can run back to Darrell Manor, and abase yourselves, and stay there forever!"

The boat was touching the landing stairs. The boy glowered at his companion, sprang up and was out of the wherry ahead of him, running quickly up the stone steps to the street. Roger had to hurry to catch up with him.

XIII

CEDRIC SEES A FACE

EDWARD VANCE was waiting for them at Mrs. Salter's.

"I received the note you left for me last night," he told his nephew.

He looked somewhat grim, and hesitated when invited to join Roger and Cedric for supper, but accepted.

"If you will tell me your story again while we eat," he stipulated.

Roger agreed, a little surprised at the lawyer's nervous intentness. Vance said nothing until the name of the lawyer's man came out, when he gave a short "Hah!"

"Do you know him?" Roger asked.

"I think so. I think he is Humphrey Sefton's confidential man."

"Does that mean anything?"

"It may. At present it means only that we are dealing with a shrewd, ingenious, but honest man," Edward Vance replied. "I opposed him once. There was a weakness in his case and I was fortunate enough to find it." He drummed on the table with his fingers for a moment, then turned to Cedric.

"Did he see *you?*"

"I think not, sir."

Roger grinned.

"Cedric was away like a rabbit as soon as the door opened."

He went on with the story to the end, and saw that his uncle seemed perplexed and discouraged.

However, the lawyer took a tablet and pencil from his cloak and wrote down in detail what Roger had told him. He questioned closely about Fenwick's final words. Roger was sure of them: "If this proves to be the end of my search, it will be a matter of some loss to Master Darrell," and the muttered, "Strange, very strange" as the lawyer's man had departed.

Vance seemed satisfied on that point, and he was interested in Roger's feeling that a slight change of expression had passed over Fenwick's face when he heard the name of Vance.

"If you are right as to that, it may mean that he and the lawyer's clerk who came seeking you by night are both Sefton's men," he pointed out. Roger said that the same thought had occurred to him.

"But he had a description of me from someone who knew me as Roger Darrell," Roger pointed out. "How could that be? Of course, Master Johnson could have described me well enough, but he knew of my fight with Wickard, and I think would say little about me."

Vance shrugged.

"That seems likely; and yet he may have been persuaded that this was a different matter, and perhaps to your advantage."

Vance then asked if there had been any hint of an interest in Cedric, even a mention of the boy. Roger assured him there had not been, and Cedric agreed.

Vance turned the leaves of his tablet to some pages of finely written script.

"I have set down carefully from my notes," he said, "as exact an account as I can of every occurrence that seems to have any relationship to this business. I want to read you what I have written. This may be a case of some good labor lost, but I find that sometimes, by studying all the evidence I have explicitly set down, I can find a clue to something that other-wise might escape me."

The others nodded in agreement.

"I will begin with the first encounter with Wickard," the lawyer announced, and read what was a surprisingly accurate and detailed account of that episode. He paused now and then to ask about an action or something said. The others made a few corrections. Vance next took up the encounter with the law clerk outside Mrs. Salter's house, and then the visit of Bragdon's retainer to the Johnson shop the morning Roger had taken Cedric's portrait there. When these had been read and corrected, he nodded with a certain satisfaction.

"Does it make any sense to you, sir?" Roger asked. "Frankly, the more I think of it, the more puzzled I am."

"There is one possibility," his uncle answered slowly, "which explains the contradictions if it is assumed, but as yet explains nothing else to me."

"Which is—"

"That Sefton may have no connection with Bragdon at all," his uncle replied.

"You mean there are two mysteries and not one?"

"No. If we assume that Sefton has no relationship to Brag-don or Wickard, then Bragdon and his crew present no mystery. They are merely after Cedric. It's Sefton who is after you."

"But, sir, why *should* he be after me?"

His uncle shook his head and smiled a wry smile.

"That's the weakness of the assumption. It takes us no-where. But," he pointed out, "he does seem to be after you."

Roger nodded gloomily.

Vance turned to Cedric.

"Does anything in all this mean more to you than you have already said," he asked, watching the boy closely.

Cedric shook his head.

"Very well, then. Within the week my agent can start for Surrey. You have written again to your brother?" he asked the boy.

The youngster nodded.

"I told him to write to you or to seek you out if he came to London," he explained. "For if I—or we—took new lodgings, then he would not miss finding us."

Edward Vance murmured approvingly, asked some questions about Bragdon's and Cedric's estates, and at length seemed satisfied.

"As we learn more of Bragdon, we may learn more of Sefton," he remarked. "I shall try to find out where your guardian lies in London, if he is still here, and learn what he does. Do you think he has gone back to Holcombe?"

Cedric shrugged.

"He was urgent about the marriage. It seemed monstrous important to him. He may still be looking for me here. And even if he has gone, I think he may return for the King's progress through London: he has a great love for such shows. But he may have gone to the country and left Wickard and others here. He's not a man to neglect his estates. He watches all very closely there."

"We'll soon know," Vance remarked almost absently; then looked at Cedric with a rather searching glance.

"I have thought you knew some things about this business that you have not told me," he said.

Cedric colored slightly, then paled.

"Remember, if you have kept back anything—anything," the lawyer emphasized the word, "it may affect the whole outcome of this suit, if we can attempt one. It might even stop us from making the attempt, and thus alter your entire life. So speak up if there is something untold."

There was a brief silence, the lawyer looking steadily at Cedric, and the latter returning the look, large-eyed and pale. Finally he shook his head.

"Only that my last name is really not Wales, but Hardie, like my brother's," he said.

"That I had assumed."

Edward Vance looked at the boy again. He still seemed unsatisfied, but finally sighed, put away his tablet, and rose.

"Very well," he said.

Roger asked if he could walk a part of the way home with him.

"I am to call on Master Shakespeare and get a copy of his new play," he explained.

"Master Shakespeare? He dwells near here?"

"At Silver and Monkwell Streets."

"Would it be an intrusion if you brought me to him? I have been much moved by some of his plays." He added quickly, "I should like to greet him and tell him so—no more."

Roger said he thought there would be no harm in it, and the two went out together into the night.

The days were getting longer, Roger told himself as he came down from the loft where he had been doing the last of his work on the properties for the plays which the King's Men would use the first week of their reopening. The sun still hung in the sky, gilding the top gallery of the playhouse, he had noted from the window of the third story.

He had apparently settled into a satisfactory routine now; Burbage and Heminges both seemed to regard him as a fixture, although he had been with the Company only a few weeks. But what, he wondered, would they think of the designs he had started for Shakespeare's new play? The playwright had encouraged him to be bold: "Give your imagination the rein, and, when she soars, the spur," he advised. "Then the force of what you do will be felt, even if it offends." Roger needed no urging. He was shaping a new kind of scenery, he thought, for the Globe or any playhouse. He planned to carry out for the entire play his idea of combining the perspective of an Italian set with the greater flexibility of the English theater and its numerous playing areas.

He stepped out onto the main stage, walked down the length of it, and turned to examine the tiring house front. Yes, what he planned could be done. He could alter the entire rear wall with two painted cloths, and focus the attention of the audience on a single scene. Shakespeare, he felt, would like the idea. So would others, once it was bodied out as scenery. His uncle, for instance. He remembered the meeting of the two. It was brief, for Edward Vance would not stay, although urged to do so. But there had been an immediate sympathy between the playwright and the lawyer. Perhaps, Roger thought, because each had the instincts of a precise and complete craftsman, although they worked in different fields. Well, men like that would understand what he did.

He went back into the lobby and was taking down his cloak when he became aware of a group of his fellow workmen beside him, with Hodge foremost.

"Leave on your carpenter's clothes, Master Dainty," said the latter with a grin. "It's a clear day, the light will last long enough for a bout, and there's a smooth bit of turf nearby. Give me no talk of appointments in the City. The reckoning's past due, and I mean to teach you better wrestling than Master Burbage will show the groundlings in a few days."

Roger saw the smiling faces of the workmen and apprentices, and knew that, regardless of Hodge, he could not disappoint them.

"Why not?" he asked. "I've something in hand for the evening, but can spare you an hour. As to the teaching," he concluded, "let's talk of that when we see who can do it best."

An appreciative murmur greeted this reply. Hodge gave a short laugh.

"Come on, then," he said. "By Hercules, as the players say, I'll bring you down to mother earth and make you tell her you've found a master!"

"Not tonight, Hodge."

All turned at the sharp words and saw Burbage standing there, cloaked and hatted. Roger thought he had a glimpse of Cedric darting behind the far corner of the inner stage, but could not be sure.

"Not tonight, or any night," repeated the actor. "I'll not have Master Vance brawling with you. We've one man with a broken leg: that's why he's here. A shoulder out, a wrist lamed, and the whole company will suffer for it."

Hodge gave no ground.

"It's honest sport, sir," he retorted. "I'll do no more to him than ruff his hair. Besides, what's done away from the playhouse is the business of those that do it."

"Not so," snapped Burbage. "If we suffer from it, it's ours, too. I know what can happen in the heat of such rough and tumble. I want Master Vance sound and whole for the work he has in hand, and if we continue to play, he'll have enough of it. I'll have workmen here that work, and leave sports to fairs and holidays. Besides," he added frowning, "he's a nobleman's son and should be free of annoyance from such as you."

"No, sir," spoke up Roger. "We work together and are on a level while we do. If he wants it, I'll try a fall with him gladly."

"Aye, well spoken," muttered Hodge almost gratefully.

"You'll try none." Burbage spoke with authority. "I'll have a promise now from both of you to forget this nonsense wholly, or you may get your wages from Heminges and go your ways."

He stared at the two with hard eyes, and Hodge at length shifted his, and said it should be as Burbage wished.

"And you?" the latter asked Roger.

"Gladly. Though it was no wish of mine to deny him what he wanted."

"When we close for the King's progress, if we do, suit your own pleasure," said Burbage. "But for the present, no more of it."

He turned on his heel and made for the door. Hodge went after him, grumbling, and Roger looked about for Cedric, who suddenly came through the door from the main stage.

"Did you hear that?" he asked, glancing shrewdly at the youngster.

Cedric replied that he had gone out to practice the routine of going forward from the mid-stage to its outer edge as he would have to do for his speech after the play, and asked what had happened.

"I think you know," replied Roger. "Burbage came upon us and broke up a bout that Hodge planned to have with me. It was neatly timed, his coming upon us. Not that I'm sorry he did. I want to work tonight, and an hour with Hodge of mauling and being mauled would leave me too spent for it."

"Oh, was Hodge after you?" asked Cedric innocently, but with a gleam of amusement in his eyes.

"You know he was," challenged Roger, and Cedric smiled but did not deny the assertion. Instead he said quickly: "If we hurry, we can see something of the arches being built for the King."

"Good!" exclaimed Roger, who was really eager to examine

the growing structures. "Come along. We may find some of
the workmen still about who will talk of what they are doing."

When the two reached the first arch at Fenchurch Street
on the other side of the river, the artisans and laborers were
putting away their tools. The great rectangular structure
towered above the street some fifty feet, and was as broad as
high, with a central gate eighteen feet in height and a smaller
one to one side. The framework was now fully up, and piles
of stone and lumber for the finishing of the arch lay about.
Roger approached a man who seemed to have some authority,
and asked him about the project. The artisan was friendly,
and said that they were making good time, and could finish
in a week if it were necessary.

"We wait only word of the day of the King's coming, sir,"
he explained, "and I have news that it will not be ten days
from now. We shall have the stone facing up in a few days;
then the painters will busy themselves, and the artists will
install their work and do such final painting as may be necessary. It will be a brave thing," he added proudly, "and no expense is being spared for such work as we do, or for music,
or wine, or the costumes of those who have parts to speak. Aye,
it will cost the city a fortune, but we do not welcome a new
King every day."

"Does the City have the whole expense?" asked Roger.
"Don't some of the great nobles with houses here pay a part
of it?"

"Not a penny, sir," answered the tradesman. "All is paid
by the companies or guilds of the City—the carpenters,
mercers, ironmongers, stationers, and the like. The Dutch
and Italians, it is true, will erect arches of their own, and bear
the expense. Some men of rank there are who will open their

purses; but they are all our own citizens who have been en-
nobled. Why, London has no need of knights or earls to help
entertain her king," he went on. "We're older at that business than any fine family in England. There's not one of
them—De Vere, Herbert, Dudley, Montague—that held land
or power before the Conquest, and London welcomed kings
before the days of Alfred the Great. Aye, the town is as old
as the Romans, sir, they tell us. Some hold that it's older.
Such call the place New Troy in their orations and verses, for
they say it was a band of Trojans who built the first walls
here."

Roger nodded, for he knew the legend. He thanked the
craftsman, saying that he and Cedric would go on to the
other arches, and the two sauntered on through the sunset
light. They could see the shapes of at least four more structures
rising into the golden air: one beyond St. Paul's, outside the
wall, seemed to tower the highest. Several were still in skeleton
stage; others lifted solid bulk against the sky. A few days
before some had lacked both height and shape; now they
stood like the symbols of an imposing promise.

They passed the second arch in Grace Church Street, which
the Italians were building. "If Master Bartolomeo had lived,
he would have worked on this, and I, too, perhaps." Roger
looked at the rather simple lines of the structure, noting that
the lettering had already been blocked in for the motto that
ran above the gate. He spoke to one of the few remaining
workmen, but the man smiled and shook his head, and
stumblingly declared that he spoke little English.

So they hurried on to the third arch, which the Dutch
merchants and craftsmen were building near the Royal Exchange on Cornhill. This was well on its way to being completed, with a central gate, two smaller ones at the sides, and
a great chamber above, where presumably living figures

would present some kind of a tableau. Higher still was a smaller alcove with four pyramids, two on each side.

The decorations were ornate. Pillars, wreaths, lions and dolphins writhed up and down and across the elevation; but little painting had been done as yet. Several workmen who spoke English well enough told Roger that this would now be started, and that the great alcove just above the gate would display seventeen girls, daughters of tradesmen or craftsmen, each bearing a shield of one of the Dutch provinces. On the other side of the arch would be painted various scenes showing life in the low countries.

"And by night, sir," declared one of the men, "the four pyramids that you see near the top will have lights within them. These will show through their walls, which are transparent, so that people can see by night as well as by day."

It was dusk now, and the two made for their lodgings. Roger was silent for a while. "I wish I had had a part in it," he muttered finally.

"It would have been even more glorious if you had," asserted Cedric. "But there will be other great work to be done, and you'll do it!"

"A new king doesn't come every day," Roger quoted the artisan at Fenchurch Street.

"But a new king gives masques and plays, and pays for brave notions on which to spend his gold," persisted Cedric.

Roger laughed. He did not believe too much in such opportunities now, having been brought down to what seemed more like a natural level. But the great arches stirred him. A vision of their final magnificence flashed through his mind. For a moment he saw the crowds, the banners, the high-mettled horses; heard speeches and songs and the roar of the multitude. He walked on through the dusk, watching the changing shape of a single arch, and feeling that the gray dome of sky around him was somehow splendid with a magic that whispered a promise to him.

Father has heart and will for hunting only, and will listen to no talk of returning to London until he hears that the King moves thither. So I must ride out with them, or sit here in the house at my needlework. It is a dull life, with only those much younger or older than I for talk and companionship. My eyes turn often down the River, and my feet shall follow them as soon as it can be managed.

Roger read on, standing by a window in the lobby at the rear of the Globe stage. The noonday light made this letter from Lucy, brought to him early that morning, easy reading. There was little news in it. Like most English girls of that day in any similar situation, she was tied closely to her father, and must come or go with him. On this occasion, Roger was not wholly sorry. The thought of Lucy stirred him, yet if she had been in London he would have had less time for his work on the designs for the new play. There was too little time as it was, yet he had made progress. Another ten days and the task might be finished.

He slipped the letter into his doublet. The performance would begin in half an hour. Cedric was dressing for the first scene, in which Rosalind was a woman, and there had been quite a to-do twenty minutes ago, when the youngster had insisted on using one of the window stages on the second story as his own private dressing room. The other boys had jeered and protested. "The prince of wails!" cried one of them as Cedric insisted, punning on his name. But Heminges had supported his new boy-heroine.

"There's none using the place," he pointed out. "If the lad wants to dress alone, he may, and the rest of you will leave him to himself."

So Cedric had won *that* skirmish—one of a number he had fought with his young companions. Between them and him there was no love lost whatever. Roger set the friction down to a natural jealousy. Who was this new boy, they must have asked, who walked in and took the chief role in the play from others with a longer experience?

Roger mounted the stairs, elbowed his way through actors busy costuming themselves, knocked, and asked Cedric how he was getting along.

"Come in."

He opened the door at the invitation, and gasped at the glowing young woman who confronted him. With a brown wig and penciled eyebrows and painted lashes, with rosy cheeks deftly deepened by art and a gown that might well have been worn at court, there seemed to be no trace of the Cedric he had known. He stood quite speechless, and the boy smiled.

"Come in, Roger. Look at my wig and see if my gown hangs well."

It was completely unreal. Roger made the inspection and pronounced everything perfect. Cedric thanked him, pivoted, and exclaiming: "Then I'm ready!" walked past his friend with a carriage that would have done a countess credit. Roger stood looking after the boy-princess, shaking his head with disbelief.

It was almost playing time, and Heminges was standing in the lower lobby with half the cast about him. He gave an exclamation of relief and approval on seeing Cedric, and told one of the boys to hurry the rest of the actors. They joined the group in a few moments. Then the manager unfolded a letter, which he glanced at briefly, refolded, and held in his hand.

"Gentlemen," he said gravely, "we shall play out the week and no more." There was a murmur of surprise which he stilled with a practised hand. "The playhouses will close then," he continued, "until such time as the Council decrees. A week and a day from now His Majesty makes his progress through London. Some of us will have duties then, and, of course, the entire City will be on holiday to greet the King. May God bless him!"

There were cries of "Aye!" and "Amen!" and then questions about the progress.

"I can tell you little more," said Heminges. "Some of the Company must walk in livery in the progress. We shall assist certain of the tradesmen in the rehearsing of the tableaux and speeches at the various arches. When I know what each must do, I will tell you. For now—ready yourselves for the play!"

The group broke up, the prompter went into the inner stage to look through its curtains at the gathering crowd, and Burbage, Shakespeare, Lowin and Condell, who appeared in the first scene, took their stations. In a few minutes the three blasts of the trumpet, blown from the huts at the top of the tiring house to announce the opening of the performance, could be heard soaring through the sunny March air.

Roger was busy both as actor and stagehand. Thus he saw and heard most of the play, his first public performance. It was somehow a little different from the private showing he had already known. The audience was much greater in size, was greater in variety; was, if anything, more exacting. But the King's Men were in good form, and the crowd was welcoming them back after many months of absence. Roger thought that Cedric outdid himself. When he was Rosalind the lady he was all young-womanly charm, grace, and wit. When he appeared disguised as the boy Ganymede, darker of complexion ("and with a kind of umber smirch my face") and saucier of demeanor, he won the groundlings with his bravado and deft sallies; when he appeared as woman again to charm Orlando, the groundlings and galleries were delighted. And at the play's end, when he spoke his epilogue, he seemed to keep the two thousand spectators responsive to each shading of his voice. "If I were a woman, I would kiss as many of you as had beards that pleased me, complexions that liked me, and breaths that I defied not." Such man-to-man talk from the heroine brought all the house to its feet cheering as the seeming princess tripped off the stage, turning to throw them a kiss before he disappeared between the curtains of the inner stage.

But there was anxiety in Cedric's eyes as he broke away from the approving actors who surrounded him, mock-curtseying to their praise. "Roger!" he whispered, and dragged his friend off to a corner of the lobby. He looked anxious and frightened.

"What's the matter?"

"*He* was there."

"Who? You—you mean Bragdon—Wickard?"

"Both. They weren't twelve feet from me sometimes."

The two stared at each other, Roger as appalled as his young friend. Then a conviction came to him, and he smiled.

"He couldn't have known you. With the wig, the penciling and painting, the dress—"

"But, Roger—"

"Coloring, gown, your carriage—all different."

"Yes, but my voice."

"A voice sounds different from the stage."

Cedric shook his head doubtfully.

"It *may* sound different." He brooded for a moment. "Most of the time I was a boy," he pointed out.

"But darker and stranger than ever. I'd never have known you."

"You're sure?"

"Of course."

The youngster sighed, and seemed almost convinced.

"Get out of that gown," urged Roger. "I'll help you. Where's your own habit?"

"Upstairs. You needn't help me. I can manage alone."

"Well—if you can. Don't leave until I come for you."

Cedric nodded, and went up the stairs to the second story. Roger walked over to the far side of the lobby, away from the street door, wondering if he should go to Burbage or Heminges with the situation. After all, nothing had happened as yet. On the other hand—. He was saved any further debate with himself. There were voices at the door, and the man acting as porter gave way as several men thrust themselves into the lobby. Roger thought that the foremost of them was the same man who had intruded at Darrell Manor on Twelfth Night.

Just at that point Richard Burbage, dressed for the street, came down the stairs and surveyed the visitors with a hard eye.

"You make a rude entrance, gentlemen," he said coldly. "What's your business?"

"To speak with whoever has authority here."

"Then speak to me. I am chief housekeeper in the Company."

"I seek a boy," declared the stranger, "a runaway boy. I think he played the part of Rosalind this afternoon."

"What's his name?"

"I don't know what name he goes by. If I can see him—"

"What's this? What's this?"

Heminges and Shakespeare approached the two, the Company's manager on his dignity as he heard the sharp sound of the conversation. All were dressed for the street, their swords under their cloaks.

"These gentlemen forced themselves into the playhouse," explained Burbage. "They demand a boy, whose name they admit they do not know—"

"Not so. I do know his name."

"Give it, then."

"To what purpose? He'll have taken a false one."

Heminges brushed the talk aside, and took a step nearer the intruders, fairly swelling with authority.

"This Company and every man and boy that labor for it," he announced, "are the servants of His Majesty and as such under his protection. By forcing entrance here you have already shown disrespect to the King's authority."

A low murmur of assent greeted his words. The actors and their employees were sharply conscious of the protection they enjoyed, and quick to resent any infringement upon it. The strangers were visibly impressed.

"We mean no disrespect to you or His Majesty," protested their spokesman. "Yet if you have his protection, so have I, for by the King's law I am guardian to the boy I seek, and by that law I insist you produce him."

Heminges flushed.

"You insist!" he echoed. "Why, are we to line up every man Jack of our crew here for your inspection?"

He glared at the intruders. Roger began to be hopeful that they would be sent packing. The Company members and hired men were apparently in a mood to back Heminges up, and toss the strangers out into the alley. Then his heart sank as Burbage spoke up.

"Nay, John," he said placatingly, "though I was the first to challenge this gentleman, yet I'll help him here. He asks only to see the lad who plays Rosalind for us. Why shouldn't

I fetch him?"

"Why should you?" snapped Heminges.

"Why, only to avoid needless dispute," answered Burbage, and apparently there was a glance between him and Heminges, for the latter grumbled, "Well, then," and the chief actor of the King's Men bounded up the stairs. There was a minute's pause, and then Roger heard two pairs of feet descending.

"Here's your Rosalind," Burbage declared. Roger was about to step forward and defend Cedric from possible capture, when he looked at the slight figure facing the strangers and blinked his eyes. It was Bob Fairfield!

Roger realized the deftness of the trick. The two boys were much of a height. Dressed and painted for the part of Rosalind, Fairfield would have looked much as Cedric looked. His natural coloring was closer to the makeup than Cedric's. Burbage was speaking.

"Is this the boy you claim?"

"No, nor nothing like him."

"Yet he is our Rosalind," Burbage declared. He turned to the boy. "Strike in with your lines." He himself plunged into a scene between Orlando and Ganymede, Rosalind's name as a boy.

"My fair Rosalind, I come within an hour of my promise."

Young Fairfield answered sharply:

"Break an hour's promise in love! He that will divide a minute into a thousand parts, and break but a part of the thousandth part of a minute in the affairs of love, it may be said of him that Cupid hath clapped him o' the shoulder, but I'll warrant him heart-whole."

Burbage became a suppliant.

"Pardon me, dear Rosalind!"

Fairfield rebuffed him: "Nay, an you be so tardy, come no more in my sight: I had as lief be wooed of a snail!"

They raced on for several more speeches. Roger realized that from the voice alone he himself could not have been certain whether Bob or Cedric was speaking. The scene was light comedy, and both boys had been coached practically to the inflection.

At last Burbage turned to the intruder.

"Are you satisfied, sir?"

The other was staggered. He muttered something about a trick of the voice, a mistake, and made his retreat. As the door closed, Burbage laid a finger on his lips, then threw his head back in a soundless laugh, and clapped young Fairfield on the shoulder.

"Well done, Bob!"

Fairfield smiled and blushed.

"It was nothing, sir."

Heminges, somewhat put out, demanded crossly: "Who was he after? Master Cedric?"

Burbage shrugged.

"Who else?"

He saw Roger, who had come forward, and turned to him.

"I saw you speaking with the true Rosalind, and she seemed fearful about something. When this fellow appeared—well, I couldn't lead the lamb straight to the butcher."

Roger laughed.

"It was masterly. When you came back down the stairs bringing a boy, I was set to step forward with a drawn sword."

Heminges, Lowin and Shakespeare were listening, with all the apprentices and stage hands. The playwright spoke now.

"You didn't tell us young Cedric was in any danger when you brought him here."

"Sir," answered Roger truthfully, "I didn't think he was. I brought him only to fill in for a dance. I don't know this man who appeared tonight," he continued. "He may have a guardian's right. But if he has, I have the right, as *prochein amy,* to challenge him for many and varied abuses. To escape these Cedric fled from him, by accident I protected the boy, and on his plea laid the matter before my uncle, whom you yourself have met, sir."

Shakespeare nodded.

"If Master Edward Vance acts for the boy, I shall assume that this fellow is no proper guardian. Your uncle's reputation as a lawyer in London stands high."

There was a murmur of approval. Roger bowed.

"Yet I would not bring trouble to the King's Men. The fellow may appear again."

Burbage spoke.

"Do you stand as the boy's protector?"

"I do."

"Then," the actor told him, "have no concern about the King's Men. They will help as they can. That's our good will to you, and——" he smiled broadly, "something of good sense, too. It keeps us a player we need. But if the business goes to a magistrate, we pass the blame to you. Be concerned then about yourself."

"I have been these past weeks." Roger grinned wryly, and those about him laughed.

"Well, if I'm right, the bloodhound has lost the scent," remarked Burbage. "If he comes here tomorrow, he'll see no Cedric, for we play *Every Man in His Humor.* As for the parts the lad takes later—well, the wig, the paint and the pencil can make a new face." He was silent for a moment. "But they might wait for you outside even now," he concluded.

Wat Somers stepped up to the actor and spoke in a low voice. Burbage nodded, doubtfully at first, then emphatically.

"Here's a shift that might answer any danger of that kind," he said. "The greater part of the Company will leave as usual, by the door here. Meanwhile you, Vance, with Master Cedric, and I and a stout lad or two to go with you—Richards, I think, and Hodge, with staves—we shall let ourselves out at the front entrance. If they watch, it should be at the rear. Yet should we who leave by the front encounter those who are unfriendly, we can make enough trouble for them. So far as we are concerned, this fellow with his claim of guardian may be an impostor. What do you say, Hodge—" there was a shrewd twinkle in the actor's eye—"will you swing a club at need for Master Vance and young Cedric and the King's Men?"

Hodge grinned; he was in his element.

"Aye, and a heavy one!"

The plan was put into effect. The front of the playhouse was clear; Roger and Cedric and their companions slipped quickly to the cover of some houses and on to the river, found a boat and were rowed across to the Tower stairs. Richards turned back there; he lived in the Bankside. So did Hodge; but he insisted on accompanying the others to Little Wood Street, and finally came upstairs for a mug of ale. He left in bubbling good spirits, swearing that Roger and Cedric were his true fellows, and that, whatever trouble might come later, they could count on him as on a brother. Roger went down to the street with him, and came up laughing.

"There's a receipt for turning an enemy into a friend," he remarked, "and Burbage knew it. He made Hodge our protector. A few days ago the man was passionate to pin me to the turf; now let anyone lift a hand against me, or you, and he'd crack the fellow's head!"

Cedric smiled rather wanly.

"You saw Bragdon," he began. "You know that he—"

"Is the fellow who came hunting a boy at Darrell Manor,

and that you were that boy," answered Roger. "I guessed as much all along. Why didn't you admit it that night on the street after we left my uncle's?"

Cedric twisted his hands and looked miserable and ashamed.

"I don't know, Roger. It—it was habit, I think. I'd sworn when I left Holcombe to trust nobody. And I thought the less I admitted, even to you—" He broke off, and exclaimed passionately: "You don't know what it is to be alone, quite alone, and hunted."

Roger looked at him with a mixture of amusement and annoyance.

"Thanks to you I know a little about it," he pointed out. "Haven't there been those who have hunted *me?*" He shook his head. "Well, after we eat, we must talk of this. It's true they need you at the Globe, yet your safety comes first. We must see what my uncle says."

"No, Roger."

"But it's a matter of danger."

"If Master Burbage truly fooled Bragdon, there's little or none," the boy insisted. "I'll stay here tomorrow. You shall find out if the others saw anyone watching the playhouse door."

"Uncle Ned should know of it."

"If there's a need, he should," the boy agreed. "Yet if there's no need, it would merely trouble him, and perhaps pen me in here again. If Bragdon thinks I'm not at the playhouse, to be there will be a kind of protection. And if I see him again, I'll tell you, and Master Vance, too."

Roger finally agreed to wait until the following night. If no one had been watching the stage door, perhaps it was a safe thing for Cedric to go on playing.

XIV

A KING PASSES

THERE were groves and forests of people, thought Roger, using a metaphor that a poet would later employ to describe the London crowds of that morning of March 15, 1604.

All the way down from Little Wood Street to the first arch he had seen men and women pressing toward the line of the progress. And now that he stood with Cedric on Fenchurch Street, a little toward the Tower from the arch, he had a sense of not all London alone, but all England being packed along the royal route.

There was a cleared central portion of the street through which the King and his escort would pass. On either side of this, except at the intersections, was a mass of standing people, pressing against the rails that confined them. And behind them, railed off again, were elevated seats. Here the tradesmen of the Companies of the City sat, with their families and guests. And farther back still, and above standing and sitting folk alike, the second-story windows of every house—the casement frames removed to give a clear view—bulged with people who leaned out waiting for a first glimpse of His Majesty.

The town was a motley of color. Wreaths, garlands and banners hung at window-frame and peak of roof or gable. The rails of the merchants' seats were draped with ensigns and streamers. And above everything, dominating the city,

187

towered the arches through which the new ruler of England would pass. All were ready now, with their pillars and carvings and heraldic devices, with their lettered mottoes in gold or silver, with their paintings, hangings and banners, with their groups of living, costumed figures. Along the route two marshals and their attendants, mounted, and gorgeous in the livery of the City, pranced up and down. They watched the crowd, keeping all men within the rails, so that the King and his companions could pass freely.

It was bright and fabulous beyond anything suggested by an embellished manuscript of mediaeval romance, flashing red, blue and gold. It outshone any tapestry woven by duchess or queen, where cunning threads captured in brilliant color a stag at bay, a knightly combat, a coronation. Yes, the city was a garden, blossoming with the glitter and chanted wonder of the chivalric past. But the flowering was also, although less clearly, that of the Renaissance: the more modern world of printed books, theaters, new continents, expanding trade, bustling schools and assertive parliaments.

It was the great day at last. It was well past ten in the morning of that day; and Roger and Cedric, from where they stood, could see the first arch to the last inch of its imposing splendor. In the large recess above the central gate, a tableau of figures, robed and crowned, sat waiting to perform. On either side of them, in smaller recesses, sat musicians. Beneath them, in an alcove, were other symbolic personages. The arch itself rose about them with its carvings and painted mottoes, exploding at the top like an intricate rocket in a cluster of miniature churches, houses, and halls—a skyline replica of London itself.

Unfortunately the two could see little more than the arch, for they were crowded against the first story of a house that stood just behind the tier of tradesmen's seats. They could only look out sideways toward the towering structure; and, of course, they had no view whatever of the street in the direction of the Tower, from which the King would come.

Their position was partly a matter of choice. They wished to be close enough to the outskirts of the crowd so that they could slip out of it when the procession passed; for they had been invited by a friend of Edward Vance to view the pageant from his house on Cheapside. It stood between the fourth and fifth arches, one of the best of possible vantage points. They must return to occupy it in time. But before the invitation had come, Roger had planned on their seeing the King arrive at the first arch. Neither he nor Cedric wanted to give up this plan. They had explained it to the lawyer: to find a post on Fenchurch Street, then perhaps follow on to the second and third arches. To their surprise, Vance had spoken vigorously against the idea.

"It will expose the boy to needless danger," he had declared.

Roger saw a certain force in the objection, but Cedric pleaded desperately for the excursion. He had a new cloak, doublet and hat. In the crowd, he pointed out, he would be obscured and disguised. Besides, all eyes would be on the King. Should he be denied the full glory of this rare occasion for a mere shadow of risk? So at length Vance had consented to the expedition if two of his retainers—one an ex-soldier who was a stout swordsman—went along. The four were now in position.

"The crowned figure must be Britain, Roger; and look— the one with the green hair and robes of green and white— that must be the River Thames!"

Cedric was staring at the figures above the central gate, trying to guess what they represented. Roger answered him absently; his mind was ranging elsewhere. By the time the four returned to the house of Master Tilton, his uncle's friend, he told himself, Lucy would have arrived there. He felt a sudden thrill of anticipation at the thought of her.

She and her father had returned to the city only three days ago. He had supped with them on the very night of their arrival. Thomas Knowles had been somewhat cool toward him at first, but Lucy had doubtless told of an impending reconciliation between Roger and his father, and with her aid the atmosphere was soon pleasant. Sir Thomas had finally suggested that the young man join them for the pageant. A friend of his had made his house available to them, and it opened on the street near the third arch. The friend would welcome Roger, too.

"I am pledged for that day to my uncle," the latter explained quickly. He told of the advantages of the Tilton house. A view of two arches, and of a platform between them where the City Council would sit.

"And," he concluded, "I was told to bid both you and Lucy as guests."

Sir Thomas shook his head.

"I cannot break my promise to my friend."

"Yet *I* could join Roger, Father," Lucy had pleaded quickly. "It is a much better outlook, and they say the boys of St. Paul's will sing."

She made a great point of going, and her father at last agreed that she could. Roger spoke of his own plans for the morning, offering to forego them, but Lucy told him he must not; she would come with a safe escort and arrive at Tilton's at about noon. So it was arranged; Roger explained that a simple dinner would be served as they sat and watched.

A mingled cheer and roar from the crowd brought him back to the present. He and Cedric looked from behind their barrier, but could see nothing.

"If we lift the lad up and let him stand on our shoulders,

sir," suggested the tall ex-soldier, "he could see as well as those in the seats above us, and report on it, too."

Roger agreed. They hoisted Cedric aloft, and he straddled somewhat precariously, one foot on his friend's shoulder and one on the retainer's (the other man was short of stature and so not useful). The boy reported that the commotion seemed to have been caused by some apprentices who had slipped out from the rails, and were now being put back by the marshal's men.

Just then a voice from a window above them called out, "Young sir, young sir!" and as Cedric turned, a friendly householder pointed to a gable beside his window. "You can perch there and see more, and you, too, sir," he added as Roger turned his face upward.

"You can sit in front of me and I shall be well hidden," whispered the youngster. Then as Roger nodded, he thanked the man in the window and scrambled up to the gable with the aid of jutting beams that criss-crossed the plaster of the house wall. Roger followed, taking the front place.

He had found himself feeling a kind of strangeness toward his young companion in the last few days, and as he sat waiting for the procession he wondered about it. There was the playing, of course. Cedric had continued to take Bob Fairfield's former parts. He was not so happy an Ophelia or Helena (*All's Well*) as he had been a Rosalind, but under Burbage's and Shakespeare's direction he had played well. The work had made him more of a personage and less a fugitive under Roger's protection.

That was part of it, Roger told himself—that and perhaps Cedric's general anxiety about his situation, an anxiety which might have grown greater with the strain of waiting. Yet all looked more promising now than a week ago. Bragdon had not appeared again at the playhouse, so far as they knew; they had agreed not to tell Edward Vance of their having seen him at the theater. Hammond, the agent, had at last gone to Holcombe. The lawyer had not been able to find Cedric's guardian in London during the past few days, so the danger he represented had dimmed for the time at least. Of course, Bradgon might have left the city and returned for the festivities this morning.

Meanwhile, the playing was over for a time. There was only one performance at Westminster—a special appearance before the King and Court, a week from now. What, then, was Cedric concerned about, if he was concerned? And if not, why did Roger have this sense of a strangeness in the boy's behavior? If there was something unknown to Roger that he feared—

"Do you think so, Roger?"

He realized that Cedric had spoken to him, and with a start asked what he had said.

"Do you think it's near eleven?" the boy asked, and Roger was aware that the question was being repeated. He replied that it must be near that hour, and Cedric asked with a chuckle: "Where were you, Roger? With Isabella and Claudio and Antonio?"

Roger had not thought of his designs for *Measure for Measure* all morning long, but the boy's assumption that he had was convenient, and he said: "I'll finish that business next week."

Cedric had read the play and watched the progress of the work.

"Master Shakespeare will like it," he prophesied, "but Master Burbage and Master Heminges will be amazed—and confounded—at least for a time." He added: "The sketches are monstrous strong and good, and if the King's Men don't use them, something very like will be shown in other houses."

"If they aren't shown at the Globe, that will be no gain to me," grumbled Roger.

"But you could take them elsewhere," the boy insisted, "to another company. Or to the Court. With such designs, you might win a place there."

Their creator shrugged. "Who will look at them?"

The sound of a cannon fired in the direction of the Tower cut off the conversation; and the two on the gable and all in the windows and on the seats and in the railed off areas beneath them turned toward the echo of the gun. Gradually singing could be heard in the distance, and the crowd stirred restlessly.

It waited with mingled patience and excitement. All knew that the event was at hand, and were heartened; yet they were on tip-toe of suspense for the first glimpse of the procession. At length a trumpet sounded nearer, and music struck up. Then some gentlemen in royal livery appeared, with heralds flanking them on either side. The crowd burst into a gathering roar. Roger and Cedric leaned forward, shouting to each other as the splendidly garbed officers went past them and lined up on either side of the arch. Some they recognized by costume or the emblems they bore—the royal servers, the clerks of the Privy Seal and Signet, the chaplains, the royal carvers and cupbearers (all gentlemen or nobles, of course), and Cedric cried of a group following the Lord Chief Justice in his wig and robes: "There, there, Roger! Master Burbage and Master Shakespeare and the others!" Sure enough, they marched behind a troop of trumpeters, in royal red livery as Grooms of the Chamber.

But even their friends were quickly forgotten as the earls and barons of the land appeared, then the Lord Mayor of London, then the Prince—a boy of ten whom all England had already hailed for his comeliness, wit and modesty as the hope of the land. Pennons and kerchiefs waved, and the shouts mounted; but they rose to a frenzy as, under a canopy borne by eight gentlemen of the Privy Chamber, the King himself appeared, riding on a white jennet and bowing and smiling somewhat solemnly.

He was a strange figure of a king—a man in his late thirties, richly dressed, sitting easily enough on his horse, but somehow clumsy and awkward of bearing. He stared about him with large, heavy-lidded, protruding eyes—"goggle-eyed" might have been the word. He looked at once uncomfortable and somewhat bored. Roger was aware of this, but neither he nor the thousands about him were in a critical mood. They had heard enough of their monarch's heavy learning and uncouth appearance. It was said that his legs were warped and unsteady, and he could not walk evenly. Now, on his horse, a central figure in the pageantry, he looked better than might have been expected. Besides, the occasion possessed them, and the man was only a symbol. For the moment he was glorious, and they roared their delight in him.

He drew up near the arch; and from a niche in the central portion of it, somewhat above the ground, a tall, commanding figure representing the genius of the City began to speak. He was far more regal in presence than the ruler he faced. " 'Tis Allen!" "Master Edward Allen!" Roger heard voices from the seats just below him. He knew then that he looked at the chief actor of the Prince's Men, formerly the Admiral's —the troupe that Henslowe managed. He had once seen the great actor play in a revival of *Tamburlaine,* the play by Christopher Marlowe which had borne Allen to fame. Roger listened breathlessly now as the strong and flexible voice gave its message of greeting, watched the easy gestures and fine play of facial expression which helped to make the speech one of distinction. With regret he heard the actor conclude his address, and the trumpet bid the procession proceed. He saw the various units fall into place and march on, then finally, behind the smiling blonde Queen and a dazzling group of ladies, the eager townfolk bursting from the rails. They crowded the protesting marshal and his men as they surged on in the wake of the marchers.

It was no trick for Roger and Cedric and their two escorts to make their way northward out of the scattering crowd, then hurry westward parallel to the procession as it halted by the second arch. The four pressed in to see what they could of the ceremonies there. But others had arrived before them, and the outlook was poor, while the voice of someone addressing the King was a mere drone of sound.

"What are we doing here?" Roger asked at length. "Or in any street this side of Paul's? It will be no better at the Dutchman's arch. I'm for Master Tilton's! Come, we'll have a good view there at least, and may be able to hear something."

Lucy was walking toward St. Paul's, just to the south and east of it. She went with Alice, while Dick her page strode on ahead and a retainer brought up the rear. The girl was thinking about Roger. She knew well enough that the outlook for his going back to Darrell Manor was not good. She glanced at the arch just north of the cathedral on Cheapside. It was decked with greenery and rounded at the top, like an arbor. Mentally she made a face at it. The thing seemed a symbol of Roger's stubbornness. It had been the work of architects and craftsmen—men like that Italian, Bartolomeo, who had put the nonsense into her friend's head. There would be people on it, some of them professional players, acting their parts. The arch was pretty and seductive—so doubtless was the whole world of artists and actors. But that world threatened certain hopes that she had been encouraged to cherish and had accepted. She was not ready to let it take Roger from her.

She turned her eyes from the arch and saw the packed crowd lining the street ahead. At the other end of the city, Roger was pushing in and out of such a crowd even now. She was sure that he had not written to his father. Not that she had asked. Even before reaching the city she had decided not to press that matter for the time. But Roger had told her that his prospects had improved, and talked as if he would go on working at the theater. She felt sure that there had been no real change in his status there; if there had been something definite, he would have been quick to tell about it. And if he had written to Sir John, he would have mentioned that, too. Instead, he had told her that the boy, Cedric, was playing women's parts at the Globe.

A frown creased Lucy's forehead as she thought of the youngster, and instinctively she quickened her pace. She did not like him. Indeed, he seemed somehow bound up with Roger's determination to stay in London. If it were not for Cedric, Roger might have listened—she broke off with a short laugh that caused Alice to look at her quickly. "I thought of something," she said carelessly in answer to the woman's questioning eyes. And what she had thought was at once pleasing and somewhat bitter. It was this: that to imagine Cedric's directly influencing Roger was preposterous, for neither man nor boy—nor woman, either, as she had discovered for herself —could persuade Roger to or from what he wanted to do. Still, this being true, it did not lessen her dislike for Roger's young companion. For one thing, she had now decided that Cedric was the boy who had bound and gagged her on Twelfth Night. She had pretended to accept Roger's assurance that the two were not the same. *But they are. The coloring is the same*

*to a shade, there's the same audacity, and what is a youngster
like that doing in London alone? Is is merely an accident that
such a one appears at Darrell Manor, pursued by those seeming to have a right to him, and another turns up here with
Roger, wholly footloose?* No, there was much more here than
had been explained, and she meant to find out what it was.
Somehow she felt that the boy was an antagonist. An absurd
feeling, yet it persisted. And for all Roger's going his own
way, if the boy were not with him, he might be easier to
manage.

"Look, Mistress Lucy! The streets are lined with people
through Ludgate clear to the Temple, and the arch over Fleet
Street has a globe of the world in it!"

They were beyond St. Paul's now, and ready to cross the
line of the progress and turn northeast. The street was massed
with people on both sides, but the intersection where they
would cross was clear.

"It moves, it moves!"

Alice clutched her mistress's arm, and pointed to the arch
beyond the gate, where the great globe was indeed slowly turning. Then gradually it ceased to revolve.

"They are testing the mechanism," said Lucy calmly, "and
seem to have found it in order. Come, we must not waste time.
When we are at Master Tilton's house, we shall see things
more marvelous than we can here."

They crossed the street, and passed on around St. Paul's.
Lucy felt an impatience with all these people dumbly waiting
for the pageant, and for Alice, as giddy as a girl with the excitement of the day. She herself had matters of greater moment
to think of. Not that she was sure just now as to what she could
do about them, except to watch carefully, and wait. She must
study Roger and know fully what he was doing and feeling.
She must find out more about the boy. She felt certain that if

she were patient, something would happen to tell her what she should do next. There would be an opportunity. She did not intend to miss it when it came.

There were two large windows in Isaac Tilton's house, both useful for watching the progress.

One faced east. It gave a full view of the length of Cheapside, looking toward the Tower. The most imposing feature of the scene was the fourth arch, not a hundred yards away. Through this the procession would come, moving toward Paul's.

The other window overlooked the cathedral and the fifth arch just beyond a tall vine-and-tree-decked structure which Londoners had already named "the arbor." An extraordinary variety of foliage and fruit hung from its tall sides and wreathed about its arches and columns. It was the very emblem and bower of growth and fruitage.

Between Tilton's house and the fourth arch stood the platform on which members of the City Council would sit, together with certain aldermen and officials who would pay their respects to the King.

Isaac Tilton was a big, hearty, but quiet man of sixty who, Roger learned after he and Cedric arrived, had once followed the goldsmith's trade, but had retired from it with more than means enough for the comfort of his wife, his daughter and himself. Apparently Edward Vance had been of great help to him in managing his properties; the one-time craftsman spoke and listened to the lawyer with the greatest deference. Mrs. Tilton was a smaller, feminine edition of her husband, with ruddy cheeks and bouncing energy. She was busy with preparations for the repast, and after greeting all three of her young guests cordially—for Lucy too had now appeared—told them to look at the sights.

All had crowded now into the window facing south, and were studying the details of the arbor arch. In two bowers, one above each of the two great gates which led through the structure, costumed figures were already seated. Others were placed in smaller niches. There was Fortune, recognizable by her wheel. Edward Vance identified some of the others: Peace, Plenty, Gold, Silver, Pomona (goddess of fruits) and Ceres.

"There, too, are the seven arts," he pointed out. "You can know Astrology by the globe of the world he carries. And the third to the left of him is Geometry, I think, with the design of a building."

Lucy listened and questioned with animation, as if the whole tableau were of the greatest interest to her.

"It's a brave pageant for any king, is it not, Master Vance?" she asked finally, adding: "And we are fortunate to have one like you to explain it to us."

"Aye, it's fine enough," the lawyer answered, passing over her compliment, although pleased by it. "Perhaps too fine. Yet it is the choice of the citizens of London, and I do not question its fitness." He paused a moment and added, "I trust His Majesty, God save him, will justify the great cost with his wisdom and particularly with his regard for the English law."

"But is he not learned," Lucy asked, "and well fitted to understand and approve the law?"

"Learned enough, I hear, but strange to English liberties and the forms of English justice," answered Vance. "Why, even before he was crowned, while on his way from Scotland, he tried and hung an accused man, himself acting as judge and jury in one. No king has the right to do that in England, a fact which none dared point out to His Majesty at the time. I hope he has learned it now."

Apparently the lawyer was not too happy about either the

character of his King or the lavish reception that London was offering. But just then music struck up in the distance, and all turned to the other window, drawing up stools to watch what happened in greater comfort. However, Tilton recognized a Danish air, and remembered that a music gallery had been set up just beyond the third arch to play the airs of her former country for James's Queen. Since it was past noon, Mistress Tilton told her servants to bring in the dinner. They were soon passing pewter plates and bowing to the guests with silver platters of golden-brown fish. Tilton bade all eat heartily.

"It will be a light repast," he said. "There's only a roast and a salad to come, and a sweet afterward."

They ate, listening to the music and watching for the procession. Lucy and Edward Vance were seated nearest the window, with Cedric, Roger and Tilton behind them. After a time the girl insisted that Cedric take her place. She wanted to sit beside Roger, she said. She rose with the word, and all but pushed the boy into her place, then took the stool he had left. As if to soften the act, she asked about his work at the playhouse.

Cedric spoke of it briefly, but courteously enough, saying that he had taken part in revels at home, and it was not wholly new to him, and that he was well instructed when there was need.

Lucy nodded.

"You will be idle now, and miss the playhouse."

Cedric said that it might soon open again; at any rate they played before the King next Thursday at Westminster.

"I shall be there myself!" Lucy exclaimed. "We are guests to a friend who has bidden us. Will it be a new play?"

"We've played it before. We rehearse it next Tuesday; that will be all."

Lucy turned to Roger and was soon telling him of an experience during her recent stay in the country, when she had ridden out with the hunters. Her father and his host had followed a stag for hours. Near a little village they were pressing it closely, and had hopes of making a kill. But a workman, a smith, was walking with his dog on his own property, which had some meadow and woodland on it behind his cottage. The deer skirted the edge of the trees, and the smith's dog, a powerful mastiff, leaped on the animal and brought it down. Naturally the hunters were vexed. They came up, and some of the retainers would have taken the deer, but the blacksmith bade them stand back, claiming that the stag was his both by right of the kill and by ownership of the land.

"And what did your father and Sir Fernando do?" asked Roger.

"Why, father and the retainers were for taking the deer by force if need be, and having the law on the smith." Lucy smiled. "But Sir Fernando said no, that the right lay with the blacksmith."

"And so it did, so it did!" exclaimed Vance almost gleefully. "Ha! While there are Englishmen of mean estate like that smith to speak for their liberties, and gentlemen like your father's friend to approve them, the future is bright for this land!"

"As to that I can't say," said Lucy somewhat dryly, "but I confess I was so wearied with listening to talk of stags and dogs, and of the true courtesies and proper strokes to be practised in dispatching a tired deer, that I smiled to see the smith bear off the horns and the meat."

"The King!" exclaimed Cedric suddenly. "Look, you can see the procession through the open gate!"

"Aye, and a fountain there will be spouting wine and milk!" Tilton told them with satisfaction, for as a Company member, he had some knowledge of what had been planned. Beyond

the arch they also discerned the King's canopy and his white
horse, and soon there was silence, and they heard the clear
voice of a boy telling in verse what had happened. The figures,
it seemed, were symbolical of Britain. They had been inert
and slothful; the arrival of the King had brought a new Spring
to the land:

> For joy whereof, nymphs, senses, hours and fame
> Echo loud hymns to his imperial name!

Then music struck up—violins and other instruments—
and, as these softened, the voices of two boys floated acrosss the
space in song. The crowd was breathlessly silent, the enuncia-
tion of the young singers was excellent, and most of their words
came clearly to the group at the window. Roger had heard of
the boy choristers of St. Paul's, trained to the finest pitch, able
to outdo any vocalists in Europe. He had thought the praise
too great, but now as he listened he was enchanted. The words
had the magic which many poets of that age seemed to command naturally, and the rendering was exquisite:

> Troynovant * is now no more a city;
> O great pity! Is't not a pity?
> And yet her towers on tiptoe stand,
> Like pageants built on fairy land,
>   And her marble arms
>   Like to magic charms
> Bind thousands fast unto her,
> That for her wealth and beauty daily woo her;
> Yet for all this, is't not a pity?
> Troynovant is now no more a city.

The song ran on, comparing London to a summer arbor in
which four kingdoms held festival, and again to a bridal chamber with roof of gold and floor of amber, and finishing:

* New Troy—a poetical name for London.

Hark, what the echoes say!
Britain till now ne'er kept a holiday!
For Jove dwells here; and 'tis no pity
If Troynovant be now no more a city.

Jove, of course, was their James, and the crowd shouted and huzzaed. The trumpets sounded, the progress went forward. It paused at the platform where the City dignitaries sat, and the recorder (Sir Henry Montague, Vance told them) began a speech. After the first minute or two Cedric's eyes wandered about, looking at the crowd, turned toward the platform. Many had risen in their seats. Suddenly he drew back sharply, and exclaimed to Edward Vance: "My guardian, sir! Bragdon!"

The lawyer started.

"Where? Where is he?"

"Yonder. Almost directly across the street, just under the largest window. To the left of the man in the green doublet. That's Wickard."

"In a black and red doublet? Is that Bragdon?"

"Yes, sir. I think—I don't think he's seen me."

Cedric shrank back against the side of the window frame. Edward Vance nodded at length.

"We have another acquaintance there," he remarked.

Roger leaned forward.

"Who, sir?"

"My friend Sefton." He watched for a moment. "Change places with Roger," he told Cedric quietly.

The boy did so. Roger glanced at Lucy as he left her. She smiled a little at him, and as Cedric sat down beside her she murmured: "You do not seem pleased to see your guardian."

The youngster gave her a cool stare, and replied in a tone as low as hers:

"Nor would you, Mistress Lucy, if you knew him as I do."

Lucy smiled again, but said nothing. At the platform the King, the Queen, and the Prince were being handed golden goblets, and soon, to the trumpet-note, they moved on. The girl glanced at her King, riding with a rather bored and tired air under his canopy, then looked closely at the men Cedric had indicated. Soon the procession halted again; a satyr pranced forth to greet the royal visitor; and then led him toward the next arch and St. Paul's. He passed from view.

Tilton rose and suggested that they move to the other window. The servants, who had rushed to it and looked for a moment, gave place, and Mistress Tilton briskly ordered them to bring in the main course. In the confusion, Lucy drew her page to her with a touch of the hand.

"Did you hear what Master Cedric said?" she murmured, smiling as if she spoke of some trivial matter. "Did you see the man in the black and red doublet?"

"Yes, my lady."

The girl slipped a half sovereign into his hand.

"There will be twice that for you, if you do well what I say."

She spoke a few sentences, and the boy nodded. Lucy turned calmly and rejoined the others at the south window. She took a seat there, and watched the ceremony at the arbor arch. The allegorical figures were posed before the King, and a boy actor was explaining the significance of the tableau. Then another boy's voice soared up in song, a chorus of young voices joining him at points. The soloist sang:

> Shine, Titan, shine;
> Let thy sharp rays be hurled
> Not on this under world,
> For now 'tis none of thine.

The chorus chimed in, giving the quatrain a full-bodied signature:

> *No, no, 'tis none of thine!*

The single voice lifted again, velvet-smooth but penetrating:

> But in that sphere
> Where that thine arms infold,
> Turns all to burnished gold,
> Spend thy gilt arrows there!

And the mingled voices underscored the plea:

> *Do, do, shoot only there!*

Then came several other verses, carrying the fancy along to a final stanza:

> And make Heaven ring
> His welcomes shouted loudly,
> For Heaven itself looks proudly
> That Earth has such a King!

The full medley of voices corrected that statement with a last exultant cry:

> *Earth has not such a King!*

It was as delicately yet clearly rendered, thought Roger, as any song he had ever heard, and as the procession moved on he was almost glad that he could not be present at the two remaining arches, for it seemed that he had heard a triumphal ending to the progress.

The others moved away from the window; for them as for him the pageant was finished. The servants set up a table on trestles, laid a "carpet" on it, as the cloth was called, and set out custards, cakes and tarts as the dessert course.

Edward Vance spoke approvingly of the ceremonies.

"The procession was well ordered, the speeches nobly given," he pronounced.

"And the songs even more masterfully sung," Roger added

with a smile.

"One king honoring another could not have done better," declared Lucy.

"Well said," approved the lawyer. "A great city *is* a kind of a king." He looked around the table and seemed slightly startled. "Where's your boy?" he asked Lucy.

"Oh, Dick," she answered carelessly. "He wanted to follow along with the crowd, and I gave him leave to do it."

It was an incident natural and trivial enough, and nothing more was said about it. After the meal was finished, Roger offered to see Lucy home, but she made excuses and refused. He and Cedric were soon on their way back to Little Wood Street.

"Did you see Dick in the crowd?" asked the boy.

Roger replied that he had not.

"I did," his companion went on. "I noticed Mistress Lucy saying something to him, and saw when he slipped out a few minutes later. Then, Roger, when the crowd broke up after the ceremony, I looked for him, and—well, I found him at last."

"What of it? He went to join the crowd, and it was natural that he should be in it."

"Yet perhaps not so natural either," replied Cedric rather stubbornly. "You see, Roger, I was watching Bragdon and Wickard, too. I wanted to see what *they* did. They went on through St. Paul's, so it didn't seem as if they had noticed me."

"Good. A good thing."

"But," the boy concluded, "not five paces behind them walked Dick, and I think, Roger, that he was following them."

XV

BRAGDON ATTACKS

IT IS never an easy thing for a boy of twelve to convince two men that they are completely mistaken about a point, particularly if it concerns a woman.

Cedric persuaded Roger to go with him to Edward Vance's house that night; and there he argued stoutly that Lucy had sent her boy Dick to communicate with Bragdon. But as the three sat around the table in the lawyer's study, both of the others smiled at him.

"Why, Cedric, Lucy Knowles is all but affianced to Roger," Vance pointed out. "She is an attractive and I am sure quite loyal young woman who would never work against one so close and dear to her."

"But, sir," Cedric remonstrated with boyish seriousness, "it is not against Roger that she works, but against me!"

"Against you!" exclaimed the man of law, his smile broadening. "But why should she?"

"It is not an easy thing to say," began Cedric hesitantly. "She does not like me—"

"Nor you her," interrupted Roger quickly.

Cedric nodded.

"I grant it. But, Roger, that doesn't change the—the truth of the business!"

"And what is the truth of it?" demanded Edward Vance.

"Why, sir, the bigger part of it is that she does not wish

Roger to stay in London. And though she holds me of no great consequence, yet she may think that my being here keeps him from Darrell Manor and his father. She's a very determined young woman, sir, though she may have a soft manner and can please and flatter if she has a mind to."

"Now you aim a shaft at me, I think," the lawyer remarked with a smile. "Yet I will not think the worse of her for a few pleasant words to an older man."

"No, sir—but—but you should not let them mislead you, sir." Cedric spoke eagerly in his desire to make his point. "Then there is the trick I played upon her at Darrell Manor on Twelfth Night," he blurted out.

The lawyer sat up with a jerk.

"You were at Darrell Manor? But Roger says he had never seen you until the duel with Wickard."

Roger looked uncomfortable, and Cedric eagerly broke in before his friend could speak.

"He *thought* he had not, sir." He explained what he had done on Twelfth Night, how Roger had suspected his identity, and how he himself had not admitted it when questioned.

"So you tied her and gagged her and took her costume and played the part," the lawyer mused. He looked at Cedric with a half-startled expression for a few seconds, then chuckled. "But how then did Roger learn that you *were* that boy, if you denied it?"

"Because," answered Cedric promptly, "Roger had seen Bragdon that night at Darrell Manor, and when he saw him again today from Master Tilton's window he realized—"

He spread his hands, having avoided speaking of Bragdon's visit to the Globe.

"Yes—er, of course." Vance studied the matter for a moment. "Well, I can see that if she were sure you were the boy who trussed her up, she'd not feel any great friendliness for you. But *does* she know? She can only guess."

"I think she has no doubt of it, sir."

"Well, say that it's so. I still question if she would do any-thing in a matter affecting Roger—"

"But it's partly because it *does* concern him," insisted Cedric. "She thinks that with me away that—well—that there would be one less thing to keep Roger in London."

"She wants him to return to his father, yes," conceded Edward Vance. "And a very natural feeling. Are you of a mind to do so, Roger?" His nephew shook his head.

"No, sir, I shall stay on here. Lucy must accept that. Though I think Cedric is right that she doesn't—not as yet. Perhaps she will not. But I shall stay. The designs I am doing for Master Shakespeare may open up a prospect for me. If not, I shall go on as I have gone, hoping for something else. Of course," he added, "it puts off for some time any question of our being affianced."

"Naturally." The lawyer, it was plain, was getting a defi-nitely clearer notion of Lucy's hopes and attitudes. "Well," he asked, "what do you think of Cedric's suspicions?"

Roger laughed.

"Oh, Lucy might suspect that Cedric trussed her up," he conceded, "and she's determined when it comes to pushing a point, but I still can't believe she would try to get in touch with Bragdon. She may not even have heard his name or have been sure who he was. The boy, I think, was just drifting along with the crowd, following the progress. Bragdon and Wickard and Sefton were going with it, too. Everyone was moving in the same direction. So I don't read into that what Cedric does."

The boy shook his head, but was silenced.

Vance spoke again.

"Besides," he pointed out, "there will be no public performances at the Globe. And did you not say there will be but one rehearsal there for your appearance before the King on Friday?"

"Yes, sir," said Roger. "There's little work to be done on the properties and the actors are almost ready. We do nothing until next Tuesday as to rehearsing, and I myself may finish my work before then. I hope so; I want a few hours to complete the designs for Master Shakespeare's new play."

"Well, then," said his uncle, "I see little risk in any case. Suppose Bragdon goes to the playhouse on Monday? He'll find no players about. But if he comes, you'll know he's been there. If you learn of it, we can decide what to do. And on Tuesday I'll send Travers with you in any case."

Roger nodded, and Vance went back to the matter of their seeing Sefton, the lawyer, with Bragdon.

"That seems to show there is only one mystery in this business," he pointed out. "I don't understand it any the better, yet at least everything seems to be clear as to that point. Well, we shall soon be ready for action, I hope, and the puzzle will straighten itself out. Meanwhile, go about your business, be alert, but I think you need not be unduly fearful."

Cedric was half convinced, and shrugged his shoulders.

If he could have seen Lucy as the moment, he would have felt fully justified in what seemed to the others his unreasonable suspicions. She was in her room in the lodgings she had with her father, writing a letter.

Sir, it ran, *as one who has an interest that happens to accord with yours, I write to give you news of your ward. If you wish to find him, go to the Globe Playhouse this coming Tuesday where the Company rehearses for a performance this Thursday next before their Majesties at Westminster. The boy plays*

*with them. He goes by the name of Cedric Wales. You will
find him there, and I trust have the means to prove and en-
force your authority.*

She hesitated, then signed the letter "A Well-wisher." She
laid it under a little tablet on the table at which she sat. She
could not send Dick out with it until the next day. But he
knew where to take it.

Lucy had no doubt whatever about what she had done.
There was no mistaking that Cedric was the boy who had taken
her place in the masque on Twelfth Night. She had not seen
Bragdon then, of course; she might not have recognized him if
she had. But he was Cedric's guardian; the boy himself had
said so. Nor could she believe that there were two boys so alike
in appearance, and both eager to escape those supposed to
govern them. Therefore Bragdon had a right to Cedric, and
she herself was justified in restoring his authority to him. And,
of course, she had a definite satisfaction in paying off what she
regarded as a grievance.

To send the letter might well further her plans about
Roger. It was not that the boy exerted any direct influence
upon him. Yet, having taken some responsibility for Cedric,
Roger would be influenced indirectly by that fact. Without a
companion who lived and worked with him, he might the more
easily be turned away from London and what he was doing.
And if he were turned back to his father, that, she felt, would
be good in the end for him as well as for his family and for her.

Of course, Lucy admitted to herself, Roger would not like
what she was doing if he knew about it. *But he will never
know,* she told herself. *Neither Dick nor I will tell him.* She
had rehearsed the boy on being wholly ignorant about Bragdon if questioned. It was unlikely that he would ever be asked;
Roger would not imagine or believe that she had had any part
in what would happen. It did not occur to her to call what

she was doing deceitful. She felt that she had a right to inform on Cedric; it was just evening a score. Also, she regarded it as a very practical step that might open a way out of a difficult situation. It would work out well for all concerned, probably even for Cedric. As she put the letter aside, she had argued herself into feeling the downright satisfaction of one about to do a useful and worthy deed.

Roger stood by the open door leading from the lobby to the main stage, watching the rehearsal. Everything was going well enough. The properties were now in order; the play seemed to be in hand. They would finish early today, he was sure, and go to Westminster tomorrow. He would be able to complete his designs tonight, perhaps bring them with him to Westminster for Shakespeare to see.

He looked towards the door that led to the street. Travers was lounging near it with the man whose business it was to stand there as a guard. Roger had given his uncle's servant instructions to stop Bragdon if the latter came, but he was not expecting any intrusion. Bragdon had not put in an appearance up to now, and if Cedric had been right, he should have done so.

There was a break in the rehearsal, and some of the cast came back into the lobby, Cedric among them. He and Heminges went over to the cask for a drink, talking about a point in the play. Roger went over towards them.

"You draw a sword too much like a man," the actor was insisting. "A girl would botch the business." He referred to the scene in which Viola is about to be forced to fight the cowardly Sir Andrew Aguecheek.

"Even if she were playing a man?" Cedric demanded, unconvinced. "Wouldn't she have practiced?"

Heminges was doubtful.

"Perhaps," he conceded, "yet for the play it would be better if she were strange to it. She's afraid, remember that."

Cedric agreed, and stood off to demonstrate. But he paused, his hand on the sword he wore for the rehearsal.

For there was a commotion at the stage door, and even as he stood staring, three or four men pushed back Travers and the guard and broke into the lobby. Travers had drawn his sword and stood facing them. Roger leapt to the wall where he had hung his own, belted it about him over his carpenter's apron, and joined his uncle's man. Bragdon, Wickard (his arm no more in a sling) and two other men stood just inside the door, their swords at their sides. They moved forward, and two more stout looking fellows, armed also, followed them in.

"That's the boy," said Bragdon, pointing to Cedric.

"And there's the young cockerel who pinked me," muttered Wickard to his master. "He with the apron."

Heminges spoke up sharply.

"Are you the master of these men?" he asked Bragdon.

"I am; and I come with an order from the court for the return of my ward, who—"

Heminges broke in.

"Sir, you must have made forcible entry to a building under the protection of His Majesty," he said crisply. "Before I speak with you I will ask you to withdraw these armed men, and then state your business in a peaceable manner. I will not speak with you at all under the threat of force."

Bragdon hesitated, but Wickard spoke rapidly to him in a low voice. Bragdon nodded.

"I must have the boy," he said. "If you will look at the order—"

"When you have removed these men from the playhouse I will speak with you."

Bragdon looked at Cedric, then at Wickard, then nodded. Instantly the swords of all six of the invaders were out of their scabbards, and the men moved forward. Heminges was caught unprepared, and stood scowling with Wickard's blade at his breast. But Travers and Roger stood on guard against the three foremost men. Cedric also drew his sword, but Roger spoke quickly to him.

"Get away," he said, in a low voice. "We'll hold them."

He parried a thrust from Wickard, as he spoke, and Cedric, after hesitating a second, darted through the stage door to his rear and out onto the main platform.

"Get the boy!" shouted Bragdon to one of his men, while Wickard and the two others pressed Roger and Travers. The man, strange to the playhouse, did not at once see the door in the wall of the inner stage. As he finally did, and made towards it, he found it locked. He threw himself against it, but it would not yield.

"Through the side curtains, fool!" shouted Bragdon.

The man caught the idea, and dived through them. At once there was a sharp crack and the fall of a body, and almost on the instant a shout, "Clubs, clubs!"

It was the cry of the apprentices meaning "Come along with your staves. Come to the rescue!" It had chilled more than one swordsman unfortunate enough to quarrel with those who worked for London merchants. With it Hodge burst in, followed by Richards, Smith and Somers.

"Clubs!"

Yelling with sheer delight, the master brawler of the hired men swung a stout cudgel at the rearmost of Bragdon's men, catching him a paralyzing blow on the sword arm as he turned. Richards finished him with a smart clout on the head that sent him reeling backward.

"After them! After them!" shouted Bragdon, turning his

sword toward the intruders and forcing them back while his retainer staggered against the wall, blinking to clear his brain. Wickard and his two companions stormed forward at Roger and Travers, but they were cramped for space, and one took a glancing blow on the arm from Travers. Hodge bellowed at him, and the fellow turned two ways successively, now toward the hired men on his flank, now toward the more deadly foemen in front. In a second he and his companions lost the offensive. Roger lunged furiously at Wickard, Hodge and his companions bellowed, and suddenly the four swordsmen were on the guard against their five opponents, for the quarterstaffs could not be ignored. In the confusion, Travers nicked a second opponent, and the invaders, swept by a common impulse, began to retreat. Wickard shifted to the dangerous flank, cut quickly at Hodge, parried a thrust from Travers, and so enabled his wounded companions to edge back toward the door. They slipped out, then Bragdon. Wickard deftly met a lunge by Roger, cut at the hired men, and would have got clean away but for a swift stroke by Hodge that took off his hat and sent him reeling. He found the door, his blade a whirling arc, and stumbled down the stairs and away. The Globe crew crowded to the opening, jeering at the invaders. Hodge retrieved the hat from the floor and waved it in triumph at the end of his stick.

"A trophy!" he shouted. "Blood and booty for the King's Men!"

Burbage came in from the outer stage and smiled on seeing the intruders gone.

"Why, it was a rout!" he exclaimed.

Several of the other actors brought in the man who had been felled as he entered the inner stage, gave him a drink of ale, and told him to be on his way.

"And don't come back, my fine slasher," warned Hodge,

swaggering up to him, "if you want a whole head on your shoulders. I'll hit the clout full center next time!"

Glowering at him, the retainer slipped out. Cedric came back from the outer stage, looking somewhat pale and shaken.

"I think you've had enough for the day, lad," said Heminges, regarding him closely. "Now we'll see about getting you home."

That was a business rather elaborately managed, with a landing at the Tower stairs and scouts to the front and rear to make sure that Bragdon would have no knowledge of where Cedric had gone.

"You and we must part company soon," Burbage told him before they started, "but we can't spare you until after this Thursday and must work very shrewdly to see that you aren't taken. Then, I think, you must fight in the courts and I trust win your case there."

But the elaborate precautions were apparently needless. Bragdon and his men were watching another landing stairs or, knowing that a brawl in the London streets would be of doubtful value to them, had retired to work out a quieter and safer way of getting what they wanted. Roger and Cedric walked the last block alone, and let themselves into Mistress Salter's door. Roger lit a fire, and insisted that the boy take a drink of sherry to restore him. Cedric had been very quiet on the way home. He put sugar into the cup and sipped the wine with a little shudder.

"Come, drink it," Roger urged him. "It will put heart into you. Why," he went on, "we routed the rascals, but you look as if Bragdon had caught you."

Cedric did not answer his friend's smile. He pushed the cup aside and stared at Roger with desperate eyes.

"You don't understand. It isn't just Bragdon."

"If it isn't, I don't know what it is," the other countered briskly. "We've come through this, and we'll soon have the business before a court and finished."

"We can't go to court," Cedric insisted. "Your uncle can't be ready. I've wrecked it. I've been a fool. I meant to tell him, then I couldn't, and I've ruined everything!" His voice rose with excitement. "Do you understand? Everything!"

"I don't understand any of it," replied Roger, "and can't see why things aren't as good as they ever were. What are you talking about? Why can't we go to court? Why can't Uncle Ned be ready?"

The eyes that looked into his seemed very old for a twelve-year-old boy's. Then they dropped and Cedric suddenly gave a little moan, bent forward to the table and buried his head in his arms. His shoulders shook with sobs. Finally his voice came, desperate and muffled. The words left Roger gasping.

"Because I'm a—a girl!" it said.

XVI

CONFESSION

ROGER looked at the bowed head with astonishment, exasperation and alarm. He took a turn about the room, and wound up before the table again to find his companion looking at him with an uncertain smile, winking the tears from her lashes. Her faintly flushed face, the glance of her eyes, the quality of the smile were all suddenly feminine.

"I feel better now," she said in a faint voice.

Roger stared at her: confused, moved by a certain sympathy, but annoyed and aggrieved.

"I don't," he retorted. "What kind of a dance have you been leading me? What will they think at the Globe? What will my uncle say—or Mrs. Salter?"

Cedric's smile broadened and her eyes sparkled.

"Oh, as for Mistress Salter, I told her long ago," she replied. "I couldn't hope to go on fooling *her*. She's several pounds the richer for it, and, as I pointed out to her, can say that I deceived her—as I did for more than a week."

"And me for many of them!"

"Well, Roger, if it's any comfort to you, I worked hard at doing it," his companion answered somewhat wearily. She sighed. "I'll be glad to stop trying to act like a boy, and four years younger than I am."

"You're sixteen?" Roger demanded in amazement.

"A week ago." She leaned forward earnestly. "Roger, don't

be angry. I want your—your friendship and good opinion more than—Roger, you *must* believe me. I had no choice. None in the world."

She shuddered; and, looking at her, the young man had a sharp realization of what she must have suffered.

"Well, tell me about it," he said gruffly. "The full truth, this time."

The girl nodded. She sat for a moment as if uncertain of how to begin.

"I told you my last name was not Wales but Hardie," she said finally. "And, of course, my first name isn't Cedric. It's Diane. And you shall judge if what I did was one whit more than I had to do." She paused and saw that Roger had begun to walk about again. "Do stop striding back and forth and sit down, Roger," she said sharply.

Roger stared at her in surprise, then sat.

The sudden effectiveness of her command made her laugh out; then with a look of apology she said quickly:

"I'm sorry, Roger. It's only that I don't find speaking of this an easy thing, and with you pacing about distractedly—" She completed the sentence with a shrug. "I'll try to be brief and clear. I told you before about Bragdon's making this marriage a thing of profit," she continued. "I can't prove it—I've warned your uncle about that. Yet I'm sure that both Ralph's and my estates have been tampered with. Bragdon had only a small property when my father died—a hundred acres, perhaps. Now he manages five hundred and draws tithes from more than twenty tenants. He's shrewd, but from his own holdings alone he could never have done it."

"Uncle Ned's man will find evidence about that."

"I hope he will, hope he can. But since I didn't tell Master Vance my true name—" She shrugged doubtfully.

"But he may get evidence in any case."

"He may, but—where was I? Oh, yes—the estates. I've only suspicion there, as I said. It was the marriage that forced me to —to this. You see, Roger, it's the trick on which he has hazarded everything. Why, the husband he chose for me is a widower with one daughter almost old enough to be my mother. He's a hideous old man. But the marriage would save Bragdon. He may get several hundred pounds. Or he'd keep some advantage he has gained from my property. Ralph will soon be of age. If Bragdon pledged part of *his* estate, as I'm sure he did—"

"Then he could make that good by something from yours. There'd be no question about yours because your husband would have it."

Diane nodded.

"Of course; it was pat for his purpose. But the marriage—" She shuddered again. "Roger, imagine *your* being matched with a woman of fifty. Oh, worthy enough, but fifty. Only with me, he'd take not only me but all I have, and I—"

She threw out her hands in a desperate gesture, and Roger nodded slowly.

"What would *you* have done?" she demanded. "I tell you I'd have made an end to everything first, and I will yet if I must!"

"Why didn't you tell Uncle Ned?" Roger asked.

Diane shook her head.

"I was going to tell him. But at first there was no need of it. I thought to wait until the agent had started for Holcombe. Finally he went, and—well, I couldn't bring myself to it. I was happy at the playhouse. It seemed safe. I was going to tell him the day after Hammond left, then the next. It was partly the habit of being secret about everything. And I didn't know what Master Vance would do. I— Oh, I was going to tell him tonight—"

"You *are* going to tell him tonight," Roger assured her, smiling, but with a certain grimness.

She nodded.

"Of course," she gulped. "I must—I know it. But—can you not say something, Roger? Tell me that you understand it, that you believe me, that you'll help me!"

Roger looked at her, and whatever was left in him that was aggrieved and hard suddenly melted. He could not doubt what she had told him, could not be angry with her.

"Of course I believe you, Ced—Diane."

Her eyes twinkled.

"Better call me Cedric for a while, Roger."

"Cedric, then. I'll help you all I can. We'll tell him about it together."

"Thanks, Roger." Her voice was husky and she gave him a smile very different from any he had ever had from Cedric. Then with a sharp realization of what their situation was, both felt constrained and embarrassed.

"We—we can't go to his house yet," Diane said at last. "It will be safer after supper."

Roger agreed. Then a thought came to her and she rose, pushing back her chair.

"The designs!" she exclaimed. "I want to see all of them again. You've only one scene to finish—isn't it so?"

"Yes—only two hours' work. I thought of taking them with me to Westminster, but—"

"Oh, yes. Oh, you must. But let's look at them."

Roger rose and brought the sketches to the table and began laying them out.

They were different in quality as well as in idea from the hurried drawings he had previously made for Burbage and Heminges. Roger had brought to this work all the skill and finish of execution that he could command. First he took up one of the stagefront showing the opening scene of the play as it would appear to the audience. It was a room in the Duke's palace, set on the smaller stage just behind the main one.

"I finished this only last night," he explained, "and it shows the whole purpose I have in mind."

Diane gave an exclamation of pleasure.

"The scene stands out like a jewel," she declared. "What have you done? Why, of course—the other stages are curtained off—all in one color. They are wholly a background—"

"That's it," Roger rushed in eagerly. "Of course," he added, "Heminges and Burbage may speak against the expense. For as you see I have these warm gray curtains all of a color except for an edging of scarlet to cover the upper stage and its framework, and both the window stages. Everything is a framework for the inner stage, and the red and green hangings will bring the eye at once to the scene and keep it there. It will be the same throughout the entire play."

He laid out the prison scene, with wings representing stone walls instead of the usual curtains, and a stone wall and high, barred window instead of curtains at the rear.

"Here too there will be expense."

"But it's worth it! And 'tis simple—easy to set up."

"Easy enough. Then the scene for the outer stage—here's the effect Master Shakespeare wanted—no curtains across the rear, but a gate. Above, the effect of a wall."

"They are masterly, Roger! The King's Men would be fools not to use them. In fact—"

Diane stopped as if an idea had come to her.

"In fact, what?"

She colored and shook her head.

"Oh, nothing. I—I was going to say that the scenes would win them larger audiences, but they play to full crowds already."

Roger had a feeling that her reply was an evasion, but could not guess why.

"Yes, they usually do," he admitted, slowly. "That may be the trouble. 'Why spend more, then?' Heminges will ask."

Diane was about to reply when there was a knock at the door. Roger asked who was there; and when his landlady answered, told her to enter. She opened the door and spoke softly.

"Mistress Knowles and her woman are below, sir," she said.

Roger frowned, then began to gather up his drawings.

"Let her come up," he said.

Lucy and Alice came in not a minute after his words. They were dressed for the street and the mistress walked with a buoyant air. Then she saw Cedric and her face underwent a subtle change which Roger did not miss. It was only for a second; then she smiled.

"I came to bid you to supper, and I will not take a 'no'!"

Roger looked at her calmly and shook his head.

"I can't come, Lucy," he told her. "I have business at hand that will not wait."

"Is it so urgent as that? A conference with the players? Some work to do for them? Are you not all in readiness for Westminster?"

Roger looked at her steadily.

"The matter is important," he replied. "As to what it is, I think there's no need to discuss that."

"What do you mean? Is it so secret?"

"Possibly. But the point is—after what happened this afternoon I cannot talk freely about my affairs."

"But I don't understand, Roger. What happened this afternoon?"

"I think you have some idea as to that."

"What do you mean? How should I?" Lucy looked surprised

and aggrieved.

"If you don't, I'm glad of it. And in that case it's something I can't speak of."

Lucy shrugged, but managed a smile.

"Why, Roger, you are as close-mouthed as a lawyer's clerk or a King's agent!" she exclaimed.

"I'm sorry. I must be."

"Why, then, I'm sorry, too, and my father will be. Shall you be free tomorrow evening?"

"We go to Westminster tomorrow."

"Of course. We shall follow you the morning after. I shall see both of you then, I trust."

Roger bowed.

"If I can find you among the quality there."

"Oh, make a point of it!" Lucy shook a finger at him and smiled.

He said nothing, and after a moment she turned. "Then I must be going. I shall see you both at Westminster."

She went toward the door, and Roger followed.

"I'll see you to the street."

He came back a few minutes later looking unhappy. Diane was sitting at the table again and gave him the ghost of a smile. He sat down himself, sighing. Finally he flung out:

"Oh, you were right. There was no way of his suspecting except through her."

"Or of his knowing the day of the rehearsal," murmured Diane. "I told her about that."

Roger nodded gloomily.

"For all I know, she'll send him here," he muttered.

"No," Diane corrected him. "I think not. It would be sure then that she was helping him, and she doesn't want you to know *that*."

Edward Vance looked very grave when the two were ushered into his study that night. He asked them to be seated and pointed grimly to some papers lying on the table.

"I have a report from Hammond," he told them, looking searchingly at Cedric. "This is a very strange business. I can only conclude, Cedric—if that's your name—that you are a complete rascal—or a young woman."

Diane blushed, but looked steadily at him.

"I am Diane Hardie, not Cedric," she told him. Then with Roger's help she went over the full story, including what had happened that day at the playhouse and Lucy's visit.

The lawyer did not respond to her account as easily or fully as Roger had done, but finally seemed to feel that he had the full truth.

"You will still aid me, Master Vance?" Diane pleaded. "I know you are justly offended. I should have told you. I—I hope Master Hammond has managed to do something, in spite of not knowing the full truth."

"Hammond has gathered all the facts he could about the estates of both Ralph and Diane Hardie. He is a shrewd and able man. When he has finished, things may look brighter for you and the worse for Bragdon. I hope so."

"Then you *will* see it through!"

The lawyer looked at her severely.

"Why I should, I don't know," he replied, "except that I believe you have now told me fully what happened, and the principle involved remains the same. But," he continued, checking the girl as she tried to speak, "if I continue with the case, I must have complete obedience from you as to how you expose yourself to danger."

"What about the performance at Westminster the day after tomorrow?" she asked. "The players cannot find anyone now to take my part."

Vance looked troubled at the thought of her appearing again.

"They might borrow a boy from the Queen's Troupe—the Children of St. Paul's," he pointed out. "Those youngsters are highly gifted and I'm sure learn their parts quickly."

"But *is* there danger, Master Vance?" Diane urged. "We leave the city; Bragdon is not likely to be invited to *that* performance. And once at Westminster I shall be much safer than here—wholly so, in fact. And sir, the King's Men cannot hope for much from a boy with only one day's training. They count on me, Master Vance. I am still a member of the Company. Remember, it is for the King."

The lawyer sat for a while studying the matter.

"Well, I think we may hazard it," he began, "but if we do—"

"Oh, thank you, sir!"

"—it must be with the utmost care. I shall prepare such papers as will give you some protection; then if the case comes to court, we can ask such time as will enable Hammond to gather more evidence. I shall write him tonight. And you, mistress, from now on shall be my guest."

"Stay here?"

"Stay here. If then Bragdon were to learn you lodged with Mrs. Salter, it would do him no good."

Diane nodded. "As you say, Master Vance."

"There is one point I do not understand," the lawyer continued. "Why has Bragdon always spoken of you as a boy? Why did not he declare to Master Heminges who you really were?"

"I think I know the reason," said Diane. "He wants no risk of the marriage failing. He probably told my husband-that-would-be that I'm away from Holcombe on a visit. If there were too much ado about my running away and putting on a boy's habit, if it were widely known, the old grandfather might think again before taking me."

"That's it, sir," Roger agreed. "Bragdon wants to get hold of her quietly."

"Yes, that is probably the case." Edward Vance nodded thoughtfully. "Well, this performance at Westminster must be your last. And it must bring us no new difficulties. Meanwhile we may hear from your brother. Hammond is busy searching into *his* affairs, also."

"We shall manage the trip to Westminster very well, sir," Roger assured his uncle.

"I hope so," the latter replied. "I have a feeling that Bragdon is desperate and may lay all on one last attempt. If he knew of the rehearsal, doubtless he knows also of this performance at Westminster."

"But we shall be a big company," Roger remonstrated, "and under the King's protection."

"That may not be of as much value as you suppose," his uncle replied. "But I myself will go with you, with Travers. If the law is invoked, I shall have something to say about that. If violence is attempted, well, we shall be better able to meet it if we must."

Vance sat a moment longer, then rose.

"Roger and Travers will go get your gear," he told Diane. "You will remain here. You can arrange with my housekeeper about some suitable clothes, which she will soon provide for you. I want you to have full protection until this business is before the court. You shall be under this roof by night and in my sight by day."

He struck a bell and was soon giving Travers and one of his servants directions about going to Little Wood Street with Roger. He sent out another servant to fetch his chief clerk.

"We shall prepare the papers for a suit," he explained. "Bol-

ton can see that they are filed tomorrow and bring the court's
authorization to me at Westminster. This will take some hours.
You, mistress, should retire when Roger returns; my housekeeper will show you your room. You will need your sleep
for the performance Thursday and perhaps for other events we
cannot foresee. We seem to be moving towards a resolution of
this matter. Yet I am not satisfied. I cannot believe that all will
go as quietly as now seems possible."

Vance stood for a moment in thought, then sat down and
began making notes for the paper he was about to prepare.

XVII

INIGO JONES

"If music be the food of love, play on:
    Give me excess of it, that, surfeiting,
    The appetite may sicken, and so die!
    That strain again—"

ROGER stood at the side of the rear stage in the Great Chamber
at Whitehall, watching the opening scene of the rehearsal.

Through a gap in the side curtains he had a view of Burbage
as the love-sick Duke in *Twelfth Night*. All morning he had
worked helping to complete the platform which was more
than half finished when he arrived—thanks to the Globe's
carpenters and some workmen directed by an agent of the
Master of Revels. Now, with the noonday meal eaten, the
actors could rehearse.

The stage was simple. *Twelfth Night* required only the
main platform, the inner stage just behind it, and the second-
story stage above the latter. All the playing areas were of somewhat smaller dimensions than the Globe's, because of the size
of the hall. But except for size, they were replicas.

The first brief scene was drawing to an end. Duke Orsino,
pining for the love of the indifferent Lady Olivia, had heard
rather cheerfully that she would not receive his messenger. Although the death of her brother was long since past, she was
still in mourning for him. It was a good sign, argued the Duke.
If she could feel such love for a mere brother, how gloriously

would she give her heart (to him, of course) when finally she was ready to bestow it! He waved his courtiers out.

"Away before me to sweet beds of flowers;
  Love-thoughts lie rich when canopied with bowers!"

The prompter gave the signal; the curtains of the inner stage, which had represented a room in the Duke's palace, slid together. Outside, the second scene opened. Cedric, playing the part of shipwrecked Viola, came in from the side, escorted by a sea captain and followed by sailors carrying chests.

"What country, friends, is this?"

"This is Illyria, Lady."

The young woman stood irresolute and stricken.

"And what should *I* do in Illyria? My brother, he is in Elysium. Perchance he is not drowned: what think you, sailors?"

Roger looked at Viola—no, he corrected himself, Cedric—no, not Cedric, Diane! She was dressed as a woman, for the company was playing this rehearsal, their final one, in costume. Now that he knew her to be a girl, how much a girl she seemed! How could he or any of the Company have been so deceived? Yet the others still were. This Viola, talking with the sailors about the chance that her twin brother Sebastian, separated from her in the storm and wreck, had survived, then suddenly getting the rather wild idea of disguising herself as a youth and going to serve Duke Orsino—why, to all the Company but Roger she was just a clever boy, skilled in pretending to be what she was not!

But Roger watched her with new eyes. He found himself acutely concerned with this girl's appearance, gestures, spoken words. He fancied that he could detect a certain anxiety and strain in her acting. That was natural, and luckily it fitted the part. He told himself as he looked and listened that now she was more like the person she really was than she had been during these many weeks when she had played the role of a twelve-year-old boy. She would be much like this as he would know her in the future. Yes, she would be a woman: as much of a woman as—as Lucy. Not *like* Lucy, but a woman. One whom Bragdon wanted to seize and sell off for profit and —Roger reminded himself—one ready to die rather than to have that happen.

Well, nothing had happened yet, he thought as he watched her. He, Diane, and his uncle had got away early that morning, joining the Company at St. Paul's wharf and going up the river in barges previously chartered. Now they were in the safety of the royal grounds. There was only one difficulty: all the chief actors had been bidden to a supper near Westminster the evening following the play. As a result, his own party and Diane would not have their company and protection on the return journey. But Vance did not seem greatly disturbed by that fact.

"We shall take measures for a safe journey later," he had said.

Vance had seen them to the Great Chamber; then, on consideration, had gone back to the city to attend to the filing of the petition which would pave the way for Cedric's—or rather Diane's—freedom. He would return the next day. Meanwhile, Travers and Brown (another of Vance's men) were lounging about the stage. They were an insurance against an extreme emergency.

The night before, Roger had finished the last of the designs for the new play. Diane had asked about them with an insistence that had amused him. In the boat she had reminded him to give them to Shakespeare. So everything seemed to be going well. Diane and he and his uncle's two men would stay the night at Westminster with the King's Men. Diane would be safe there, and, Roger hoped, safer with each succeeding day.

The scene ended, and the actors jostled past him into the small lobby at the rear. The prompter signaled to draw the curtains for the ensuing scene, set for the inner stage. It showed a room in the Lady Olivia's house where the stout Sir Toby Belch, her uncle, and the pert maid Maria were discovered.

"What a plague means my niece, to take the death of her brother thus!"

It was a long scene, Roger knew, introducing the silly Sir Andrew Aguecheek as well as Sir Toby and Maria, and opening up the rollicking vein of comedy that ran through the rest of the play.

He looked about him. Where was Wat Somers? He had come up an hour ago with a story of having to find a cousin who served somewhere about the palace, and since Wat had no part in the early action of the comedy Roger had agreed that it would be safe for him to do his errand. It had taken a long time.

With some concern his eyes again swept the space back of the stages, and with a sigh of relief he saw that Somers had just returned. Cedric (as Roger still tried to think of her) came out from behind a screen where she had changed into her youth's costume, and went over to the stage-hand. Somers smiled and nodded. He must have told Diane about his errand. At the moment there seemed to be no more to the encounter than that.

The rehearsal went forward. By this time, of course, Roger knew every turn of the plot of this romantic comedy by heart. Orsino has dedicated himself to a great love for Olivia, although he scarcely knows her except by reputation. Naturally enough, he chooses his new attendant, the youth Caesario (the name the disguised Viola has chosen) to plead his cause. But Viola herself has meanwhile fallen in love with the Duke.

"I'll do my best," she tells him, "to woo your Lady," but adds to herself, "Yet a barful strife! Whoe'er I woo, myself would be his wife!" Now it needs only Olivia's falling in love with Caesario, who is apparently a handsome and resourceful young man, to make a three-way tangle. Luckily there is the twin brother Sebastian, who did not drown, and turns up to satisfy the Countess completely. As for Orsino, when he knows Caesario to be a woman, he is more attracted to her (already his favorite as a youth) than to the indifferent lady he had worshiped from afar.

As he watched this plot unfolding in rehearsal, Roger found that another drama, a wholly personal one, was unfolding at the same time. His thought of a few minutes ago returned to him—Diane and Lucy! The images of the two young women rose up before him, making a contrast and even a conflict, and with them came a discovery that startled him: Lucy no longer mattered to him at all! For an instant he felt amazement and protest: *She's done only what she thought was right: it's what she would and must do.* Yet he realized that the protest was perfunctory, for he knew now that the girl he had once expected to marry would never want him except on her own terms, and that he would never meet them. But he knew also something more important—that it was Lucy herself and not her acts that had brought this abrupt realization of indifference toward her. Under the prettiness and lively charm he saw now with complete clarity the calculating and determined spirit that had faintly repelled him at times in the past. Had he ever really loved her? The question seemed pointless. It was startlingly clear to him now that their different attitudes toward his own future had really been differences of character. These were so sharp that, whatever relationship he and she might have had, under the surface they would always have been strangers.

Roger sighed with a kind of shuddering relief, like a man who has walked in his sleep and wakes to find himself about to step off the edge of a high parapet. Lucy's own acts had, of course, helped to reveal her to him. But they alone had not done it. No, there had been a more important factor: Diane. Diane! *Why, you hardly know her,* he told himself. Or didn't he? For the girl she had suddenly become was also the boy that she had pretended to be. Acts and words came back to him, tumbling about in his mind: *I'd march up to the King himself for a friend,* he remembered, and again: *If there's a good for me that goes against what's best for you*—and still again: *Were I a woman, I would think long before I tried to force the man I loved away from what he did best and wanted most!*

The remembered sentences teased and mocked him. More than that, he found himself feeling a parallel between the play he was watching and a part of his life during the last month. For Diane was playing a woman disguised as a youth, and at Little Wood Street and the Globe she had done the same thing in actual life. The discovery brought him a kind of exhilaration. Here was a girl not scheming and contriving to get her way, but courageously fighting for it; one who could understand and even applaud the choice he had made, and bid him hold to it when he had faltered. She had said—

A recognition of what he was feeling brought him up sharply, with a wry inner laugh. *Why, what are you telling yourself? What mad promise are you playing with now? Is it so easy to forget that you are still Roger Darrell the hired man?*

He wrenched himself away from the action and voices of the rehearsal, and began checking the properties beside and behind the stage. *Keep your mind to these,* he told himself savagely. *They and only they are your business now.*

The rehearsal had ended, and Roger like the others was getting his hat and cloak, when he heard his name spoken and found Shakespeare beside him.

"Have you a moment, Master Vance?"

"Certainly."

"There is a gentleman here asking about your drawings, and since I have not looked at them myself I thought you might be willing to show them to both of us."

"Why—gladly." Roger stared in surprise at the playwright, then turned to walk with him to the rear of the hall. Shakespeare, he noticed, was carrying the portfolio that contained the designs for *Measure for Measure*. A cloaked figure was waiting in the corner of the Chamber at the other end from the stage.

"Who is he?" asked the young man, astonished and puzzled. "I cannot think of anyone who would know about the designs. I spoke to no one about them."

Shakespeare lifted an eyebrow and smiled.

"Well, you shall soon know him," he promised, and led his companion up to a rather young but assured looking gentleman with keen, light blue eyes and a small golden-brown beard.

"Sir," said the playwright, "this is the Master Vance of whom we spoke, and here are the designs he has made for me. He says he cannot guess how you heard of them, yet I think he will have heard of you when I tell him you are Master Inigo Jones."

Roger looked his complete surprise, but bowed quickly and assured the stranger that he was indeed familiar with his name and work.

"Had I dared, and known how to manage it, I would have begged to wait upon you myself," he told the architect. "Indeed, I sought an introduction through a friend at Court, but he refused to attempt it."

Jones lifted his brows, then nodded.

"It might have been difficult to manage," he admitted, "for I have been busy here, and have refused to speak with many craftsmen who have sought interviews with me. My undertakings have been quite uncertain and there seemed no point as yet in building on them. But apparently you have a friend who admires what you do," he continued, "and can write of it well. You say you did not know you have an advocate. This came to me about noon today."

He offered Roger a single sheet of paper which had been sealed as a letter and contained several paragraphs of clear script.

Sir: Roger read, *If you have any interest in the work of a young artist of exceptional talent who, I think, would give much to serve you, come to the Great Chamber this afternoon where the King's Men are rehearsing. Master Roger Vance, who knows nothing of this message, has completed some drawings for the settings of a play by Master William Shakespeare, who has them and I think will gladly show them to you if you explain your reason for wishing to see them. He too knows nothing of my writing to you.*

They are designs most unusual in character, suiting to use in an English playhouse the perspective type of scenery affected by the Italians. To do such work the maker of these drawings has parted with his father and lost hope of the estate that would naturally have come to him. I tell you this only to make you know the firmness of his purpose. He now works with the King's Men, but must look to someone of your talent and place if he is to show truly what he can accomplish. That

*you will at least take pains to become acquainted with his skill
is the hope of*

A Friend.

Roger finished reading the note and silently returned it.

"I assure you that I knew nothing of this," he said.

"But from your looks I think you can perhaps guess the writer?" Inigo Jones smiled.

"I think so—yes, I do," admitted Roger. He recalled the idea that had seemed to come to Diane as she had looked at the designs the night before. Had this been it?

His face evidently reflected a variety and confusion of feelings, for Jones said briskly:

"Well, I will call him a good friend of yours, indeed, who knows how to throw out an attractive bait. When a man in the doublet of the King's Men demanded to see me and gave me this—I confess that I felt no small curiosity, Master Vance, and—well, you perceive I am here. Am I to see the designs?"

"Why—why, gladly," stammered Roger, and untied the tapes of the portfolio.

"As Master Shakespeare will tell you," he said as he did so, "they represent a hazard; for they are not at all such settings as have been used at the Globe."

Jones smiled.

"With all respect to Master Shakespeare and his quality, may I say that I am not sorry to hear it."

"Oh, I am an aider and abetter in the venture towards something that might improve on what we do." The playwright laughed.

Roger had now thrown back the portfolio cover, and showed the overall design of the stage unit front, with the first scene set in the inner stage. Quickly he explained the effect he wished to produce.

Shakespeare exclaimed in surprise as the drawing was laid out, and looked at Jones, who nodded.

"It should have been tried long since," he remarked. "Your mind runs with mine in this drawing, Master Vance."

Roger laid out the other designs, explaining with respect to each the purpose he had in mind.

Jones watched attentively, nodding now and then, or saying a word as to color or design, then looked them over again carefully.

"Who was your teacher, sir?" he asked at length.

"A Master Bartolomeo, an Italian," Roger answered.

Jones murmured his satisfaction.

"I thought these had not come out of England only," he remarked. "Though they are English, too," he added, "English in their boldness and honesty of purpose. Sir," he continued, "if my affairs here at Court come to a flowering, as now seems most likely, I think you are a man to my taste. We must speak further of it."

Roger stammered his thanks, and the architect took down his London address, also that of his uncle.

"You'll hear from me," he promised. Then turning to Shakespeare he asked, "Have you immediate use for these drawings? Shall you and your fellows be likely to use them?"

"As far as I have a voice in the matter, we shall," said the playwright. "But it is a question for the housekeepers to decide, and I am one of half a dozen. Frankly, I think there will be some stiff objection because of expense. At any rate, there is no hurry about them. Take the designs for a day or two, if you like."

Jones looked questioningly at Roger, who nodded. The architect tied up the portfolio.

"I shall see that one of you has them again within the

week," he promised. Then he said to Roger, smiling, "If you know who sent the letter to me, give him my thanks."

As he left the hall, Shakespeare offered Roger his hand.

"I think this venture may pay you better than we dared hope," he said. "I'm glad."

Roger clasped the playwright's hand. In a confusion of feelings, he could find nothing to say. Shakespeare seemed not to notice. He clapped his young associate on the shoulder and moved off to get his own cloak and hat.

When Roger came to the entrance of the hall where supper was to be served, he found Diane waiting for him. She smiled with unconcealed delight.

"You had a visitor!" she announced.

"Sent by you!" he accused her with a smile; then added awkwardly: "He told me to thank you."

She clapped her hands.

"Then he liked them! It came to something!"

"It may," he admitted. "Master Jones wants to see me again. And I—I want to add my thanks to his."

"Truly? You're not offended?"

"How could I be?"

"I had the idea last night when we were looking at the designs," she said quickly. "But I was afraid to tell you." Her eyes twinkled. "You'd have been full of scruples." Then she asked: "He showed you the letter?"

Roger nodded.

"I persuaded Somers to take it," she explained. Then hesitantly, "I—I had a scruple myself—about mentioning your father. But it seemed to me that I must. I wanted to make Master Jones know what had gone into your work."

Roger found suddenly that he could speak out freely.

"You were right, Cedric," he said, using the old name. "It may have been what persuaded him to come. And I want you to know this," he added, "never has anyone done for me a thing that I have valued so much."

She flushed, then sparkled at him.

"Why, we are quits, Roger. For I never did anything that pleased *me* more!"

She turned smiling and marched through the door, and he followed her, at once confused and elated. A half an hour ago he had told himself to push all promises away. But as he walked beside Diane he knew that one went with him. He did not try to spell it out, but neither did he repel it.

Roger was busy preparing for the performance the following afternoon when he became conscious of someone standing beside him in the little lobby back of the stages, and looked around to see a once familiar figure and hear a ringing laugh.

"Anthony! By all that's impossible!"

He gripped hands with his brother.

"So here's the master showman!" Anthony laughed as he looked curiously about him.

"And here's the gentleman!" Roger retorted, tapping the other on the chest; for his visitor was dressed to the part, with a lace-edged hat and cloak, tooled kidskin gloves, and a sword that swung carelessly as he moved.

Anthony shook his head, grinning.

"That's your doing," he reminded Roger quickly. "Sir Ralph has come to London at last, and I'm with him. I found the Knowleses in the city this morning," he went on, "and by leave of their host have come along with them for the play. It occurred to me that if I made myself known to your doorkeeper, I might break in here, and so it proved."

Roger urged him to be seated, but his brother declined.

"I know you begin soon, and I must go back to the Knowleses. Lucy seems hopeful of your patching things up," he added quickly. "Will you try it?"

"Why, in one sense, gladly," Roger answered. "I'd give much to have the bitter part of this forgotten, and enjoy Father's love again, and good opinion. But—"

"But you hold still to the purpose that brought you here."

"I do, Anthony, I must." Roger looked at his brother earnestly. "It is what I set most value on," he explained, "and now I have a hope of advancement. Only yesterday I had something like a promise from Inigo Jones himself."

"Inigo Jones?"

Anthony's face was so wholly blank that Roger laughed.

"I'd forgotten," he said, "you don't know of him. But you will soon. He's an architect and artist—an Englishman, but already famed abroad, and somewhat the talk of the Court. They say he will manage masques and other entertainments for their Majesties."

"So that's the way of it." Anthony nodded regretfully. "Well, Roger, I'll not say I'm wholly pleased. It's easy enough to slip into your place, and, should I keep it, I'd trust to fill it honorably—"

"You'll fill it better than I could."

"Say rather in a different way. More Father's way, perhaps. But the place is yours. I can't shake off the feeling of *that*. Give the business more thought. Let me speak for you. I'll move everything to get you back."

"It's late for that—"

"Not too late. I know Father and his ways. Lucy and I could bring him around, I think."

Roger shook his head.

"I must stay on in London. But if you'd speak to Father about his feeling more kindly toward me—"

Anthony shrugged, and took Roger's hand.

"Of course I will, if there's no more to speak of." He paused, then added: "I'll come for you after the play. You'll go back to the city with us?"

"No; that's impossible."

Roger spoke emphatically, thinking that he saw Lucy's hand in the proposal. She might have sent word again to Bragdon. To detach Roger from Cedric at the same time would be a skilful trick.

"No," he repeated. "Another time I could, but not this afternoon."

"Well, then," said his brother, "I'll come for you anyway. You can speak a word to the Knowleses."

It seemed only courtesy, and Roger agreed.

Edward Vance arrived just after Anthony left, and seemed pleased with what he had accomplished in the city. He had not been able to get the suit filed until that morning, but now it had been attended to and they had a certain legal status.

"Our chief care must be to get back safely to London after the play. I am concerned about that. Several barges of men could push off from either shore between here and Paul's Wharf, and take us outright."

As if in answer to his fears, the hired man Richards appeared just then, and told Roger he had seen a man in Bragdon's livery down by the river stairs. It seemed a confirmation of the lawyer's suspicions, and he spoke out decisively.

"We shall go by land."

"When the properties go by water?"

"Why not? There are workmen and boys enough to go with them. We can cut off to the north east, skirting the royal park. In a mile there is a road that turns west, then north to St. Giles-in-the-Fields, then west again to London. We can come in by Moregate or Aldersgate."

Richards spoke up.

"Aye, Master Roger," he said. "Hodge and Somers and I can go with you, and Smith and the others by boat."

It seemed a neat solution, and Roger agreed.

"I'll speak to Smith," he said. "Say nothing about it."

They broke up to make final preparations for the play; the first ladies and gentlemen of the Court were coming in.

These were ushered to their appointed seats by royal officials. Toward the rear, platforms had been so placed as to make several different levels, the highest the farthest from the stage. In this fashion all the spectators would have a fair view of the performance. Roger could hear the tinkling laughter of the women and the deeper bass of the men as the audience grew.

Retainers in royal livery came to light the tapers in the candelabra that hung from the ceiling above and in front of the stage unit. There were also two gilded standards of candles, one on either side.

Roger was too busy to give more than a few glances at the splendid audience. There was, he saw, much silk and satin; there was the glint of jewels; there was the sound of bantering talk, of laughter. But he could not miss the royal entry; a sudden silence announced it, and the actors and apprentices crowded to the curtains of the inner stage and to the side-doors, opened a crack for observation.

The entire audience was standing, the men uncovered,

as the King in his stuffed doublet walked forward awkwardly, almost toddling to the special seat provided for him. He was a quaint figure; in contrast, the blonde Queen, proud and jeweled, sustained the dignity of her station fully. Courtiers led them to their seats and took their places beside them, some in chairs, some lounging on cushions. The buzz of talk was again audible. All was now in readiness, and soon from before the curtains on the upper stage a trumpeter blew the customary blasts that preceded the opening of the play.

Through the first several scenes Roger stood or worked in a kind of daze. They went well, he thought, but he seemed almost feverishly busy supervising the change of furniture after the first one to prepare for the third.

But with the fifth scene, in Olivia's house, when Viola appeared to plead the Duke's cause with the Countess, he found himself steadying and following the familiar action closely. Diane was superb—bubbling with wit, sparkling with a grace and proudness which, he thought to himself, would stir any countess's heart. There was the moment when she persuaded Olivia to unveil herself, and the lady jested about her beauty. The disguised girl could see that it *was* great beauty (what chance now had she, masquerading as a youth, to outshine it?) But she put such thoughts aside, and Roger felt an almost personal pride in Viola's resolute attack:

> "I see you what you are, you are too proud;
> But, if you were the devil, you are fair!
> My lord and master loves you: Oh! such love
> Could but be recompensed, though you were crowned
> The nonpareil of beauty!"

It was as if Diane had planned it herself. And no less than Olivia was he swept along as Viola told eloquently how *she* would woo the reluctant lady. He chortled when, in the suc-

ceeding scene, the Countess's steward, pursuing the disguised
girl, tried to return a ring he asserted the supposed youth
had left behind.

As the steward departed, the heroine stood wondering.

I left no ring with her: what means this lady?
(*Amused and alarmed*) Fortune forbid my outside have not
    charmed her!
She made good view of me; indeed, so much
That sure methought her eyes had lost her tongue!
(*Full realization*) She loves me, sure; the cunning of her pas-
    sion
Invites me in this churlish messenger . . .
I am the man!

Again Roger reveled in the romantic double meaning of the
scene in which the Duke converses with his attendant:

DUKE: How dost thou like this tune?
VIOLA: It gives a very echo to the seat
        Where love is throned.
DUKE: Thou dost speak masterly.
      My life upon it, young though thou art, thine eye
      Has stayed upon some favor that it loves;
      Hath it not, boy?
VIOLA: A little, by your favor.
DUKE: What kind of woman is it?
VIOLA: Of your complexion.
DUKE: She is not worth thee, then. What years, in faith?
VIOLA: About your years, my lord.

And then, later, when Orsino scoffs lightly at women's love—

VIOLA: Ah, but I know—
DUKE: What dost thou know?
VIOLA: Too well what love women to men may owe;
      In faith, they are as true of heart as we.

My father had a daughter loved a man,
As it might be, perhaps, were I a woman,
I should your lordship.
DUKE: And what's her history?
VIOLA: A blank, my lord. She never told her love,
But let concealment, like a worm in the bud,
Feed on her damask cheek; she pined in thought,
And with a green and yellow melancholy,
She sat like Patience on a monument,
Smiling at grief. Was not this love indeed?
We men may say more, swear more, but indeed
Our shows are more than will, for still we prove
Much in our vows, but little in our love.

The situation tore at Roger's heart. What a girl she was, he exclaimed inwardly, thinking of Diane and not Viola, and forgetting for the moment the part of one William Shakespeare in all this. And when the Duke, quite as moved as Roger, asked,

"But died thy sister of her love, my boy?"

how magnificently she extricated herself, speaking the truth as she knew it (for she supposed her twin brother Sebastian drowned) yet confusing her questioner:

"I am all the daughters of my father's house
And all the brothers, too; and yet I know not."

Then the triumphant question which diverted the nobleman's attention from her own situation:

"Sir, shall I to this lady?"

Roger stood enchanted, forgetful of the play. He stood so while the Duke eagerly assented, and with a start saw the curtains draw together. Even then he could not wholly feel that this was make-believe and not reality.

It was over at last, and Anthony drew Roger outside to speak with Lucy and her father. The audience was breaking up; many were leaving. Roger exchanged civilities with Sir Thomas, asking how he had liked the play. The latter was enthusiastic.

"And you, Lucy?"

"Oh, it was monstrous well done."

"Then you give some praise to Cedric at last?" he could not resist asking. She smiled grudgingly.

"Oh, he spoke his lines well."

Roger chuckled.

Lucy renewed the invitation she had earlier sent by Anthony, that Roger return with them, and Sir Thomas seconded it.

"Sir, I cannot," Roger replied. "I have responsibility for the properties. Besides, my uncle is here, and we have matters to discuss that will not wait."

Lucy started to speak, then paled and was silent. Roger thought he could guess the reason. She made a fresh start, asking if they would see him tomorrow in town. He answered that he trusted so; tomorrow seemed a long time distant, and he could send a note.

Anthony then declared that he would remain with his brother.

"But you are promised to us," Lucy remonstrated.

Roger for his own reasons urged his brother not to wait.

"But I shall," the latter insisted. "Lucy and Sir Thomas have dined with me often, and will again; but it may be long before I see you."

Roger did not know what to say, and watched the Knowleses make off, Lucy looking almost stricken.

"I wonder she takes it so hard," remarked Anthony.

"I have a notion why," answered Roger rather grimly.

"What do you mean?"

"It's a long story. You'll not change your mind? Then I'll see you later. We shall be packed in twenty minutes, and still have light for supper when we get to London."

XVIII

AMBUSH

ANTHONY went out to walk a short distance with the Knowleses and to take leave of them, and Roger turned back to the stage somewhat troubled. He took his uncle aside and explained what had happened.

"I think we should warn Anthony that there is a certain danger," he pointed out. "After all, this is no affair of his."

Edward Vance agreed, and a few minutes later the two were disclosing the situation to their unexpected companion. Roger told his brother of Cedric's part in the masque at Darrell Manor on Twelfth Night, and how he had later encountered the latter in London. He did not tell him, however, that Cedric was really a girl.

"We are both convinced that he had good reason to run away," he said, "and Uncle Ned has filed a suit on his behalf. But Bragdon's a desperate man. There's little doubt that he knows we are here. If he should learn the route we take back to London—though I cannot think he can or will—there may be trouble."

"Will you resist if he attempts force?"

"We'll make a show of it. We have four swords, counting Uncle Ned's, and three lads with staves who I think will stand with us."

"You have five swords," Anthony corrected him. "I'll take your word for the boy. He played his part today famously.

If there's trouble, why, it will season me for Ireland," he concluded with a grin.

Roger grinned back at him.

"Is this putting two and two together and coming up with
the right answer, as you say a sensible man should?"

"It makes a perfect four," Anthony replied promptly.
"When did a Darrell ever fail to stand by a Darrell?"

Roger had no answer to that.

The road ran north and west, with the glades of the royal
park beside it on the right, and with meadows, woods and a
few tilled fields on the left. After a mile, it turned west,
somewhat north of the park. They had covered perhaps a
mile and a half, and had turned toward St. Giles-in-the-Fields.
The sun was still well above the trees, and threw a checkered
light across their way. Then Hodge moved up to Roger's
elbow and told him in a low voice that he had seen a man
move in a clump of trees some hundred yards ahead.

Roger halted the group.

"It may be a forester or a farmer's lad," he speculated.

"No, Master Dainty," answered Hodge, using his old nick-
name for Roger, "I saw a cloak and a scabbard's end, and I'd
swear the fellow's not alone. They may have had a lookout
somewhere about the King's grounds," he added. "If they
got a signal in such a way, they could have made quick work
getting across country, and so lay here to wait for us."

"We'd gain nothing by turning back now," said Anthony.
"And," he pointed out," they may be no stronger than we are."

"I think we must go forward," Vance agreed. "Keep to the
rear, Master Cedric. If there's trouble, we'll retreat to that
edge of stone in the meadow just off the road, and make our
talk and if necessary our defense there."

So they resumed their walk. As they came to the clump of trees and bushes where Hodge had seen a figure move, eight or ten men suddenly burst out and threw themselves across the road. Then Bragdon appeared in company with Sefton, who waved a scroll of heavy paper.

"Master Vance," he said pleasantly, "I know you are an observer of the law, and I have here an order for the boy called Cedric Wales."

Vance motioned his group behind him.

"Let me see it."

Sefton stepped forward and handed him the scroll. Edward Vance looked at it for a moment, then handed it back to him.

"For reasons which you yourself should know, this has no force whatever," he said crisply.

Bragdon scowled and his men murmured, but Sefton lifted a hand to quiet them.

"Why not?" he asked.

"Because suit was filed on behalf of the person concerned only this morning, and I am responsible for him. Besides," he added, "he stands under the protection of the King himself, since he serves with His Majesty's players."

"But is not one of them," Sefton pointed out, meaning that a boy could not be an actual Company member.

"The protection extends to every man employed by the Company, of whom there are five here," Vance maintained.

"I do not so assume," Sefton retorted, "nor do I think it has ever so been held by any court. If a hireling or apprentice—"

"A plague on apprentices and players and lawyers, too," broke in Wickard, who had come forward to Bragdon's elbow. "Here's the boy, and a good court order for him. Let's take him, I say, and see who can part him from us."

"One moment!" Sefton commanded.

But the opportunity, and Wickard's words, and perhaps most of all a movement of Roger and his group off the road toward the ledge, seemed to sweep Bragdon to a decision.

"Take him!" he commanded.

There was a ragged rasping of steel as swords came out on both sides, and Roger's party, Vance with them, retreated further.

The latter waved his blade and expostulated with his fellow-lawyer.

"Calm these men, Master Sefton!" he half begged, half commanded. "We will not bow to force!"

"Gentlemen, gentlemen!" the other pleaded in response. "Wait but one moment. Master Vance is a reasonable man, and he and I—"

The smack of steel drowned his words, together with the yells of Hodge and Somers, who pranced about on the flanks of their party, brandishing their staves.

"Richards!" shouted the former. "Stand close to Wat yonder. Look you—why, the coward's gone!" he exclaimed. "Scuttled away like a rabbit. Aye, perhaps it was he—"

"No matter, no matter!" Roger threw at him, knowing that there was no point now in speculating on whether their companion had fled in mere cowardice or had betrayed them. "Stand to it, man, and the devil take him!"

"Aye, Dainty my lad," Hodge assured him, giving a swift cut that caught one of his opponents on the wrist and brought out a curse. "Clubs!" he roared with a terrific voice as the man gave ground.

Roger and his group were now close to the ledge, which was protected from behind by thick bushes, and Cedric stooped down and picked up a jagged piece of rock that had flaked off. Bradgon's men were pressing in, nine swords to five.

Just then, with a tattoo of hoofs, a half dozen horsemen burst into the little clearing from the north, and were on the opposing groups before they could check their horses. The swordsmen paused, startled; and one of the riders dashed between them. The newcomers were all richly clad and caparisoned, and were clearly of rank and authority.

"Put up your swords, sirs!" cried the nobleman who had pushed between the combatants. It was the voice of one accustomed to being obeyed, and as the swordsmen hestitated he thundered:

"Put up! Will you fight on in the presence of His Majesty?"

With his words all glanced at a single horseman who hung back from the others, and then quickly sheathed their weapons and doffed their hats.

The nobleman glared at them with an angry satisfaction.

"Hah, better," he cried with an oath. "What have we come to when the King of England cannot ride a mile from his house without finding his subjects in armed conflict? Are you thieves, cutthroats?"

The King, seeing that all weapons were sheathed, pushed his horse forward cautiously, and blinked at the two opposing groups. Then, his curiosity rising as his alarm subsided (for he was almost fantastically disturbed at the sight of naked weapons), he rubbed his hands together nervously and remarked:

"Weel, my Laird, ane o' the twa bands, I think, are the lawless men, and the other honest."

Roger was startled to hear this broad Scots on the lips of the King of England, but recalled having heard that James spoke in such fashion.

"Put up your swords, sirs!" cried the nobleman who had pushed

between the combatants. It was one accustomed to being obeyed

Edward Vance stepped forward quickly and knelt.

"We, Your Majesty," he said, "are the party attacked; and the one most wronged is this lad, who, by the badge on his doublet, you will recognize as one of Your Majesty's players."

James's eyes seemed to start from his head.

"Is it so, now?" he demanded.

"You yourself can judge, Sire, for you saw and heard him this very afternoon, taking the chief woman's part in the play performed before you."

The King's face softened into a smile, and he regarded Cedric with something like downright affection.

"Weel, lad," he remarked, "ye made as sweet a lass as ever I hope to hear or see."

Diane bent low in acknowledgment, but said nothing.

But now Sefton stepped forward and knelt beside Vance. He had no intention of yielding the case by default.

"Your Majesty," he pleaded, "I must speak out on behalf of these men," indicating his party, "whom I represent as advocate, and whom you have just heard maligned. We came today with an order from one of Your Majesty's justices, to take lawful possession of this boy, who fled from his guardian."

He held up the scroll he had earlier offered to Vance.

"If you will look at this paper, Sire—"

One of the horsemen took it and handed it to the King. He studied it for a minute.

"Aye, it's written fair and plain," he muttered. Then he raised his voice. "Which of ye is Giles Bragdon?"

"Here, Your Majesty."

Bragdon knelt beside the others.

"Weel, it says beyond doot that ye are the man," the King muttered.

"And yet, my Lord King, the paper has no force, as I can

quickly prove to your satisfaction," asserted Edward Vance.

"Can ye, noo?" James was at once challenged and pleased, for he loved nothing so much as a good dispute over the letter or spirit of a text or law. Then he looked at the three kneeling men, and regarded their somewhat absurd postures with distaste. "Nay, stand up," he commanded. "Ye look like a parcel o' rogues bent doon for to hae their heads choppit off. Up, all o' ye. We may perhaps talk this matter out in a friendly way and to a gude end."

The kneeling men rose somewhat sheepishly, and James studied them for a moment. Then he pointed a finger at Edward Vance.

"Now, Maister—er—"

"Vance, Your Majesty."

"Aye, Maister Vance. We will hear why the order of ane of our own judges has nae force."

"Not, Your Majesty, because of any fault in the judge," Vance replied promptly, "but because of two facts at variance with what is stated in the order. The first is, that the guardianship of Giles Bragdon is under challenge, suit having been filed by me this very morning as *prochein amy* for the infant, or ward."

"Your Majesty, we have no evidence of that whatever," snapped Sefton.

"The evidence is here," replied Vance calmly, drawing a paper from his wallet.

James waved the document aside.

"We shall look at this paper in gude time," he remarked. "And the second of the twa facts ye mentioned?"

"Only that the ward in question is misnamed in the order you have seen as Cedric Wales, a boy," replied Vance calmly, "when in actuality she is a girl, and by name Diane Hardie."

The remark might have been an exploding bomb. Anthony, Hodge, Somers, most of Bragdon's men, the King and his escort all gaped at the lawyer, and then began to exclaim.

"Your Majesty may ask Master Giles Bragdon himself if this is not the case," Vance asserted, pushing his advantage.

James looked at Diane's guardian.

"Weel, what hae ye to say to it, mon?" he demanded.

Bragdon grudgingly admitted that it was so. Sefton leaped to the rescue.

"Your Majesty will note that the order refers to the boy who *calls* himself Cedric Wales, and this he has done, as Master Vance must admit if asked. The ward was so designated to avoid scandal."

"And to serve a very ill purpose of Master Bragdon's!"

Diane's voice rang out clearly.

James stared at her and rubbed his hands.

"Ah, the lass hersel' can speak to the purpose!" he exclaimed. "A lass!" he repeated as a thought struck him. He beamed with satisfaction. "Noo, my lord," he said to the nearest of his companions, "I dinna mind me that ever before a lass was known to play wi' a company of players."

"With your permission, Sire, heaven forbid!" Sefton hastened to remonstrate. "By common custom it is considered an ill thing that any woman should perform in a playhouse, much less one of gentle family, as this girl is."

The King gave a grudging nod.

"I didna say it was a fit thing," he pointed out; "but rare and uncommon it is nane the less."

Sefton bowed his agreement, but persisted in making his point.

"Your Majesty is right, of course; yet the very strangeness of the event shows the need for the proper control and restraint of this young woman," he declared.

"May be, may be," muttered the monarch, "but I maun know mair o' this matter before I can render judgment upon it."

Edward Vance spoke up courteously but firmly.

"In the end it is not Your Majesty who can render judgment in this matter."

The effect of his words was explosive. James's face purpled and his eyes widened with surprise and anger.

"Canna render judgment?" he demanded. "Do ye deny the power o' the King o' England, mon?"

"No, Sire," said Vance, staunchly. "I only affirm the power of the *laws* of England, made and confirmed by both her parliaments and her kings."

The two stood facing each other a moment—the opposing forces that in another generation would divide the land into two camps, one supporting parliamentary authority, the other the rights of the crown. Then Vance, perceiving that he had gone too far, said quickly:

"But I think I speak for my client, and I do for myself, when I say that we will gladly leave this question to Your Majesty alone, as the highest judge as well as the ruler of this land."

James's face softened at once.

"Weel, weel," he said. "That was spoken fair and free, and I dinna doubt that I ken eno' the right o' things, and the law, too," he added a bit dubiously, "to sift out the right and wrang o' this matter. What d'ye say, Master lawyer and Master Bragdon?" he demanded of the opposing group. "Will ye take the King o' England as judge, or no?"

The two looked at each other. There was nothing else they could do, and Sefton spoke up promptly.

"We will gladly put the entire business in Your Majesty's hands," he declared, "but there is certain evidence we would submit—"

"And I, too, Your Majesty," said Vance quickly, "for we trust to make the better case."

One of James's attendants spoke to him almost impatiently.

"Sire, the day goes, and you are already past due for supper."

It was an important point with the King, and he nodded dubiously, with an "Aye, aye."

"But the case could be heard by you tomorrow morning, Sire," urged Vance.

"Tomorrow the French ambassador waits upon you," the noble reminded his master.

It seemed a point of decision with James.

"He can e'en wait another day," he said somewhat peevishly. "We maun hear aboot the lass and the why o' a' this business," he continued. "Is there no some likely lad at the bottom o' it?" he asked slyly, looking at Diane.

"No, Your Majesty, but—"

"Say nae more!" the King exclaimed hastily. "Say nae more! It maun a' be presented wi' due form and order. At half eleven o' the clock the morning," he continued practically, "baith o' ye shall appear at the Grand Chamber."

He looked questioningly at the opposing factions. Vance bowed, then Bragdon and Sefton.

"A-weel, then—"

Sefton took a step forward.

"But the custody of the ward, Your Majesty," he suggested. "My client being her guardian—"

"Nay, under challenge of a suit already filed," remonstrated Vance.

James shook his head and frowned.

"Noo, noo," he protested. Then a sly smile lit his face. He turned to Diane.

"What does the lass say aboot it?"

Diane dropped to her knees.

"Oh, Sire," she said earnestly, "do not put me in the hands of that man for one hour!"

James's eyes twinkled, then sobered.

"We canna say but we will deliver ye to him for mony a day, let alane an hour," he remarked gravely. "If he can prove his right, he must have it. But for the night," and he twinkled again, "ye shall make your ane choice."

Diane murmured her thanks.

"My Laird," continued the King to one of his escort, "ride to the city gates wi' these men, see that they have entrance, and gang their ways decently, in peace."

The nobleman bowed. James gave a last look to the disputants, then spoke to his horse and trotted off with his escort toward Westminster.

XIX

TRIAL BY ROYALTY

THE boat pushed smoothly up the river, propelled by two diligent watermen. It was a large one; and Edward Vance sat forward in the craft with his agent, Hammond, and a clerk from his office, while Diane, Anthony and Roger occupied the stern end.

The day was crisp and clear. On the shore to the right they were just passing the group of buildings called the Temple. A long line of houses, walls and turrets, broken by trees, stretched ahead of them, with the towers of the royal buildings at Westminster visible almost a mile away, at the bend of the river. The water, its motion barely discernible, reflected objects on the shore almost like a mirror. To the south, on the farther bank, there were fewer houses, but there, too, clumps of trees on the land looked down on twin clusters in the stream, almost as perfect. To Roger there was a brightness and quiet about the voyage that was unreal, as if he were passing over an imaginary river and through a dream landscape.

Hammond had returned the night before, and had met them this morning at Blackfriars Stairs, where they took the boat. He was a pleasant, responsive man; although Roger, after talking with him for ten minutes the previous evening, had realized that he knew little of the agent's personality and practically nothing of his recent work.

Diane was speaking in a low voice.

"Your uncle's clerk Bolton is not here this morning," she said.

Roger shook his head.

"No. He was at the house this morning, though. I saw him leaving as I came."

"Uncle Ned and he talked together with a great air of mystery and excitement," said Anthony, who had arrived at his uncle's house earlier than Roger. "I heard something about the man's returning to Westminster, and how he could win admittance to the Great Chamber."

Diane sighed. She was dressed in a simple gown of aquamarine which Edward Vance's housekeeper had managed to have made for her during the last two days, and looked at once older and prettier, Roger thought.

"They are very secret about it," she remarked, making a little face to show her annoyance. "I contrived to have a moment's talk with Master Hammond this morning. He was like a handbook of courtesy, but as to what he had found—" She broke off and shrugged. "Did you learn anything of what he had brought back, Roger?"

"Nothing at all, except that Uncle Ned seemed disappointed in it. And worried about having to plead the case on such short notice. That was the only thing he talked of at length."

"What did he say?" asked Anthony.

"Why, that it was a question of law, and should have gone to the courts, where he would have had the time he lacks now."

"He told the King himself that the courts should have it," Diane murmured with a smile.

"Yes." Anthony agreed, laughing softly. "If he'd made less of a point of that, he might have managed better."

Roger nodded.

"Maybe," he conceded. "But you'll remember the King began to talk of making a judgment. That was too much for

Uncle Ned. 'I could not see one man, even though crowned,' he told me, 'take on himself to override the law.' "

"The law, the law!" scoffed Anthony.

"Are you so scornful of it, Master Darrell?" asked Diane with a quizzical smile. "Then you and I must quarrel for sure."

"Quarrel?"

"How can you ask?" she retorted. "Why am I here today?"

"Why, to demand your rights under the law, to be sure." Anthony grinned. "And," he added, "to grant me pardon for forgetting it."

"On condition," she parried with mock severity.

"Which is—"

"To speak respectfully of this law you sniffed at until it gives me a new guardian. Of course," she added, "if it fails there, you may speak against it freely."

"Agreed," laughed Anthony.

"Diane's a living proof of what all we English are," remarked Roger. "We forget the law easily enough; then, when the pinch comes, we remember and cry out for it. It's in our bones."

"But it's more than that to Master Vance," Diane objected.

"It's as close and real to him as his house or his doublet," Roger agreed. "He never forgets it for a moment. That's why he spoke to the King yesterday as he did. But he saw that to push his point would only work harm."

"Did he concede that?" asked Anthony.

"Oh, fully. He'd have liked to press the matter—'even at the hazard of punishment,' as he put it. 'But,' he said, 'His Majesty confuses the law with the Crown, and the risk in this case could not be mine alone. My client shared it. I should have put her cause in peril.' "

"It was a gallant thought!" exclaimed Diane.

"A just one, at any rate," Roger corrected her. "That's why

he 'bent to the wind,' as he described it."

"Hating to do so," chuckled Diane.

"No doubt. But he gave another reason, and a shrewd one, for tossing the case into the King's lap. 'I have grave doubts,' he told me, 'as to how good a ruler His Majesty will prove for England; but I believe that he is a kind, just, and even scrupulous *man*.'"

"And now he's concerned about the scruples, I think," Diane said slowly. "And it may be that he's right. I can imagine our King holding very hard to the letter of a point, which might lose all for us."

"It's a danger," admitted Roger.

"Yet I think our uncle will move mountains to meet it," said Anthony. "Look at him."

Their eyes went to the other end of the boat, where Edward Vance was talking to his assistants in a low voice, and making notes. Beyond doubt he was bending all his mind and will to the work before him. If his face was grave and even troubled, no champion at a tournament barrier, waiting for the trumpet and dedicating his strength and skill to a high cause, ever showed a keener eye or an air of sterner resolution.

The Great Chamber at Westminster wore something of an official, something of a festive, air. The stage had been removed, and the King's chair had been set at the end of the hall where yesterday the play had been performed. Two tables and a number of chairs had been placed near the walls on either side, apparently for the contending parties and their witnesses. A third table stood to the right of the royal seat; here sat a law official in wig and gown, apparently from the King's Advocate's office, and several clerks. A Bible lay before one of the latter. On the other side, somewhat forward, a single chair had been placed, which Roger took to be for the use of witnesses. Anyone occupying it would face the side wall, toward which it fronted, and would be visible both to the King and to the audience.

For there was an audience—the festive aspect of the scene. Evidently word had gone about that James would play the part of a judge. As a result, some twenty-five or thirty gentlemen had gathered, and at least half as many ladies. The air smelled faintly of their perfumes. The men lounged lazily in their carved chairs, their long hair falling over cloaks that were silken-lined and laced or jeweled, their well-trimmed beards wagging as they leaned to talk with each other or to women companions whose fingers glittered as they twirled their gold or ivory-handled fans. None of the gallants was smoking. Roger remembered that the new monarch had spoken out wrathfully against tobacco, and that he was supposed to have penned with his own hand a tract denouncing it, soon to be published.

Servants in royal livery were lighting the tapers in several candelabra at the end of the Chamber where the proceedings were to be held. This measure was apparently designed to give the greatest possible light for the reading of documents and the making of such notes and records as might be required.

Sefton, Bragdon, Wickard and several clerks (among whom Roger recognized the shrewd but responsible-looking Fenwick, who had come to the Globe asking for him) had already taken their seats about the side table to the right; a gentleman usher led Vance and his party to the other. One of the functionaries at the central table came over and spoke with the lawyer, taking notes. When he retired, Edward Vance spread out his papers and glanced at his tablet.

While he was still busy with these matters, a voice at the door called out that the King approached. Everyone stood;

and in a moment Roger saw the now familiar figure walking with his uneven gait down the hall on the arm of a friend. Finally he reached his chair, almost falling into it. In one hand he carried a little rod which apparently he planned to use if he had occasion to rap for order.

He looked about him in a hesitant fashion. One of the clerks at the nearby table stepped forward, knelt, and handed him a paper. It seemed to contain information about the trial, for James studied it a few moments, and held it in one hand as he looked up and began to speak. Roger quickly recognized that, in spite of the physical awkwardness, shyness and naïveté which the royal judge exhibited, he was really a shrewd, well-informed and, in his own fashion, competent person. It occurred to the young man that there was a lifetime of experience behind the rather gauche posturing and broad Scots accent of his Sovereign.

"We have come to hear a dispute between certain parties who forced the matter, it might be said, upon our attention," the King began, speaking as if with an effort to use the minimum of Scots accent. "The control and guardianship of Diane Hardie is in question, a lass whom most of ye saw and heard but yesterday in the chief woman's part of the play, *Twelfth Night*."

There was a murmur at these words, particularly among the women, but it subsided quickly as James stared at them.

"This is no an ordinary court," he continued, dropping more and more into his usual manner of speech, "and we shall not preserve the formalities which attend the law on maist occasions. We will hear first a preliminary statement from—" he consulted the paper—"Master Robert Sefton, speaking for one Giles Bragdon, who asserts his right to the control of the girl Diane Hardie as her lawful guardian."

Sefton stepped forward, knelt, and asked respectfully:

"Is it Your Majesty's desire that we be put in the position of plaintiff in this case? I would point out that it is not we who challenge, but rather the opposing counsel and his client, who question an authority delegated by one of Your Majesty's courts."

James waved the protest aside somewhat peevishly.

"Ye may be right, Master Advocate, ye may be right," he said. "But to my mind it will gang better if we begin wi' your argument and evidence, since your client's being in the post and place of guardian was the start o' the whole business at hand, as ye yoursel' will agree. Ye shall hae every opportunity to answer what may be urged against ye."

Sefton bowed and replied cheerfully:

"Then we gladly accept Your Majesty's command, and indeed take satisfaction in presenting our case first, and in making it, we hope, the very base and foundation of this hearing and the judgment to follow it."

He then went on to assert that he would prove both by document and testimony the full authority of his client over the infant in question. He would establish, too, that the said infant, Diane Hardie, had fled from the custody of her guardian for no just reason; and that it was as a matter of right and duty that the latter had pursued her.

"We shall show," he declared, "that in violation of the law an agent of Giles Bragdon was on one occasion prevented by violence from assuming custody of this Diane Hardie, and that later my client himself was so prevented. Your Majesty is already aware that in a third attempt the use of force was undertaken only when an order of a proper court was ignored.

"Our case rests wholly upon the law," he concluded. "We stand ready to disprove any assertion that it does not. It will therefore be necessary, in our opinion, for those opposing us to show some right beyond the law which shall persuade Your

Majesty of its superiority to your established courts. This, we believe, they cannot do."

It was a forceful presentation. The audience murmured a kind of approval, and the King nodded. Again he looked at his paper.

"Master Edward Vance," he announced, "as *prochein amy* for the said Diane Hardie."

Vance rose and spoke as briefly and clearly as Sefton had. He would not contest the fact that Giles Bragdon had been lawfully constituted the guardian of his client. He would show, however, that the infant in question had suffered abuse at the hands of her supposed protector, that she had fled from him for just cause, that she did not wish to return to his authority, and that she had the sanction of the law in her effort to seek a new guardian.

"If the rights of a guardian are law," he announced, "so are the rights of an infant, for the courts of England, and her statutes, give every man, woman and child in this land a protection against injustice that is by intention perfect. Therefore we too rest our case wholly upon the law, but more, we believe, upon that equity which the law serves than does the plaintiff. It will be for Your Majesty to examine and weigh the law and the right in this case, and to judge in accordance with both."

Again there was a sympathetic stir among the spectators; James silenced it with a frown, and told Sefton to present his case.

The lawyer came forward with a paper which, he explained, was the original order appointing Bragdon as guardian. He asked that it be examined, and that the opposing counsel accept or reject it.

James waved him toward Vance, who studied the order for a moment and returned it to his adversary.

"We accept it, Your Majesty, as proper and valid at the time of issue."

Sefton deposited the paper on the central table.

"I will now bring as witness my client, Giles Bragdon."

Bragdon came forward, took the oath, seated himself in the witness chair and, was soon being examined as to his identity, place of residence, and appointment as guardian. His relationship by marriage to Ralph Hardie, Diane's half brother, was established, and the fact that he held the guardianship of Diane because Ralph, as a minor, could not hold it.

Sefton then reviewed Bragdon's actions as guardian. He had maintained his ward in suitable residence? Continued such education and training as she had received from her own father? Managed her properties and servants? Bragdon affirmed he had done all these things. This led to the question of marriage. Yes, he had arranged a marriage for her.

"Was it a suitable marriage?"

"I believed it to be. The man is of gentle family, of no small wealth, of excellent reputation."

"What is his name?"

"Isaiah Hart."

"His age?"

"In his forties, I believe. But of good appearance and perfect health."

"You believed this marriage not unpleasing to your ward?"

"I did not think it would be unpleasing to her. It was pleasing to *him*."

A titter ran through the room, which the King silenced with a lifted hand.

"Did the infant protest against this marriage?"

"Yes, she did. But I held it my right—"

"One moment," Sefton broke in. "Did she give reasons for her objections?"

"She would have a part, she said, in choosing her husband."

"But she made no exception to his character or station?"

"She could not."

Bragdon then explained that Diane had attempted to run away; was caught, then seemed to accept the marriage. After a time she had then run away a second time. He had been obliged to tell the prospective bridegroom that there had been a death in the family in another shire, necessitating the girl's absence; later, that Diane was ill. Meanwhile, he had pursued her to London. Wickard had found her there, and had been wounded by a young stranger when he attempted to take Diane into custody. He described his visit to the Globe, the refusal of the manager of the playhouse to examine a court order, the violent expulsion of him and his men from the theater.

"Who seemed to be the leader of those who did violence to you? Was it one in charge of the players?"

"No, sir; a mere hired man, whom Wickard asserted was the one who had wounded him."

"Do you see this person here today?"

"Yes, sir. He sits at the table yonder with Master Vance." Bragdon pointed to Roger. "The tall dark fellow. I am told he's a Vance, too, and the lawyer's nephew."

Sefton announced that he had finished. Roger's uncle rose and began questioning Bragdon quietly. He brought out that, according to the original order appointing him Ralph Hardie's guardian, the latter would be of age on April 24th next.

"This being the case, since there was an unwillingness on the part of your ward to make this marriage, did it not occur to you to delay the matter until her brother might help to decide this question?"

"It was a matter for *my* decision."

"You feared he might not approve of the match?"

"There was no question of his approving it or not."

"You had the authority and proposed to use it regardless of the feelings of your ward or of her nearest kin?"

"I had the authority and felt it was right I should use it."

Vance took a few steps back and forth, then suddenly shot his next question.

"What consideration were you to receive from the proposed bridegroom for this marriage?"

Bragdon flushed, and Sefton leaped up, protesting. This was not a point at issue. The question was designed to build up a prejudice against his client. In all marriages where property was involved, there might be certain arrangements made; they were not relevant here.

The King interrupted him.

"I dinna know as to the relevance, Master Sefton," he said, "but I have a sartain natural curiosity aboot the business." The audience tittered, and James was pleased. He turned to Vance. "The question, as asserted, is prejudicial as ye hae asked it," he pointed out shrewdly. "Would ye like to rephrase it, to cover a fact, aye or no?"

Vanced bowed, and turned to the witness.

"Were you—or are you—to receive a consideration from the proposed bridegroom as a result of this marriage?"

Bragdon scowled, and answered emphatically.

"I was not to receive a penny from him."

"I suggest that your ward's estate has been impaired under your management, and that the profit you gained in this fashion you were to keep."

"I have managed the estate under the authority provided by law. If it were impaired on marriage, the ward and her husband would have ground for action."

"But it was understood and agreed that no action would be taken?"

"There was no agreement about that at all."

The King was annoyed, but interested.

"Come, mon," he remonstrated, "ye have not made a straight answer to the question."

Bragdon gave him a look of injured innocence.

"Your Majesty, I have made the best answer that I can."

Edward Vance spoke quietly to the King.

"Sire, I believe it *is* the best answer he can make."

There was a ripple of laughter, in which James joined.

"We are satisfied to leave this matter for the present," Vance concluded with a smile.

He questioned Bragdon about the proposed bridegroom. Had he children? Bragdon agreed. Older than the girl he wanted to marry?

"I believe one of them is."

"Has he grandchildren?"

Sefton was again on his feet. Such questioning, he asserted, was absurd. A man could be a grandfather at forty, even at thirty-five. The matter was not relevant.

James shook his head, a smile in his eyes.

"We will again—in pure curiosity, if ye like, Master Sefton —hear the question answered." He looked at Bragdon and waited.

"I believe he has a grandchild," muttered the witness.

Vance nodded pleasantly, and the entire courtroom smiled.

"He is an old Hart, then, and well-used if not well-worn," the lawyer punned, clearly not to the judge's displeasure. Then Diane's advocate turned to the Wickard episode.

Had Bragdon not learned from his deputy, he inquired, that the young man who protected the supposed boy had suggested taking Cedric to a provost, so that his status might be proved? Bragdon denied knowing anything of this.

"But you have no knowledge that such an offer was *not* made?"

"It may have been made for anything I know."

Vance then took up the attempt to seize Diane at the Globe. With some difficulty he forced Bragdon to concede that a forcible entry had been made, although the playhouse was under the King's protection. He brought out that Heminges had demanded the withdrawal of the armed men who accompanied the witness, and that the latter had refused to comply with this request.

"You were then twice at fault in offering violence, is it not so?"

Again Sefton objected, and there was a long wrangle. Vance finally ended it by declaring: "We are satisfied to leave the point for His Majesty's consideration. We *do* ask, however, that it be considered." Then he added, "I have no further questions."

Sefton skilfully re-questioned his client. He emphasized the *intent* behind Bragdon's actions. In the case of the marriage, there was a purpose to fulfil a duty to the ward which was a guardian's legal right also. In the case of the disturbance at the Globe, there was an effort to assert a natural and proper authority, no more. Gradually the lawyer changed the climate of the courtroom. Roger could see some of the courtiers nodding agreement. Most of them, as was the fashion in noble families, had studied law for a time. They knew that any guardian had broad powers. They knew that by long custom he was supposed to make some profit from the task he discharged. Sefton dwelt skilfully upon Bragdon's responsibilities and obligations; that he should have some advantage from them was implied. After all, for centuries men had been making money through the control of wealthy minors.

Dismissing Bragdon, the lawyer fortified the strong impression he had made by producing witnesses who testified in support of his client's character as a guardian. Doubtless he had prepared these during the preceding weeks: they were impressive. They pictured a careful, diligent, and dependable person. The balance seemd to swing back far in Bragdon's favor.

Wickard was now called, and gave his account of his meeting with Roger. This pictured the witness as the aggrieved person.

Vance questioned the retainer. He seemed satisfied to press the question of Roger's proposal to find a provost. Wickard admitted it, but pointed out the possibilities for delay and confusion. He had no evidence of authority about his person; the matter might have ended in a lot of legal hocus pocus; his master wanted the boy, as he then supposed him to be, at once.

"And you were prepared to wound, perhaps to kill, a stranger who merely asked for proof of your authority, rather than to satisfy him?"

"I was prepared to do my duty as I saw it."

"By violence and defiance of law?"

"No, sir."

"But you attacked this man?"

"I don't know if I attacked him or he me. At any rate, I took a wound which lost me the use of my right arm for some weeks, and he was not scratched. So, as to the issue, I suffered, and not he."

A ripple of laughter approved the reply. Vance persisted in seeking an admission that Wickard was the aggressor; the witness would not admit it. When the lawyer concluded his questions, Sefton arose. He gave his attention to the points that had been established, adroitly whittling them down and smoothing them away.

At length Sefton completed his case, and Vance called Diane to the witness chair. Roger knew that his uncle had spent some time in discussing her testimony with her. He found himself somewhat disappointed by its simplicity and brevity. Vance brought out only a few facts: that the proposed marriage had been highly repugnant to her, that she had begged in vain for time and her brother's judgment upon it, that she had questioned the management of her estates, that she had fled in order to learn her rights under the law. However, Roger finally perceived what Edward Vance was trying to do. He was seeking to present a sensitive, modest and thoughtful girl who had merely tried to protect her own future.

Sefton was quick to see what was being attempted, and as he began to question her, he set out to wreck it.

Did Diane not know the authority her guardian possessed? Had she tried earnestly to understand that his purpose aimed at her own good? Why had she made a pretence of compliance, if she had been so deeply opposed to the marriage? Had she any actual evidence of the mismanagement of her estate?

The questions were shrewdly phrased, calculated to put her in the wrong, or, in some cases, to provoke an outburst of anger. But Diane answered them respectfully, yet with a resourcefulness that almost or fully matched the lawyer's.

Sefton on his part never lost his temper, never modified the considerate manner which he had adopted. He seemed regretful, as if truth forced him to his unpleasant task.

"Did you think of your reputation when you disguised yourself as a boy?" he asked. "Did you not know that you might gravely injure the good name of your family, and your own character among men?"

"I was more interested, Master Sefton, in preserving a character that I myself could respect."

"You took a false name?"

"I could not find safety under my own."

"You dwelt in a house with this young man whom you had never seen before?"

Diane flushed.

"I dwelt under the same roof," she replied somewhat sharply, "but as a boy, and in the other side of the house. My hostess knew my sex."

"And you believe that this young Master Vance did *not* know it?"

"I am sure of that. He and dozens of others accepted and worked with me as a boy."

"You admit that you deceived both this young man and your lawyer?"

"I was in a position where I could not tell the full truth at once."

"But you had put yourself in that position?"

"That, Master Sefton, is a matter for judgment. I may remind you that yours is not the final one."

The lawyer smiled and bowed.

"This young man," he continued shifting his ground, "had no means of support except what he earned as a hired man at the playhouse?"

"That is true."

"Did you never suspect that both he and his uncle may have guessed your sex, and saw an opportunity for a marriage different from what your guardian proposed, which might be profitable to *them?*"

There was a gasp from the audience as the meaning of the question was recognized. Diane paled, flushed, then said quietly:

"My experience with those who had abused me made me confident that these men, whose behavior was ever honorable and kind, had no selfish purpose whatever in befriending me."

A slight murmur of approval swept the room. Sefton smiled again.

"I myself have no knowledge," he said, "that either had a selfish interest in serving you. I asked the question to remind you and the court what possibilities for danger were the issue of your defiance of your guardian. You confess that these existed?"

"I do not think they did."

"Yet they could have, and may have?"

"I am sure they did not."

Sefton bowed.

"I must leave you with your opinion," he conceded with something like pity. Then he paused a moment and added: "I have no more questions."

Diane came back to the table looking confused and troubled. She smiled faintly at Roger, then fixed her eyes on the table. He noticed that her hand trembled.

Edward Vance sat frowning a moment, then quietly called Roger, using his correct name.

A murmur ran about the room as the word "Darrell" was pronounced. Sir John was not unknown, even at Court. The King stared at Roger.

However, Edward Vance quickly brought out his witness's family background and former residence, and the reason for his coming to London. These facts were sympathetically received. They established him as a gentleman in an assembly where social status counted; and if they suggested rashness and even folly, they also showed the courage to follow a conviction. Vance proceeded to the duel with Wickard. He emphasized both the offer to seek a provost and the fact that Wickard had made the attack.

"You had some fears as to what might happen as the result of this encounter, did you not?"

"Yes, sir."

"Were they soon afterward intensified?"

"They were."

Roger described his encounter with the lawyer's man on

Little Wood Street, and his taking the name of Vance. He explained that this action was taken partly with a desire to protect Cedric, as he then thought of Diane. He told of the retainer who some days later followed him to Johnson's shop, and of Fenwick's still later appearance at the Globe.

Vance came back again to Roger's first encounter with Cedric.

"As to your protecting this boy, as you supposed him to be, what did you do when you had heard his story?"

"I brought him to you."

"At that time, and for some time afterward, you had no idea that this boy was actually a woman?"

"No, sir. None whatever."

"Had you known that fact, what would you have done?"

"What I did when I finally learned it—brought her to you at once."

"And since learning it, have you said anything to her about a marriage with her?"

"No, sir. I could not have done so had I wished to, my position being what it is."

"Have you mentioned such a possibility to me?"

"Never."

"Have I at any time suggested it to you?"

"No, sir."

"You say these things with a full realization that you are under oath?"

"I do."

Vance indicated that he had completed his examination, and Sefton rose slowly from his table.

His first question surprised Roger and the entire courtroom.

"Master Darrell," he asked, "were you acquainted with one Raphael Bartolomeo?"

"I was," Roger replied promptly after a start of surprise. "He was an artist, and for several years my teacher."

Sefton nodded sympathetically.

"You came to London to work with him, did you not?"

"That was my hope. But I found that he had died. The house was boarded up. I—I then set about finding other employment."

Sefton nodded again, started to speak, then checked himself and began to examine Roger as to his reasons for helping the supposed Cedric after hearing the boy's story.

"Did it not come to your mind that you were putting yourself in a dangerous position by stepping between a guardian and his ward?"

Roger agreed that it had.

"That is why I took him to my uncle," he explained.

Sefton pushed the point. Did Roger not perceive that Bragdon's authority existed until it had been set aside?

"I did not see how it could be set aside if the ward did not have an opportunity to challenge it."

They fenced along, Sefton courteously insisting on the fact of Bragdon's authority and Roger's obligation to it, Roger insisting as firmly that he had acted by his understanding of the law as expounded to him by Edward Vance.

After pressing this attack sharply for some time, Sefton suddenly announced that he had ended his questions. Roger rose to return to his table. He had been asked nothing as to his intentions toward Diane, and clearly both the audience and the King were surprised.

"Have ye no more questions?" the latter asked.

Sefton bowed and shook his head.

"No more for the present, Your Majesty; but with your permission I will say a few words now respecting the questions I have already been asking."

James nodded his consent, and the lawyer began an eloquent protest based upon the failure of Diane, Roger and his uncle to appeal at once for the change in guardianship which they now desired.

"In such cases," he urged, "the infant has always sought the protection of a relative or friend, and through him has promptly appealed to a court. He has then been put in the temporary custody of this relative or friend, or has been returned to that of his original guardian. I do not now recall an instance like the present, where the infant has placed her interests in the hands of strangers. But this being the case, is it not particularly censurable that an immediate appeal to lawful authorities was not made? This was surely a breach of proper procedure. Is it not more? Does it not forfeit the right of the infant and her counsel to further consideration in this action? I will point out that, because of the failure of the opposing parties to act promptly, my client has suffered great loss of time and sustained great harm to his affairs, that several men have been wounded and many put in danger of their lives."

The plea was a strong one.

"It is a point," conceded the King, "and I would like to hear what Master Vance can say against it."

Vance had already risen.

"I could say much," he replied. "As to delay and violence, the chief responsibility must rest with the plaintiff. His agent, attempting to seize the infant in question, refused to submit his claim to an officer of the law. Later, as we have shown, on each occasion where violence occurred, it was begun by Master Bragdon himself. Again, with respect to delay, my belief was and is that a certain amount of it was necessary to establish highly important facts. But since it is our purpose to set these forth, I suggest that the question will be better argued when we have done so, as shortly we will."

The King turned to Sefton with a questioning look. The latter, seeing that Vance had effectively countered his move, replied somewhat disdainfully: "We agree to defer full argument until the opposing counsel has produced the evidence he promises to submit."

However, he retired to his table with a smile, for he had made an important point.

Vance next called Hammond, his agent, and began to examine him carefully as to his visit to Holcombe. It was now almost one o'clock, and the King was beginning to be restive. Roger thought that his uncle worked somewhat heavily, as if against time. He brought out the amount of Bragdon's holdings in land when he assumed his guardianship of the two minors, and showed that in five years it had grown fourfold.

Sefton attacked immediately. It was ridiculous, he asserted, that a man should be reproached for his industry and prosperity. The increase in property was a common occurrence. There were a dozen possible causes for it. His client might easily have possessed a certain amount of money for the buying of land at the time he became guardian.

James suggested that Vance confine himself to facts that were more clearly pertinent. The lawyer agreed; and brought out, by Hammond's testimony and supporting statements in writing, that fifty acres of Diane's land were under mortgage and would be lost in two weeks unless repayment of a loan were made.

"My client will pay!" snapped Sefton.

Hammond then testified that he had been told by various persons that the impending marriage was financially a necessity to Bragdon, and that he had been heard to say he would be ruined if it could not be made. He offered one signed statement in support of these assertions, and declared that other

witnesses would give strong color to the charges if compelled
to testify; they were now fearful of doing so.

Sefton protested vigorously.

"This is a tissue of rumors and falsehoods which my client
has had no opportunity to meet. That he can meet them I
have no doubt whatever. Yet if this action is to be settled today, such allegations cannot be properly sifted, and if not
sifted can have no force."

While he was speaking Edward Vance, who had been holding rather doggedly to his task, suddenly straightened up and took on an air of briskness and confidence.

"One word, Your Majesty," he broke in. "I am satisfied to leave this point, with one stipulation: if you should decide that Master Giles Bragdon is otherwise in your eyes a fit guardian, he shall nevertheless be forced to make a prompt and full accounting of the estates of both his wards before he assumes his former duties, for the sole point of this testimony has been that an accounting is needed."

"It seems a not unreasonable stipulation," pondered James. Sefton was in a difficult situation.

"May we reserve argument on that question also?" he asked finally.

The King looked questioningly at Vance, who hesitated, then agreed. He waved Hammond from the witness chair.

"I have one more witness," he said. "I will ask Master Ralph Hardie to step forward and take the oath."

The room burst into a storm of exclamations. Diane rose from her seat crying "Ralph!" and rushed to meet a tall young man with a soldierly air who strode forward smiling, a scroll of papers in his hand. Bragdon scowled and whispered furiously to Sefton.

As brother and sister embraced, the King banged sharply with his rod on the arm of his chair. The noise died away, Ralph Hardie patted his sister's shoulder and came forward to kneel before the King and go to the table to take the oath.

He sat quietly in the chair, regarding Vance with steady eyes which dominated a face framed in dark auburn hair. Yes, he was serving with His Majesty's forces in Ireland. He had heard from his sister, but the letter had been long in coming to him. On receiving it, he had asked for special leave, then had started for London at once, arriving only yesterday.

"Is it your desire that your sister be married to Isaiah Hart, the man chosen for her by Giles Bragdon?"

Sefton leaped up to object: the young man's opinion was not relevant.

"Still we will hear the opinion," said James, "bearing in mind the objection made to it."

Ralph Hardie replied that he did not approve of the proposed marriage.

"Had I been here, I would have moved everything to prevent it. I favor a husband for my sister nearer her own age, and approved by her."

"Do you feel yourself now in a position to prevent this marriage?"

Sefton was on his feet with a furious objection. Surely the question was a fantastic one.

"I assure the opposing counsel that it is not," snapped Vance. "If he will contain himself, he will soon concede the point."

James sat upright, goggling at the witness.

"He may answer," he ruled promptly. "Repeat the question."

"Do you now feel yourself in a position to prevent this marriage?"

There was a brief, expectant silence, and then Ralph Hardie replied:

"I think I shall have the power to prevent it."

The room buzzed, Sefton shook his head and spread his hands in a gesture that indicated a conviction that the trial had disintegrated into complete absurdity. Edward Vance's voice cut in on the subsiding murmurs.

"Does your reply refer to your own position as future guardian to your half-sister?"

"It does."

"In what way?"

"Because, as I understand the law, I shall be eligible to become her guardian tomorrow."

The audience gasped. Sefton half rose from his seat, then fell back into it as Vance asked:

"What evidence can you offer to support your belief?"

"An attested statement as to my christening on March 25, 1583."

"When did this evidence come into your possession?"

"Only within the hour."

"If you had obtained it sooner, you would have presented it to His Majesty at once?"

"Surely. I should have felt it my duty to do so."

"Tell us the circumstances which led you to the evidence you have."

Ralph Hardie explained that the matter went back to the time when his father was a young man. Richard Hardie had attended the university for several years; he had then been permitted to travel abroad. He had ranged far, making one trip with Italian merchants to the Orient. He had come back with a reputation for wildness; it was only with reluctance that his father had permitted him to study near London, at one of the inns of court. While there, he married, but feared to tell his father what he had done.

"But in the end he was forced to confess the marriage?"

"Yes, sir. My grandfather was gravely injured while hunting. My father was called home. When he arrived there, the end had almost come. He then told what he had done, was forgiven. That very day he found himself without a parent."

"And at that time, no one at Holcombe except his father, now dead, knew of his marriage?"

"That is true. My father returned to London. Because of his own reputation among many of his neighbors, he believed that his wife would be better received if he let it be thought he had married after he had inherited his estate and not earlier in secret. He wrote from London to his friends at Holcombe of the ceremony as if it had just occurred. Then he discovered that a child would be born sooner than the news he had sent would warrant."

"And you were the child?"

"I was."

"And what did your father do then?"

"On pretext of visiting his wife's relations, then of her wishing to bear her child at her parents' home, he stayed on near London."

"And you were born there?"

"Yes, sir; and remained near the city for several months. Then, returning to Holcombe, my father gave my birthday as a full month later than was indeed the fact. I had grown slowly, there having been difficulty in the matter of nursing; therefore the matter was never questioned. My supposed age accorded with the supposed date of the marriage. None at Holcombe knew the true date of birth. I did not know it myself."

"But nevertheless it was on record in the church where you were christened."

"Yes, sir."

"And how did you yourself come by the knowledge of the true time of your birth?"

"My father told me not long before his death, binding me to secrecy. I was then sixteen. In a few years I scarcely remembered the matter; but on reading my sister's letter I recalled it, for I could see that it might be of some moment to her. On coming to London yesterday, I went to your house. You were not there. I left word for you and you came last night to my lodgings."

"Where you told me the facts just related?"

"Yes, sir."

"But also told me that you had forgotten the name of the church where the record of your christening might be found?"

"That is true. And this morning, with your assistant, I began to examine the registers of those churches which seemed most likely to have been used for the ceremony, for I knew the general locality in which my father had resided."

"And you found the record?"

"Yes; at a little after eleven of the clock. The attestation of the entry was made and witnessed; I came at once to Westminster and now submit it as evidence."

He offered the scroll which he had been holding in his hand to Edward Vance, who in turn offered it to James.

"Your Majesty will observe that the date of christening is March 25, 1583. It can be assumed that Ralph Hardie was born at least a day earlier."

The King examined the document, then offered it to Sefton, who acknowledged grudgingly that it seemed to be in order. Vance begged to be heard.

"I submit that in accordance with this evidence a petition may be filed tomorrow for the appointment of Ralph Hardie as the lawful guardian of his half-sister, Diane Hardie," he said quietly. "I ask Your Majesty to direct that in the time intervening a proper person be authorized to discharge the duties of that office until the said Ralph Hardie can assume them."

The King beamed broadly on everyone.

"We accept the suggestion," he informed the room, "and if our own affairs did not press upon us, we would assume the office ourselves. Ye shall take it, Master Vance," he finished, "if the brother and sister approve."

Diane and Ralph assured him quickly that they did.

"It was a rare case," declared James, breaking into broad

Scots, "wi' some verra neat points that were weel argued, and if my heart was aye wi' the lass, I canna say how it wad hae gone but for the lad's comin' in wi' a fair proof o' the record."

Edward Vance spoke up quickly.

"Your Majesty has not forgotten the question of accounting by my client's former guardian. I submit that a prompt statement should be offered by him as to both estates."

James nodded.

"It is nae maïr than fair to the bairns," he agreed. He turned to the law official at the table. "See that within the week an accounting is made and rendered to Master Vance. Master Sefton, do your part to see it rendered weel and on time."

Sefton bowed.

"I will, Your Majesty."

James beamed.

"Then I will buss the lass and gae to dinner," he announced, scrambling up from his seat.

The King had given Diane the promised kiss and gone. Roger, with Anthony at his side, stood looking after him, feeling suddenly empty and alone. Then he felt a light hand on his arm, and saw Diane gazing up at him, and holding her brother with her other hand.

"This is Roger, Ralph. But for him I might have been— no, I'd *never* have married that old man!" she finished with a flash of spirit.

Everyone laughed, and the two young men clasped hands. Roger presented Anthony.

"You may see him again in Ireland," he told Diane's brother. "He's taken a year of service there off my hands, I having been stubborn to swing a paint brush rather than a sword."

"Which is something you pay high for, as I hear," Ralph Hardie answered. "And I learn, too, that it's not for lack of skill with a blade."

"He's a better swordsman than I," Anthony declared. "Perhaps you and your sister can persuade him to a soldier's trade, and so back to the place that should be his."

"I shall persuade him against it if there is need," said Diane promptly. "And I think I may find a fellow-advocate," she announced, looking past Roger.

"Perhaps an advocate, and certainly a host."

Roger turned and saw Inigo Jones at his side. The architect explained that he had heard of the trial, and, having seen Diane perform the day before, had slipped in to hear part of the proceedings.

"And," he went on, "since infants, guardians, soldiers and even artists must dine, I am bold to ask all of you to share such meat as I can offer. It will be plain, but enough. I think you must come with me, for I do not know where else you can dine hereabouts."

Roger thanked him, and said he would ask his uncle, who was busy with Sefton arranging a settlement in accordance with the King's instructions. He returned soon with his uncle and accepted.

"Well agreed," said the architect. "I have already sent word that I shall bring some friends. And I have news for you," he told Roger, "which will give a better color to your affairs than you seemed to think they had this morning. Have you finished your business here?" he concluded.

"Before Master Darrell goes I should like a few words with him."

It was Sefton, who had gathered up his papers and followed Edward Vance.

"Of course," answered Roger. "Is—is it a private matter?"

"I think not." The lawyer smiled. "Your friends, I am sure, will soon learn of it. It is business touching your former teacher, Bartolomeo."

"Bartolomeo!" Roger echoed.

Sefton nodded.

"You may have wondered why I put some questions to you about him today, and then left the matter. I asked for my own satisfaction. For you must know that I was Bartolomeo's attorney long before I was Master Bragdon's. I have duties with respect to the Italian's estate, and of course they have no relation whatever to the hearing today. To be brief, Master Darrell, you are heir to all he left!"

Roger stared at him, and the others exclaimed. Sefton regarded them all with high good humor.

"It deserves a plain statement," he went on quickly. "The lawyer's clerk who sought you out that night on Little Wood Street was my man," he explained. "So was Fenwick. Neither knew about your brush with Wickard, though I can see why you feared that they did."

Roger, Vance and Cedric exclaimed anew.

"Aye," Sefton laughed, "it must have seemed strange and dark to you. But we came to you as much happier agents than you supposed. Bartolomeo, you must understand, received your letter telling of your differences with your father. It distressed him. When he knew he would die, it was the more on his mind. He had no kin in England—none abroad that he esteemed. He left all to you."

"And may it be asked what this 'all' included?" inquired Anthony.

"Why, as much as many have possessed who have gone seeking the arms and the name of gentleman," replied the lawyer. "Two houses, the colors, canvasses, books, and instruments of Bartolomeo's craft. A certain amount of gold.

I swore before witnesses to put it into your hands," he told Roger. "We had no information as to your father's estate, if near London or remote from it, or in what direction. We therefore sought you in the city, in the house where you told Bartolomeo you proposed to lodge. The woman there sent us to your new lodgings."

Roger thanked him warmly.

"No thanks," Sefton protested. "Your uncle will tell you I have a character and reputation in London, if my serving a certain client today would make you doubt it. I do not know how matters stand between you and your father," he continued, "but if—"

"I shall seek my father's love and good opinion, and tell him he has another son who can serve him better as an heir," Roger broke in. "Now less than ever," he added gravely, "can I break faith with Bartolomeo by abandoning the work he believed I could do."

Sefton bowed.

"He has made you a man of respectable substance, then, although your means will be modest in comparison with what you stood to have."

Roger thanked him again, and said he had several questions to ask, if he could presume on Sefton's patience.

"It will be no presumption."

"Well, then, to begin, how did Master Fenwick learn something of my appearance? For he said that I resembled Roger Darrell as described to him."

Sefton smiled.

"Why," he said, "when we failed to locate you in London, bearing in mind your intended work with Bartolomeo, we made inquiries where we believed you might have sought employment. First at the shop of the Johnson brothers; but although we suspected that they knew something, we could get no information."

"I could not believe they would give any!" Roger exclaimed.

"Next we asked at the Fortune playhouse, and Master Henslowe recalled you, and described you well. However, he then became wary, and would not tell us, if he knew, where you lodged. However, having found a trace of you at one theater, we then went to the Globe."

Roger nodded.

"And with respect to Mistress Hardie," he asked, "how did you learn that she was at the playhouse?"

Sefton hesitated, and then said that Bragdon had received an anonymous letter assuring him of that fact.

"I had reason to suspect as much," said Roger. "Did he receive a second letter about our playing at Westminster?"

"Yes, he did," the lawyer replied, "but by that time we had other means of information. You may wonder how we knew you would go by land back to London instead of by water?"

"Why, from the behavior of Richards, one of our hired men, we thought he might have informed you," Roger answered.

"That was the case," Sefton agreed. "We made contact with the fellow on the day of the fracas at the Globe—or rather one of Bragdon's men did, for I had not been told of that attempt until after it was made. I was away from London, and my client made his own decision. Yes, they followed Richards, persuaded him that the law lay with them, and for a guinea and the promise of more he agreed to inform them. We were ready to meet you by water, but preferred land. He made you suspect a river attack, then got word to us of the route you would follow on foot. It seemed fair enough to gain such information in this way, although I have no liking for informers. Are there more questions?"

Roger shook his head.

"I think that explains everything."

Sefton laughed.

"It was a tangled business. It will be long, I hope, before I find the like on my hands again."

He turned to Diane.

"Mistress, although I was late in learning it, I believe that my client has done less than his duty toward you. He must amend that, and I shall do all I can to see that he does."

"Master Sefton, I shall most gladly have you as a protector instead of an adversary," she assured him, smiling.

"It is a pleasure I share. And as to your marriage, I know that it will not be such as Master Bragdon planned. I am happy in that knowledge, too. Indeed," he added smiling, "I myself, with what I have now learned, could suggest a far happier one!"

He turned away, bowing, as he spoke, and retired.

Ralph Hardie looked first at his sister, then at Roger. There was a gleam of laughter in his eyes.

"Why," he remarked, "I think he could. He and I might even be of one mind as to that."